SAVAGE ECSTASY

"Does the white man please you as I did?"

Loralee gasped, outraged that he would dare ask such a thing. Hot color rushed to her cheeks, and she turned away, refusing to answer him, refusing even to look at him.

"Do you call his name and claw his back as you once did mine?" Zuniga demanded. He took her chin in his hand and forced her to look at him. His eyes were like liquid ebony, deep and dark and angry. "Do you?"

"Shut up," Loralee hissed. She tried to pull out of his grasp, but his hand was like an iron vise, holding her immobile.

"Do you whimper softly when he strokes your sweet thighs, Loralee?" Zuniga taunted angrily. "Does he know the hills and valleys of your body as well as I do?"

MADELINE BAKER proved she knows how to please readers of historical romance when she created *RECKLESS HEART* and *LOVE IN THE WIND.*"
Whispers (B. Dalton Romance Club)

Now Madeline Baker weaves another wildly passionate tale of the forbidden love between a white woman and a fierce Apache warrior.

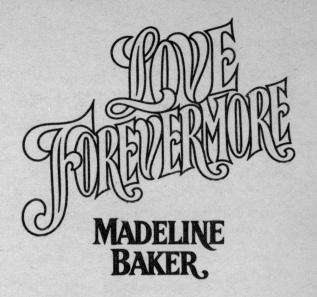

LOVE FOREVERMORE

MADELINE BAKER

LEISURE BOOKS   æ   NEW YORK CITY

To
CAROL CLEMENTICH
LOU LANSING, JANIE CRAWFORD
KIMBERLY ONUFROCK, TAWNI HENDRICKS,
RUBY ARTHUR
and
PATTY ESPINOZA
for their kind words and good wishes,
To
PESHA FINKELSTEIN and WENDY McCURDY
who encouraged me to keep trying
And to
JANE THORNTON and ALICIA CONDON
who made the dream come true.

A LEISURE BOOK

Published by
Dorchester Publishing Co., Inc.
6 East 39th Street
New York, NY 10016

Printed in the United States of America

Preface

He sat astride a big dun stallion, watching her hang a load of wash on a line stretched between two scrawny pine trees. She was young for a schoolmarm, only twenty-two or twenty-three, and more beautiful than any woman he had ever seen. Her hair was the color of sun-ripened wheat. Her face was oval-shaped, the skin smooth and clear, unblemished by freckle or mole. Her nose was small and delicately formed, her mouth as pink as a wild rose, her brows slightly arched above eyes that were a deep, deep brown. She was tall and thin, but not too thin. Her breasts were high and proud, her waist narrow, her hips nicely rounded.

In the old days, he would have ridden

into the yard, grabbed the woman, and taken her to his lodge in the hills. He would have kept her there until he tired of her, and then he would have given her to another warrior, or sent her back to her own people.

But not now. His people were no longer warriors and fighters, but farmers and drunkards, their once proud spirit subdued by too many years of living on the white man's reservation and too much firewater. Often he yearned for the old days, the days his grandfather spoke of, days when the red man rode wild and free across the vast prairies and plains. But those days were gone, forever gone, and the world was changing.

Rapidly changing. At the fort, he had heard talk of two men in a place called Kitty Hawk, North Carolina, who had built a machine that could fly like an eagle. There were horseless carriages that could go an incredible ten miles an hour. He himself had seen one such motor car at the Indian Agency and had been amazed by the odd-looking contraption. It had clattered loudly as it rolled down the dusty street, smelling of oil and smoke, spooking every horse and cow it passed.

He could see no advantage in such a machine. It was useless in the hills. It could not navigate a narrow, twisting deer trail through a forest, or swim a river, or climb a steep arroyo, or forage off the land. You could not use such a thing for hunting, for the noise alone would scare away every deer and rabbit within miles. No, he could not imagine why anyone would want such a loud and ugly thing, and yet it was said that the people in the East were buying them by the hundreds.

Yes, he mused ruefully, life was changing, and he was not ready to change with it.

He sighed heavily as he turned his horse for home. In the old days, he would have ridden into the yard and taken the woman who had sparked his desire and fired his imagination.

But the old days were gone . . .

1

Summer 1905

Loralee Warfield sat behind the large oak
desk, her fingers absently stroking the
smooth wood. She was here, she mused,
really here. Even after a month, it was hard
to believe it was true. Her friends back East
had been appalled when they discovered she
was going to teach school to Apache children at the Fort Apache Indian Reservation
in Arizona territory. Crazy, they had said.
Ridiculous. Dangerous. But Loralee had ignored their dire predictions and warnings
and eagerly packed her bags. She was going
West!

In preparation for her trip, she studied
numerous books and maps, learning about
the history and geography of the territory of
Arizona, reading about cities like Tucson

and Yuma and Tombstone, cities rich in history and folklore. She learned about the flora and fauna, and how to identify the prickly pear and the cholla, and the saguaro cactus, which could reach a height of over fifty feet and was said to live for two hundred years.

She read and studied right up to the minute she stepped onto the train in Philadelphia, all her earthly belongings packed in a single black satchel, her eyes sparkling with excitement. She was going West!

The trip had been long, arduous, the last few miles seeming the longest of all. Would she ever get there?

She had shared the cost of a rented coach with a young couple on their way to Globe on the last leg of the journey. Meals and lodging en route to the reservation had cost an exorbitant two dollars a day.

They had traveled thirty miles the first day, staying overnight at a little Mormon town called Snowflake. It had seemed a pleasant enough town, the streets neatly laid out, the brick houses well cared for, the people friendly. She had gone to bed early that night, hoping to sleep away the long hours before they would be traveling again. But sleep had been a long time coming, and she had lain awake for hours, her mind racing with excitement at what lay ahead.

After breakfast the following morning, Loralee and her traveling companions con-

tinued on their journey, passing two small
Mormon towns called Taylor and Shumway.
Some twenty miles from Snowflake, Loralee
and her companions had gazed in awe at
huge lava beds and rock formations. There
was nothing like that in the East, Loralee had
mused. Nothing at all.

The next day, they covered the last twenty miles, as Loralee's excitement grew
stronger with the passing of each minute.
The coach seemed to be traveling so slowly,
she was certain she could run faster than the
horses were moving. She wanted to shout up
at the driver and urge him to hurry. Didn't
he realize how long she had waited for this
day, how many miles she had come to be
here?

And now she was here, Loralee mused.
A schoolteacher. She had a large schoolroom to teach in. There were twenty-eight
desks in four neat rows. The east wall had
three large windows, open wide to admit the
late afternoon breeze. The west wall also
had three windows for cross ventilation, and
below the windows were long shelves filled
with books and stacks of paper, boxes of
pencils and chalk and erasers, slates, an
encyclopedia set, a dictionary.

There was a chalkboard on the wall
behind her desk, as well as a large map of the
United States. The boundaries of the Apache
reservation were outlined on the map in red
ink.

Loralee sighed heavily as she cradled her chin in the palms of her hands. She had books, she had maps, she had a vast store of knowledge, but no bright-eyed children eager to learn. It was most discouraging. She had gone from lodge to lodge in the last four weeks, introducing herself to the people of the tribe, trying to persuade the Indians to send their children to school, but to no avail. The Apache were polite. They offered her food and drink. They listened attentively to what she had to say. But they did not send their children to school.

When possible, Loralee had talked directly to the children. But no matter how she coaxed or cajoled, she could not convince the boys and girls to come to school. She promised them treats, she promised to make them laugh, she even told them they could come just once to see what it was all about and that, if they didn't like it, they wouldn't have to come again. But it was all in vain.

Moving about the reservation, Loralee had been surprised to see a number of small log cabins. When she questioned one of the soldiers, she learned that the cabins had been built back in 1895 in an attempt to encourage the Indians to move out of their wickiups and into more modern homes. The attempt had failed. Most of the log cabins had been abandoned after a day or two, the Indians preferring their wickiups to the square wood houses of the white man.

There were both Mescalero and Chiricahua Apaches living on the reservation. The Chiricahua lodges were brush-covered, dome-shaped structures, while the lodges of the Mescalero were tipis similar to those made by the Sioux and Cheyenne.

Loralee sighed again. She had not expected teaching to be easy. She knew the Indians clung stubbornly to their old ways, resisting the Army's efforts to turn them into whites. In 1901, the Commissioner of Indian Affairs had instructed all Indian Agents to direct their male charges to cut their hair. Men and women were to adopt the white man's form of dress. Traditional feasts and dances were to be abolished, and the Indians would instead celebrate the white man's holidays. But the Indian men had refused to cut their hair. A few took to wearing cotton shirts and trousers, but for the most part, they refused to change.

Holding to traditional ways and values, the women continued to do most of the work. An Apache squaw gathered nuts and berries, acorns and sunflower seeds, pine nuts and mesquite beans. She drew the water from the river. She did the sewing and the cooking and the washing and the mending. She took care of the lodge and raised the children. If there was a garden, she prepared the ground, planted the seeds, weeded and watered, and harvested the crop.

Loralee had been shocked to discover

that the women did not eat until after the men, and that if the husband had guests and they ate all the food, the wife did without.

Loralee gazed out the window. The Indians had so much to learn. How could she teach them if they would not come to school? On the reservation, they were living as they had a hundred years ago. The grandfather still instructed the young boys in the ways of the tribe, teaching them the ancient songs and rituals. An Apache man still avoided contact with his mother-in-law, turning his back when she passed by, never going to her lodge, leaving his own home if she came to visit.

And yet, there was hope. The young men were not so averse to change as their fathers, and the women were in favor of anything that would make their lives easier. The women liked the brightly colored skirts and blouses sold at the general store. They appreciated being able to buy flour at the trading post instead of having to grind their own.

But the future belonged to the children. If only she could find a way to get them to school . . .

With a shake of her head, Loralee stood up and walked out of the schoolhouse. Lifting her skirts, she wandered across the yard, her eyes unconsciously moving toward the distant hills.

He was there again, sitting astride a dun-colored horse. An invisible current seemed to flow between them, and Loralee felt a shiver along her spine, of apprehension or excitement, she could not say. Who was he? Did he mean to do her harm? Or was he merely curious about the new white woman who had come to live on the reservation? She had seen him many times, always from a distance. He seemed always to be there whenever she stepped out of the schoolhouse. Once, while walking along the shallow river, she had made an abrupt about-face and saw him following her, from a goodly distance, of course. Boldly, she had started toward him, determined to confront him face to face and discover who he was and what he wanted. But before she had gone a dozen steps, he had vanished from sight behind a tangled mass of brush and cactus.

The man never came near enough for her to see his face, but she knew it was the same man each time by the horse he rode, and by the way he sat the dun, proud and regal, almost haughty. His skin was the color of old copper and he had long black hair —more than that she could not discern at such a distance.

Who was he? The thought haunted her like a mystery she could not solve, and she had taken to looking for him whenever she went to the fort to purchase supplies, or when walking through the reservation trying to make friends with the Apache children. She had seen many men—young and old, tall and short—yet she knew intuitively that none of the men she had met was the man she was looking for.

The sound of hoofbeats drew Loralee's attention and she glanced over her shoulder to see Sergeant Michael Schofield riding toward her. Glancing back at the hill, she saw that the Indian was gone. Would she ever find out who he was, she wondered absently, and then forgot about him as she turned to watch Mike Schofield dismount.

Mike was tall and blond, with dark blue eyes, a deep tan, and a winning smile. He looked wonderfully handsome in his Army uniform. Mike had warned her weeks ago that she was wasting her time on the reservation. The children would never come to school, he had told her, not in a million years. No doubt he had come today just to say, "I told you so," Loralee thought, but she didn't care. She was glad to see him, and it showed in her smile of welcome.

Mike removed his hat as he stepped toward Loralee. Damn, he mused, but she made a pretty picture standing there with the sun shining in her hair and the hills stretched behind her. Her golden hair was a perfect frame for her lovely face, and when she smiled up at him like she was doing now, it warmed him clear through.

"Hi, Mike."

"Hi." He glanced toward the empty schoolhouse. "Still no luck, I see."

"They'll come," Loralee said, but her voice lacked conviction. She wouldn't have admitted it for the world, not to Mike, not to herself, but she was getting discouraged. She had tried everything she could think of, and everything had failed.

Mike shook his head ruefully. "I admire your determination, Loralee, but I think you're butting your head against a brick wall. Most of the Indians don't want any part of the white man, or his teachings."

"Don't try to discourage me, Mike," Loralee replied wearily. "I'm discouraged enough as it is."

"Sorry." He was instantly contrite. She did look a little downhearted today, he thought, and immediately put himself in charge of cheering her up. "Would you care to go for a ride? I brought along an extra horse, just in case."

"Thanks, Mike," Loralee said, smiling again. "I'd like that."

A short time later they were riding side by side across the flat sandy ground. Loralee hadn't ridden much back East, although she knew how to sit a horse, but Mike had taught her how to ride Western-style, and she had taken to it like a duck to water. Riding for pleasure was a wonderful way to beat the blues, Loralee had discovered, and had started saving money to buy a horse of her own.

Usually, riding took her mind off her

troubles, but not today. "If I could just get one or two of the children to come to school, I know the others would come, too," Loralee mused aloud. "I just know it."

Mike shrugged. He didn't particularly want to spend the day talking about the Apaches and their problems, but it was a subject dear to Loralee's heart.

"You could be right," Mike allowed.

"I know I am. Isn't there someone the children admire?" Loralee asked as an idea began to form in the back of her mind. "Someone they all look up to?"

"One of the older kids, you mean?"

"Anyone."

Mike let out a long breath, opened his mouth to speak, and abruptly changed his mind.

"You were going to say something," Loralee coaxed. "You know someone, don't you?"

"Well, yes, but. . . ."

"But?" Loralee leaned toward Mike, suddenly excited. "Who is it? Tell me, Mike, please. This is so important to me."

"Forget it, Loralee," Mike said with a shake of his head. "He's nothing but trouble. Bad clear through."

"Who?" She almost shouted the word.

"Shad Zuniga."

"Is he a leader? A chief?"

"Zuniga!" Mike laughed derisively. "He's a rebel, an outlaw of sorts, but all the

Indian kids look up to him like he was some kind of hero."

"Really? Why?"

"Beats me. Why did people admire Frank and Jesse James?"

"Where is he, this Zuniga?"

Mike gestured at the hills rising to the south. "He lives up there with his grandfather. Refuses to live on the reservation with the other Indians. Refuses to take what he calls charity from the whites. Won't accept a beef ration, or clothing, or blankets, or anything else he's legally entitled to. He refused to give up his rifle when he came in."

Mike grinned goodnaturedly. "The Army has searched his place for weapons at least a dozen times, but we can't find a thing. We know he's got at least one rifle, maybe more, and we know he steals ammunition from the sutler's store, but no one's been able to catch him at it. Yet."

Mike let out a sigh of exasperation. Sooner or later, he was determined to catch Shad Zuniga breaking the law and then he was going to put the man behind bars where he belonged.

Loralee looked thoughtful. Zuniga did not sound like the sort of character she would want to associate with, but she was at her wit's end, and if Shad Zuniga could help get the children to school, she was desperate enough to let him try.

"Perhaps I could persuade this boy,

21

Zuniga, to come to school," Loralee mused aloud. "Perhaps if he would come, the other children would come, too."

Mike laughed, genuinely amused at the idea of Shad Zuniga attending the white man's school, and then he grew sober. "Don't you go near Zuniga," he warned. "Shad Zuniga is not a kid. He's a man full grown and not one to mess with. Rumor has it he killed his own father in cold blood."

"No!"

"Yes. You stay away from him, Loralee." Mike shook his head, not wanting to think about Loralee even getting near Shad Zuniga. The man was no damn good.

Mike gestured at a row of small square houses located on the outskirts of the reservation. "We are making some progress," he remarked as they rode by. "A few of the single women are willing to give our way of life a try. They seem to like living under a roof, and cooking on a stove instead of over an open fire. Some even sleep in a bed. It's the men who cause the most problems. They refuse to try farming, refuse to try raising cattle. They'd rather sit around and drink and talk about the good old days."

Loralee nodded. She had seen the Apache men huddled around their lodges, their faces sullen and unfriendly. The old men wore only clouts and moccasins. They spent hours talking about the old days, the old ways. They refought old battles and talked about friends who had died long ago, victims of the white man's treachery. The old ones would never change, Loralee mused sadly. They would never forget the old hates, the old hurts.

"I guess everything takes time," Loralee remarked. "And that's one thing I've plenty of."

Mike grinned. He liked Loralee Warfield. She was bright and pretty, not easily discouraged. It took courage to take on a new job in a strange part of the country. Not many women liked living out West. There weren't many comforts on the reservation. The house she lived in was small and crudely furnished with just the bare essentials. She had only lived there for a few weeks, but already the place had changed, and he marveled at what a resourceful woman could accomplish with a few yards of cloth and a few strokes of paint. The place was still small and crudely furnished, but it had a homey quality about it now, a feeling of warmth and caring. He hoped Loralee would not give up her dream of teaching the children too quickly, for he dearly wanted to get to know her better. He planned to make the Army his career, and he thought Loralee Warfield would make a prime Army wife.

"I'm glad you decided to come West," Mike said. "Life on the post was pretty dull until you showed up."

"Why, thank you, Mike," Loralee replied, pleased by the compliment. "Tell me, what's it like, being in the Army?"

"Pretty grim, sometimes. You know, reveille at five-thirty every morning. First drill at six-fifteen; fatigue duty at seven-thirty. Fatigue duty's the worst, especially for the enlisted men. They get stuck building roads, repairing telegraph lines, cutting firewood, hauling water, all the dirty jobs. Sometimes it's drill, drill, drill, until I think I can't stand it for another day."

"Why do you stay if it's so bad?"

"I don't know. I just decided to make a career of it. I'm not fit for much else."

"Oh, Mike, I don't believe that. I'm sure you'd be a success at anything you put your mind to."

Mike shrugged, but he was pleased by Loralee's confidence in him. "Maybe. But I really like the Army."

"I hear the food is awful. Is it as bad as they say?"

"Well, you know the old saying: Army cooks have killed more soldiers than Indians."

Loralee laughed merrily. "You make Army life sound just wonderful," she remarked dryly.

"It's not so bad, not when you're an officer."

"Is that your goal, to be a general some day?"

"Me, a general?" Mike chuckled,

amused. "I don't think so, but I would like to make lieutenant, maybe even captain, before I retire."

"You'll make it. I know you will."

"I've got a pretty good chance of making lieutenant. Hoskins is being transferred back East in a month or two, and I'm next in line for a promotion."

"That's wonderful, Mike."

They rode in silence for a while, and Loralee thought about Army men. They were a special breed, willing to live where they were sent, putting up with orders and drills day after day, ready to fight at a moment's notice. Back in 1871, an enlisted man drew a mere thirteen dollars a month and lived on beans, hardtack, bread, coffee, and meat when he could get it. They had been a hardy bunch of men, Loralee mused, and surely their wives and sweethearts must have been just as tough, just as resilient. She tried to imagine herself back in those days, married to Mike, waving goodbye as he rode out on patrol while the band played "The Girl I Left Behind Me," never knowing if she would ever see him again. Of course, life out West was different now. The men didn't ride out to fight the Apaches or the Comanches any more, and living conditions were greatly improved, but it was still a dangerous way of life, fraught with peril. There were still outlaws and rattlesnakes. A man could be killed falling from his horse, or by a crazed Indian who'd had too much firewater and wanted to take a scalp. Such incidents were rare, but they happened.

Mike was humming under his breath, and Loralee grinned at him. "I know that song," she said. "I read it in a book."

"You're kidding," Mike replied. "Let me hear you sing it."

"No, I can't," Loralee said.

"Come on, I'll sing it with you."

"Well . . . all right."

And together they began to sing:

"I'd love to be a packer,
And pack with George F. Crook,
And dressed up in my canvas suit,
To be for him mistook.
I'd braid my beard in two forked tails,
And idle all the day
In whittling sticks and wondering
What the New York papers say."

They were laughing when they finished, and Mike thought what a rare girl Loralee was. Imagine her knowing that old Army ballad!

"You've been awfully good to me," Loralee said when they returned to the schoolhouse. "Thanks for the ride. It was just what I needed to cheer me up."

"Any time," Mike said. Dismounting, he placed his hands around Loralee's trim waist and helped her to the ground. "See you tomorrow?"

"I'll be here," Loralee answered cheerfully.

"I hope you'll always be here," Mike said, his bantering tone at odds with the serious expression in his dark blue eyes.

"Mike? Could I keep the horse for a few days?"

"It's yours," Mike answered, grinning at her.

"Really?" Loralee looked at the horse, her horse, and smiled as she stroked the mare's neck. It was a beautiful animal, with a sleek black coat and expressive brown eyes. "You mean it?" Loralee asked, unable to believe her ears. "She's truly mine?"

"Truly," Mike said, pleased because Loralee was pleased. "It's a long ride to the fort, and I don't want you to be too tired to spend time with me."

"Thanks, Mike," Loralee said sincerely. "I'll see you tomorrow."

"You can count on it."

As soon as Mike was out of sight, Loralee climbed back into the saddle and set out for the hills, determined to find Shad Zuniga and convince him to help her. He must be made to understand that the Apaches had to go forward or perish. Civilization was coming, bringing electricity and telephones, phonographs and indoor plumbing. Granted, it would be a long time before any of those things arrived on the reservation, but the Indians needed to be aware of the great strides being made in science and industry and medicine. They needed to be prepared to meet the future, prepared for the many changes that were coming their way.

Some of Loralee's enthusiasm waned as her horse picked its way up the brush-covered slope. Trees and shrubs grew close together, making the going difficult. Thorny cactus and low hanging branches snagged her clothing, scratching her arms and face, but she went doggedly onward until she saw it: a single brush-covered wickiup set in a small clearing at the top of a flat-topped rise. A thin spiral of blue-gray smoke rose from the blackened smokehole at the top of the lodge. A rough peeled-pole corral held a big dun stallion and a small bay gelding. A fresh deer hide was stretched on a rack beside the wickiup, an ancient buffalo skull, bleached white by the sun, sat on a log near the rear of the lodge.

For a moment, Loralee remained on her horse, letting her eyes wander over her surroundings. It was a lovely setting. Tall trees grew a short distance from the wickiup, flowering shrubs grew in scattered clumps. The air was dry and clear, the sky a peaceful blue.

A scrawny yellow hound dog growled at

her as she dismounted near the corral. Loralee hesitated, wondering if the dog would attack her, but apparently the growl was just for show. Lowering its head, the hound closed its eyes and went back to sleep.

With renewed resolve, Loralee tethered her horse to one of the fence posts and made her way toward the wickiup, her eyes darting warily from side to side. She was a foreigner here, she mused, an outsider. Some primal instinct warned her that she was treading where few white people had gone before, and she was suddenly afraid.

Her steps slowed as doubts began to crowd her mind. What was she doing up here, alone and uninvited? What made her think she could persuade this man, this stranger, to encourage the Indian children to attend school? Mike had warned her that Shad Zuniga was not a man to cross, that he had killed his own father in cold blood. What made her think such a man would even listen to what she had to say? Perhaps he would shoot her on sight for trespassing!

Loralee came to an abrupt halt some ten feet from the wickiup, about to abandon the whole plan. She would just have to find some other means of persuading the Apache children to come to school. She had always prided herself on her inventiveness. Surely she could think of something less dangerous than coming here to speak to a man she had never met.

Quite unexpectedly, her mind filled with pictures of howling Indians, their faces painted for war, their lances decorated with bloody scalps. At the same time, she imagined what Shad Zuniga would look like: short, with greasy black hair, a barrel chest, and ominous eyes. Mike had said Zuniga stayed to himself and did not welcome intruders. Suddenly certain he would not be pleased to see her, Loralee decided to forget the whole thing. She was about to return to her horse when a man stepped out of the wickiup.

He was tall for an Apache, standing several inches over six feet. His hair was as black as pitch; parted in the middle, it fell past his shoulders. His eyes were like shards of black glass, piercing and sharp. His skin was reddish-brown, like the earth at his feet. He wore a pair of stained buckskin trousers and a sleeveless buckskin vest. Knee-high moccasins, folded over at the top, hugged his calves and feet. There was a knife sheathed on his belt, and her eyes lingered on it a moment before returning to his face. His mouth was wide, turned down in a frown as he stared at her. His nose was slightly crooked, and she wondered if it had been broken, and how. He appeared to be in his early thirties. He was, she decided, the most beautiful man she had ever seen.

She flushed under his probing gaze. His eyes, so dark and intense, seemed to see right through her.

"What do you want?" His voice was deep, rich, and unfriendly.

Loralee coughed nervously. Why hadn't she listened to Mike? Why hadn't she stayed home where she belonged?

"Are you Shad Zuniga?"

"Maybe." He stood with his long legs spread apart, his thumbs hooked over the waistband of his trousers, his head cocked to one side.

"Maybe?"

"What do you want him for?"

"I. . . ." Loralee straightened her shoulders and lifted her chin. She had come here for a purpose, and she wasn't going to let this man scare her off now. "I'm the school mistress. From the reservation."

"I know."

With a start, Loralee realized he was the Indian who had been watching her for the past several weeks. The thought brought a rosy flush to her cheeks.

"Well?" he asked gruffly.

"I'm . . . that is, the children won't come to school, and I was wondering if—" Her voice trailed off. She could not speak, could not think clearly, not with those dark eyes staring into her own. His eyelashes were thick and sooty, ridiculously long. A thin white scar zigzagged down the left side of his nose, a tiny flaw in a face that was close to perfection.

"You were wondering what?" he asked impatiently.

Loralee swallowed hard. This man was a warrior. Only a few years ago, he had been making war against her people, raiding and killing and God knew what else. She glanced at the knife on his belt again and imagined it in his hand, dripping blood. He was watching her intently, waiting for her to speak, and she took a deep breath. Might as well say what she had come to say and get it over with.

"I was wondering if you could persuade the children to come to school." She spoke the words in a rush, felt her cheeks grow hot as he threw back his head and began to laugh. It was a deep throaty laugh, filled with genuine amusement.

Loralee bit her lower lip. Why had she come here? What had made her think this . . . this savage would help her?

"I'm sorry I bothered you," she said stiffly. Pivoting on her heel, she started toward her horse. Discouragement sat heavy on her shoulder. He had been her last hope.

"Wait." His voice reached out to stop her.

Slowly, Loralee turned around to face him. He was not laughing now.

"What makes you think the children will listen to me?"

"I was told they admire and respect you."

One black eyebrow arched in sardonic amusement. "Who told you that?"

"A friend."

Zuniga grunted. The children *did* admire him. He had not been conquered. He had not been captured. He had not been defeated in battle. He had come to the reservation voluntarily. After months of hiding out in the hills, he had surrendered his freedom because his grandfather was ill and needed him. And that was the only reason he stayed here, in a place he despised.

"The Apache do not need the white man or his teachings," he said at length.

"I think they do," Loralee retorted boldly.

"Why do you want to teach us?"

"I want to help your people."

"Why?"

"I admire and respect them."

"What do you know about my people?" Zuniga asked with a sneer. "What do you know of our ways, our beliefs?"

"Quite a bit, actually. I've read and studied and—"

"You cannot learn about people from books."

"Is that so?" Loralee snapped, irritated by his rudeness. "And just how many books have you read?"

"None."

"Can you read?"

"No."

Loralee took a deep breath. She could not afford to offend Shad Zuniga. He was a proud man, a warrior. One wrong word could ruin everything. "Would you like to learn?"

Shad Zuniga frowned. He did not have any interest in learning the teachings of the white man, but he was interested in learning more about the schoolteacher. She had the courage of a she-wolf, to come to see him alone, and he admired her for that, and for the way she stood up to him. She was looking at him expectantly, her luminous brown eyes hopeful as she waited for his answer, her rosy lips slightly parted. He wondered what she would do if he swept her into his arms and plundered her mouth with his own.

"I would be glad to teach you to read and write," Loralee offered. She licked her lips nervously, wondering if he could hear the rapid beating of her heart as she waited for his answer.

"I am a warrior," Zuniga replied proudly. "I cannot go to your school with children."

"Of course not," Loralee agreed quickly. She swallowed hard, overwhelmed by what she was about to suggest. "I . . . I could teach you at night. I'm sure the children would agree to attend class if they knew you were also learning to read and write."

"We would be alone, just the two of us?" Zuniga queried. "No one else would be there?"

Loralee pondered that for a moment. No decent woman ever met a man alone at night. It was scandalous to even consider such an arrangement, but then, she wasn't "meeting" him at all. She was going to teach him to read and write.

"Just the two of us," she agreed.

Zuniga nodded. Perhaps it would be wise to learn the teachings of the white man. It was always a good idea to learn as much about your enemy as possible. A wise man learned his opponent's strengths and weaknesses . . . he was lying to himself and he knew it. The only reason he was even considering going to school was to learn more about Loralee Warfield. Her strengths. Her weaknesses . . .

"I will come to the school tomorrow night," Zuniga decided. "After the evening meal."

It was done. There could be no turning back now.

"I'll be there," Loralee said. "Thank you."

Had she been alone, she would have shouted with triumph. He was coming to school! He would learn, and the children would learn. She longed to jump up and down and kick up her heels. Instead, she offered him her hand, unprepared for the sudden rush of heat that suffused her whole body as his strong brown hand closed over hers. He held her hand for just a moment

35

longer than was necessary, his fathomless black eyes intent upon her face, his steady gaze making her insides melt like butter over an open flame. A queer little tremor started deep in the pit of her stomach and radiated outward like the ripples on a pond.

Frightened by the unexpected sensations he had aroused within her by a single touch of his hand, she jerked her hand free of his and ran toward her horse, very much aware that he was watching her every move.

Mounted, she felt safer and she slid a glance in his direction. He was standing where she had left him, his dark eyes alight with amusement.

Loralee blushed, feeling foolish. Why had she bolted away from him like that? All he had done was shake her hand.

She was out of breath when she reached home. Her hand still tingled where he had held it, and she wondered what she had gotten herself into. What would Mike say when he learned she was going to tutor Shad Zuniga at the schoolhouse, at night, alone? What had ever possessed her to agree to such an outrageous arrangement?

She was uncharacteristically clumsy as she prepared her dinner that night, unable to hold onto anything. She dropped a glass, a fork, a frying pan. Staring out the kitchen window, staring at nothing in particular, she thought of Zuniga, and almost burned her dinner.

Later, her meal only half finished, she cleared the table, washed and dried the dishes, swept the kitchen floor, fed the cat, undressed for bed.

Sliding between the cool linen sheets, she closed her eyes, only to have Shad Zuniga's swarthy image burst into her mind. Long black hair, eyes as dark and deep as the corridors of hell, skin the color of old copper. His shoulders were broad, the muscles in his arms large and well-defined, hinting at great strength. His legs were long, powerful from years of running and horseback riding. He was unlike the other Apache men she had met. They were beaten, defeated, devoid of hope. But Zuniga was not beaten. He was still a warrior, still filled with the pride and arrogance that had once been characteristic of all Apache men.

Zuniga. Just thinking of him made her feel warm and tingly all over. It was most disturbing, and yet strangely pleasurable.

"Zuniga."

She fell asleep with his name on her lips, and in her dreams she was wooed and won by a dark-skinned man who had hair as black as a raven's wing and eyes as black as ebony.

2

Mike was furious when he found out what she had done.

"Are you crazy?" he demanded angrily. "Didn't I tell you to stay away from Zuniga? Didn't I tell you he was trouble? My God, Loralee, didn't you listen to a word I said?"

Loralee stood with her arms crossed over her chest, one foot tapping impatiently, her eyes flashing as she waited for Sergeant Michael Schofield to run out of steam. Who did he think he was, anyway, carrying on as if he were her father or something? She was a grown woman, quite capable of looking out for herself. Hadn't she been taking care of herself since her parents were killed in a carriage accident when she was thirteen?

She had earned her own way, waiting on tables, sweeping floors, washing windows, ironing clothes, tending other people's children, doing anything she could to earn a living. She had slept in drab rented rooms and eaten in grubby little diners to save money. She had learned early in life to defend herself, to ward off the unwanted advances that came her way because she was young and attractive and alone. She didn't need any self-righteous Army man telling *her* how to behave. She knew how to behave. She had gone to school and studied day and night, learning to read and write and cipher. She had watched the wealthy ladies in town, copying the way they walked and talked until it became second nature for her to move slowly and gracefully, to speak in a well-modulated voice, to comport herself as a lady should. When she turned seventeen, she had acquired a position as governess to a rich Philadelphia family with two small children. She had made friends with other young women who had to work for a living, and she had carved out a nice life for herself.

In her spare time, she had earned her teaching certificate and when she heard about the opening at the Apache reservation, she had jumped at the opportunity to teach, seeing it as a way to fulfill a lifelong dream. And now Sergeant Michael Schofield was ranting and raving at her as if she had done something criminal. Didn't he understand how important teaching was to her? Why couldn't he see that she had done the only thing possible under the circumstances?

"I just don't want you to get hurt, Loralee," Mike finished sincerely. He sighed heavily, knowing Loralee was annoyed by his outburst. He hadn't meant to yell at her, or hurt her, but he had to make her understand how foolish she had been to approach Zuniga alone. The man was a renegade, a savage.

"Are you through now?" Loralee asked coolly.

"I'm sorry," Mike said contritely. "I didn't mean to shout. It's bad enough, you living out here all alone, but when you deliberately go looking for trouble . . . dammit, Loralee, I worry about you."

"I appreciate your concern, Mike, really I do, but it's quite unnecessary. Mr. Zuniga was very helpful."

"I'll bet," Mike muttered sarcastically. "Well, you can't meet him at the school alone and that's all there is to it. I'll come out and keep an eye on things tonight, and then you'll have to make some other arrangement."

"No. I told him it would be just the two of us. He won't come if anyone else is here. And the children won't come to school unless he does."

"I won't have it, Loralee. It isn't safe for you to be out here alone with him. Not only that, what about your reputation? What will people say when they learn you're meeting him here at night, without a chaperone?"

"I am not 'meeting' him," Loralee retorted, exasperated by the whole conversation. "I'm a teacher and he's a student. There's nothing more to it than that."

Mike grimaced with defeat. Loralee Warfield was a beautiful woman, soft and sweet and feminine on the outside, and as stubborn as an Army mule on the inside. He had only known her for a few weeks, but he had lost every argument they'd ever had. Once she made up her mind to do something, nothing on God's green earth could change it.

Mike glanced up at the hills where Shad Zuniga lived. He had met the man only a few times, and he heartily disliked him. There was a wild quality in Zuniga that set Mike's teeth on edge and made him uneasy.

"Would you like to go out for dinner Friday night?" Mike asked. He'd lost the battle and there was no point in dwelling on it.

Loralee smiled prettily. "I'd love to, Mike. I have a new dress, and I've just been dying for an excuse to wear it."

"Good. I'll pick you up at eight."

"Fine. See you then."

Loralee spent the rest of the afternoon tidying up her house. It didn't take long to clean the three small rooms, but she swept and dusted meticulously, then applied beeswax to the few pieces of furniture, rubbing the wood until it fairly glowed.

It really was a charming little house, sturdily built of wood and adobe. Two people would have been crowded, but it was just right for one. She had repainted the whole house soon after she moved in, choosing white for the parlor, a sunny yellow for the kitchen, a soft powder blue for the bedroom. A sofa covered in a green print and a leather armchair took up most of the floor space in the parlor, a mahogany clock ticked cheerfully on the mantel above the stone fireplace, a small cactus grew in a clay pot on the windowsill. The bedroom was crowded with a single bed, a night table, a four-drawer dresser, and a commode. A colorful rag rug covered the floor. The kitchen was the largest room in the house. It made her feel very domestic as she slipped an apron over her head and started dinner. There was a small stove against the wall, a round oak table and two matching chairs, a cupboard over the counter, a dry sink. Yellow gingham curtains fluttered at the open window. She had made the curtains and the matching tablecloth herself.

Sitting at the table, she felt herself growing more and more nervous as the time approached when she was to meet Shad Zuniga. She had told Mike she could take care of herself, that there was nothing to worry about; but now, as the sun slowly dipped behind the mountains in the west,

43

she began to feel apprehensive. She was about to go to the schoolhouse to meet a strange man, an Indian man, alone.

Too nervous to finish her meal, she put the scraps in a pan and set it outside the back door for the big calico cat who came to visit her each night at dusk. She had tried to coax the cat into the house on several occasions, but the animal was too wild, too distrustful of people, to enter the cozy kitchen. Loralee smiled faintly as she saw the cat peeking around the corner of the house, but she was too distracted to try and win the animal's trust tonight.

She washed and dried her few dishes, put them away in the cupboard. Going into her bedroom, she stood before the mirror, contemplating her appearance. Her hair was swept away from her face and pinned in a neat roll at the nape of her neck. She didn't care for the style. It was too severe, too unflattering, but she wore it because it was neat and cool, and because it made her look older than she was, more mature. Her face seemed pale, her brown eyes very dark. Her dress was a deep blue cotton, unadorned with lace or frills. The neck was square, the sleeves were long and loose, the skirt full.

Loralee frowned at her reflection. She looked like an old maid with her hair skimmed back and her figure concealed by the unattractive dress. She wondered if she should change into something more becoming, and then laughed self-consciously. She wasn't going to the schoolhouse to flirt with the man, only to teach him to read and write.

Draping a soft white shawl around her shoulders, Loralee left the house and walked the short distance to the school. It was a large, rectangular-shaped building made of wood and painted a rusty red. A flagpole stood outside the door. She hoisted the flag to the top of the pole each morning and took it down each night. One side of the building had been cleared of brush and was meant to be used as a playground.

As she neared the building, Loralee wondered if children would ever play tag or kickball in the yard, or if the sound of children reading aloud would ever sound from within the walls of the school.

She paused a moment, enjoying the quiet of the night and the way the setting sun turned the sky to flame. It was her favorite part of the day, watching the sun set, watching the way the sky turned colors. No two sunsets were ever the same, but each one was breathtakingly beautiful.

Squaring her shoulders, she climbed the three steps to the door, determined to teach Shad Zuniga to read, determined to make him like it so that he would encourage the Indian children to come to school.

She knew he was there even before she stepped inside the room, felt her heart catch as she saw him standing at the far window, looking out. Slowly, he turned to face her, and Loralee marveled anew at how very handsome he was. He was dressed as before, in stained buckskin pants and a sleeveless vest, and she wondered if those were the only clothes he owned. He was bigger than she remembered, taller, broader, and his presence seemed to dwarf the room. She felt her cheeks flame as his eyes moved slowly over her face and figure.

"You're early," Loralee said brightly. "Let's get started, shall we? Why don't you sit there?" She gestured at the first desk in the front row. It was larger than the others, having been designed for an older child. "I'll get your book and we'll begin."

She was talking much too fast, but she couldn't seem to help herself. Dropping her shawl over the back of her chair, she pulled a beginning McGuffey's Reader from the shelf and offered it to Zuniga. McGuffey's Readers were a five-book series written in the 1830s and 40s by a professor named William Homer McGuffey. They contained short stories, verses, pronunciation and spelling lessons and were used in nearly every school in the country.

Zuniga took the book hesitantly, as if it were a snake with venomous fangs, or some kind of deadly poison.

"We'll start with the alphabet," Loralee said. She went to the chalkboard and began to print the letters on the board, saying each one aloud as she wrote it in bold strokes.

As the lesson progressed, she grew less nervous. She loved teaching, and Shad Zuniga was an apt pupil. He quickly caught on to the rudiments of reading, quickly memorized the alphabet so that he could recite it from memory. The lesson, meant to last an hour, stretched into two.

As the minutes passed, Loralee forgot that Shad Zuniga was an Indian, a warrior. She forgot that they were alone. It was so good to be teaching at last, to feel she was accomplishing a part of what she had set out to do. Zuniga had a keen mind and he quickly grasped whatever concept she was working on.

Zuniga listened intently as Loralee printed his name on the chalkboard, pronouncing each syllable. Her voice was soft, easy to listen to. His eyes lingered on her breasts as her hand guided the chalk. Her movements were graceful, feminine.

She was flushed with pleasure and a sense of fulfillment when the lesson ended. It had gone well, and she was pleased that she had finally been able to use the skills she had been taught.

"You've done very well," she said, smiling. "You'll be reading and writing in no time at all."

Zuniga said nothing as he closed the book and handed it to her. Already he could see the value of a written language. The Apache history was drawn on hides, or handed down verbally from one generation to the next. If his people could write, they could make a permanent record of their battles and beliefs, their customs and traditions, the names of their leaders. He knew that much of their heritage was being lost as the old ways died out. Secretly he had always had a grudging admiration for the white man's knowledge, for his ability to make guns and ammunition.

"Will you send the children tomorrow?" Loralee asked.

"I cannot send them," Zuniga said, rising. "I will tell the elders of the tribe that I think it would be a good thing for our people to learn the white man's letters, but it will be up to them to decide."

Loralee stared at Zuniga. She had taken it for granted that once he came to school, the children would come, too. Now he was talking about getting the approval of the elders. What if the elders didn't approve?

"But I thought—"

"I will tell the children what I am learning," Zuniga assured her with a hint of a smile. "I am sure most of them will want to come."

"Thank you, Mr. Zuniga. I appreciate your help."

"I will see you tomorrow night."

"Yes."

They stood facing each other, neither moving or speaking, for several moments. Loralee felt mesmerized by his gaze, felt her heart begin to pound wildly in her breast. He was so near, so very near. A queer little trembling filled her belly as he continued to gaze into her eyes. She had a mad impulsive urge to reach out and lay her hand on his chest, to feel the beat of his heart against her hand. She noticed how long his lashes were, thick and sooty. His lower lip was full, sensual, and she longed to explore it. Almost, she reached out to touch it with her finger. But, of course, she didn't. Instead, she pulled her gaze from his and clenched her hands at her sides, her nails digging into her palms. He was a stranger, an Indian. Likely, he would laugh with amusement if he knew what she was thinking. Still, she could not help remembering the many days when he had sat up on the hill, watching her, could not forget the invisible current that had flowed between them. It had been real, not merely her imagination. She could feel it even now. Could he?

Zuniga sucked in a deep breath, all his senses absorbing the sight and scent of her. She was so near. He yearned to reach out and unpin her hair, to run his fingers through the heavy silken mass. He felt his manhood begin to throb with desire as his eyes moved to her pretty pink mouth. What would it be like to taste her, to touch her, to possess her? He knew instinctively that she had never known a man. What would it be like to initiate her into the shared pleasures between a man and a woman? He suspected she would be warm and willing, eager to learn. But only for the right man. He longed to be that man, to wipe the innocence from her eyes and see them flame with desire.

His eyes traveled from her face to her figure. The dark blue dress was plain and unflattering. Was that why she had worn it, to hide the smooth flesh and lush curves he knew must surely lie beneath? He had watched her for too long not to know that her figure was round and ripe, had spent too many nights dreaming of what must lie beneath the many layers of clothing white women wore to be put off by an ugly dress. She might try to disguise her shape, but she could not hide it entirely. Her neck was slender, her hands small and dainty, her ankles trim.

The silence hung between them like an invisible wall. Almost, Zuniga reached out to draw her close. Almost, he bent down to claim her lips. But the time was not right, the place was not right. Abruptly, he turned on his heel and walked out of the room into the night.

The next morning Zuniga swung onto the bare back of the dun stallion and rode west toward the mountains. The day was cool and clear, with a hint of fall in the air. The stallion stepped lively, its eyes showing white as a gust of wind sent a tumbleweed skittering across the trail. Head high, tail swishing, the dun pranced, eager to run.

With a grin, Zuniga gave the stallion its head and the big stud broke into a lope, flying over the sandy ground as if it had wings. Zuniga squinted against the wind, relishing the chill air whipping through his hair and the surging power of the animal beneath him.

Sometime later, he drew the stallion to a halt at the tree line. Dismounting, he slipped a bow and a quiver of arrows from his shoulder. Placing them against a tree trunk, he gave the stud an affectionate slap on the neck; then, squatting on his heels, he rolled a cigarette.

He stared into the distance. In the old days, the tribe would have been hunting now, looking for enough game to sustain them through the winter. The women would have been repairing lodge covers, fashioning winter moccasins and robes. . . .

In the old days, he would have come to a place like this to seek a vision from the Great Spirit. Naked save for clout and moccasins, without food or water, he would have prayed to Usen for a sign to guide him through life and into battle. Nachi's vision had been of a great white eagle who had promised him strength in battle and long life.

Zuniga grinned faintly. Once, when he was eleven or twelve, he had gone high into the Dragoon Mountains. There, for three days and three nights, he had fasted and prayed, imploring the gods for a sign. Morning and evening, he had offered tobacco and hoddentin to the four directions, entreating Usen for a vision to guide him through life. On the evening of the third day, with his belly crying for food and his mouth dry as dust, a vision had come to him, as clear and real as anything he had ever seen. He had never told anyone of his vision, not even Nachi.

Closing his eyes, he saw it all again: his people going down in defeat to the superior strength of the white man. He had seen friends and relatives die in battle, or waste away from the white man's sicknesses, but he and Nachi had survived. Then, as the vision drew to a close, he caught a glimpse of himself surrounded by thick iron bars. That part of his vision had also come true, he mused ruefully, for now, living on the reservation, he often felt as though he were imprisoned, walled in by invisible bars heavier than steel, more binding than iron.

Opening his eyes, he gazed down the mountain. His cousin, Short Bear, had gone to seek a vision two years ago, at the age of fourteen. Short Bear had fasted and prayed in the prescribed manner, but no vision had come to him. Short Bear had been sorely disappointed. Even now, Zuniga wondered why the boy had failed to receive a medicine dream when he had prayed so earnestly and desired it so much. Had the boy failed because he had lacked the faith necessary to receive a gift from the gods, or had the Great Spirit stopped sending visions now that the people were no longer living wild and free? Nachi claimed Usen was displeased with his red children because they no longer lived in the ancient way, and perhaps the old man was right. Who could say for certain?

Zuniga smiled when he thought of his grandfather. Nachi had fought with both Cochise and Geronimo, with Mangas Colorado, and Victorio. They had known many victories, and many defeats. But now Mangas was dead, killed by soldiers. Victorio was dead, killed by a sniper. Cochise was dead. Of all the great old chiefs, only Geronimo was still living. He was a celebrity now, a living legend. He had ridden in Roosevelt's inaugural parade. He had appeared at the St. Louis Exposition the year before, where he had been a notable attraction for the tourists. It was said he sold photographs of himself to the whites for fifty cents. Zuniga thought it was disgusting, the way Geronimo sold photographs and souvenirs to the whites. The old warrior had sold his dignity for a few dollars, Zuniga thought, but he kept such opinions to himself, knowing that

Nachi would be displeased if he spoke badly about the old chief.

Sometimes, alone in the lodge late at night, Nachi grieved aloud for the old days, lamenting the passing of the buffalo, the loss of their old hunting grounds. He missed the war dances and the victory celebrations, the warriors he had grown up with and fought with. But then, Zuniga mused, they all grieved for the past in one way or another.

It had been Nachi who had taught Shad how to make a good strong bow out of the wood of the wild mulberry, admonishing him to choose a piece that was straight and had no knots in it. The bow was held straight up and down for close shots, crossways for longer distances. Bowstrings were made from a length of sinew from the back of a deer, or from the muscle on the back of a hind leg. It was necessary to wear a wrist guard made of leather or tanned hide to protect one's wrist from the bowstring.

Arrows were made from reeds or cane growing in the mountains or along river bottoms. The best cane was found on the Gila River. Nachi had told him that long ago, when the Apache first began to make arrows, they had used only two feathers, but the shaft flew crooked, so they tried four feathers, but that made the shaft fly in a curve. Three feathers made the shaft fly straight. Many kinds of feathers were used, but Nachi preferred the feathers of the red-tailed hawk.

Nachi had also shown Shad how to make poison for his arrows by drying a deer's spleen and then grinding it to powder and mixing it with the ground root or stalk of nettles. The mixture was put in a small sack made from a part of a deer's large intestine. When all was ready, Nachi spit in the bag, then tied it up tight so none of the bad air would escape. The bag was hung from a tree for four days, sometimes five, until the contents were rotten and in liquid form. The poison was very effective. A deer shot with a poison arrow died in a short time, even if the arrow only scratched it.

Quivers were made from a variety of hides, usually horse, deer, wolf, or mountain lion. If the hide had a tail on it, it was left on as a decoration. A quiver usually held between thirty and forty arrows.

Zuniga swore softly as he stubbed out his cigarette. Rising easily to his feet, he reached for the bow and quiver that Nachi had given him many years ago. The bow was good and strong, made from unblemished mulberry wood; the arrows were of cane, fletched with the feathers of a red-tailed hawk; the quiver was made from the hide of a mountain lion Nachi had killed in the Sierra Madre Mountains.

For a moment, Zuniga's fingers caressed the quiver, and then he cursed again. He had come to hunt, not to get maudlin over a way of life that was forever gone. Still, he could not help yearning for the old days as he started up the hill. He remembered what it had been like to live wild in the Dragoon Mountains. He had been old enough to fight in the last battles between his people and the whites. He knew what it was like to take a life, to dip his hands in the blood of the enemy. And he had loved it all, the fighting, the killing, the thrill of the chase, the excitement of victory. But the victories had been few, the defeats many. The warriors the Apache lost in battle could not be replaced, but the whites seemed to have an unending number of men to send against them, an inexhaustible supply of guns and ammunition, and in the end the Indians had lost their fight for freedom.

Zuniga had gone into hiding in the mountains, refusing to surrender his freedom, refusing to be penned up on the white man's reservation, to wear a metal tag around his neck inscribed with a number that identified him on the Agency record books. It was only when word came to him that Nachi was sick and alone that he had moved to the reservation. The Indian Agent had assigned him a number, but he had thrown it away. He did not want the white man's charity and he did not show up at the fort on ration day.

Zuniga sighed heavily. If only he had been born fifty years earlier. The Indian had been supreme then. Apache, Kiowa, Coman-

che, Sioux, Arapahoe, Crow, Cheyenne, all
the tribes that had once ruled the vast plains
and prairies west of the Missouri had been
subdued by the whites, forced off their native
homeland and confined to reservations.

Thoughts of the whites brought Loralee
Warfield to mind. He was drawn to her in a
way he could not understand or explain. His
dreams were filled with her golden image,
his thoughts were never far from her. He
wondered if she was as aware of him as he
was of her. When they were together, it was
almost as if he could touch her without
touching her. Had she noticed? Did she feel
the same?

He walked softly through the wooded
hillside, his keen eyes searching for game
while his thoughts lingered on Loralee.
What would she think of him if she knew he
had killed his father with his bare hands?
She wouldn't be so eager to teach him to
read and write then, he mused sourly, or so
willing to be alone with him in the schoolhouse at night.

He swore under his breath, gripped by
the old fear that sometimes came to haunt
him, the fear that he would end up like his
father, just another shiftless Apache buck
who drank too much and vented his frustration by beating his wife and making life hell
for everyone around him.

Zuniga came to a halt as he spied a deer
grazing on a patch of yellow grass. Taking his

bow from his shoulder, he put an arrow to the bowstring, sighted down the shaft, and let the arrow fly. The cane shaft flew straight and true, piercing the deer's throat, killing it instantly.

He felt a sense of satisfaction as he padded quietly toward his kill. Let the other Indians eat Agency beef. Tonight, he and Nachi would feast on venison steaks and tongue.

Tonight . . .

He moved quickly, draping the heavy carcass over the dun's withers. Tonight he would be with Loralee.

3

Loralee stood before the mirror, brushing out her long hair. It was Saturday, and the morning was bright and clear. She smiled at her reflection as she coiled her hair into its customary knot and fastened it in place. So many things had happened in such a short time. Shad Zuniga had kept his word. He had told the Apache children and their parents that he was learning to read and write the white man's language. The elders had decided it was a good thing. And the children had started to attend school.

Three little girls had been the first to come to class. Black eyes solemn, faces grave, they had arrived at the schoolhouse promptly at eight in the morning. Loralee had greeted them with a smile. They were darling children, she thought as she bid them sit down. All three were dressed in colorful long-sleeved blouses, corduroy jumpers, and moccasins. They wore their long black hair in twin braids tied with red ribbon.

Their names, she learned, were Red Bird, Little Blossom, and Miranda. Miranda was a half-breed. Her mother lived on the reservation. Her father had been a white man who lingered in the territory long enough to get Miranda's mother pregnant and then disappeared, never to be heard from again.

The girls had listened attentively to everything Loralee said, grinned with pleasure when she taught them how to write their names.

The next day, Red Bird, Little Blossom, and Miranda were at the school waiting for Loralee. Red Bird had persuaded her two older sisters to come to school, too. Their names were Yellow Grass Girl and Deer Eyes.

Now, five weeks later, Loralee had sixteen students, eleven girls and five boys, ranging in age from five to seventeen. The boys made it clear from the start that they did not want to be there, and Loralee knew it was only Shad Zuniga's influence that had persuaded the boys to attend school.

The boys. They were forever thinking up

new ways to devil her, and Short Bear was the worst of all. He was a handsome boy, about five feet, six inches tall, with dark skin, shoulder-length black hair, and dark chocolate eyes. Loralee was certain it was Short Bear who left the little surprises in her desk drawer each morning. A dead scorpion the first day, a half-eaten rodent the next, a live snake the third. Loralee tried not to let her revulsion show as she bravely removed the creatures, both dead and alive, from her desk and tossed them out the window into the brush.

Slowly she gained the respect of the boys. Her sincere affection for the children, coupled with her obvious admiration and respect for the Apache people as a whole, won most of the children to her side.

As time passed, the frogs and lizards and other repulsive creatures stopped making an appearance in her desk drawer, and Loralee felt as though she had achieved a major victory.

She set apart an hour of each day to let the children teach her, and gradually she picked up a few Apache words and phrases. It was a harsh, difficult tongue to master, but she learned that *ugashe!* meant go, *ciye* meant son, *cima* meant mother. *Nahleen* meant maiden or young girl, *chelee* meant horse. *Besh-shea-gar* meant iron-that-shoots.

Loralee listened to their stories, played their games, admired their drawings, and never gave up hope that more of the children would come to school.

Short Bear remained a problem she could not solve. He would not read aloud. He would not answer questions. He would not do the sums she wrote on the chalkboard. She often wondered why the boy continued to come to class at all. He spent most of his time staring out the window, a sullen expression on his face.

When she learned that Short Bear was Zuniga's cousin, she told Zuniga of the problem she was having with the boy, but Zuniga only shrugged.

"I made him agree to go to your school," Shad had said, shrugging, "but I cannot make him learn."

It was sad, Loralee mused, sad that progress and civilization had swept over the Apache, changing their way of life, routing them from their land, putting them under the thumb of the white man, whom they distrusted. In the old days, Short Bear would have become a warrior. He would have known who he was and what was expected of him. He would have learned to hunt and fight and live off the land. Now, he needed to learn to read and write and cipher. But he did not want to learn. Still, like it or not, the Indians' only hope of survival was to be integrated into the white community, to learn to live and think like the whites.

And Loralee wanted to be a part of that

change. She knew the older Apaches were reluctant to try new things, stubbornly clinging to the old ways, but she was here to teach the young, to help them learn the language and culture of her people, to help them increase their knowledge of the world, a world that was rapidly changing. Even Loralee found it hard to believe some of the things she had seen and heard in the last few years. Who would have thought that anyone could invent a machine that was actually capable of flight? And who would have guessed that motor cars would be more than just a passing fancy for the very rich? Even more fascinating than flying machines and horseless carriages was the advent of moving pictures. She had watched, mesmerized, as *The Great Train Robbery,* filmed in the wilds of New Jersey in 1903, unfolded before her eyes. Fully twelve minutes long, it had been the most amazing thing she had ever seen, and well worth the five cents it had cost for admission. Loralee had been on the edge of her seat the whole time. How ironic, she had thought at the time, to sit in an Eastern theater to watch a movie about a train robbery when trains were still being held up in the West, and men were still dying in gunfights on the streets of Western towns. But the movie was only make believe, and it had been thrilling.

Most of the Indians living on the reservation would probably never see a flying machine or a moving picture, yet Loralee thought it was important for them to know such things existed, to know what great strides were being made in the outside world, to look forward to the myriad changes that were coming instead of closing their eyes and remaining in ignorance. Teaching the children to read and write was the first step. It would not be easy to teach the Apache children, but she welcomed the challenge. Perhaps, if she could teach the children, the children could teach their parents.

Zuniga continued to meet her at the schoolhouse each weekday evening just after sundown. He had quickly mastered the alphabet and was rapidly learning to read and write. He had a quick mind and rarely forgot anything once she explained it to him.

She began to teach him basic arithmetic, pleased beyond words when he showed an aptitude for figures. So many people thought the Indians were dull and stupid, unable to learn. She was glad to know they were wrong. Zuniga was neither dull nor stupid. He was a grown man, one who was quickly learning to read and write and cipher, an Indian who was every bit as intelligent as any white man she had ever known.

There was only one problem in teaching Shad Zuniga. It was becoming harder and harder to concentrate on teaching when they were alone together. Each time she

stopped near his desk, each time she bent
down to study a problem or check his work,
she was acutely aware of him as a man, a
very handsome, virile man. His presence
filled the schoolroom. He was so very male,
she could not forget for a moment that she
was a woman, a woman who had never
known a man intimately.

Daily the attraction between them grew
stronger. Loralee did her best to ignore it,
refusing to believe she could be physically
attracted to a man who was different from
her in so many ways. And yet she spent hours
thinking of him, dreaming of him, wondering what it would be like to be held in his
arms. No other man had ever caused her
such confusion. Shad Zuniga never said or
did anything remotely intimate, yet she
yearned for him in a way that was frightening in its intensity. Why was she so drawn to
him? She had been courted by many attractive young men in the East. She had been
wooed and coaxed, even kissed by a few of
her bolder suitors, but none of them had
ever piqued her interest or stoked her desire
the way Zuniga did. She conjured up his
image in her mind and could find no fault in
it. His face was strong and masculine, his
body beautifully proportioned and well-
muscled, his hair long and as black as a
raven's wing. . . .

Zuniga, Zuniga, Zuniga. It seemed she
could think of nothing else. Slipping into her

riding habit, she saddled her horse, which she had named Lady, and set out for a ride in the hills. She purposefully took the trail that led away from Shad Zuniga's lodge. She did not want to think of him, or see him.

The day was warm, the sky a bright blue. Loralee smiled happily as she put Lady into a slow trot. Back East, she had never ridden a horse except once or twice in the park on Sunday after church. Now, she rode just about every day for the sheer pleasure of it. There was something wonderfully relaxing about horseback riding. Days when she was irritable from trying to cope with Short Bear, or simply out of sorts, were quickly put right by an hour in the saddle. Once, she had mentioned to Mike how she felt about riding, but he had looked at her as if she were slightly crazy. Horses were a necessary pain in the ass, Mike had said, and then apologized for his crude language.

With a sigh of pure enjoyment, Loralee urged Lady up into the foothills. It was cool and shady riding beneath the trees. The ground was covered with pine needles that muffled the sound of Lady's iron-shod hooves. Squirrels chattered at Loralee as she passed by. A deer, graceful as a ballet dancer, darted for cover, its tail flashing white as it disappeared in the underbrush. Later, a skunk waddled across the trail, followed by a brood of three striped babies. Loralee held her breath as the family passed by, hoping the animal would not become alarmed. She breathed a sigh of relief when the furry little creatures made their way around a log and out of sight.

Loralee was halfway up the hillside when she heard the sound of an axe striking wood. Pausing, she cocked her head to one side, listening to the rhythmic sound. It was coming from her right and was quite near. Was it possible that someone besides Shad Zuniga and his grandfather lived in the hills? Mike had not mentioned it, but it might have slipped his mind, or perhaps he had not wanted her to know.

Curious, she reined Lady toward the sound, marveling at the dainty way the mare picked her way through the brush, stepping over fallen logs as though she were a fine lady who didn't want to soil her shoes.

Some moments later, Loralee rounded a huge gray boulder and reined Lady to an abrupt halt. There, only a few feet away, stood Shad Zuniga. He was clad in a brief buckskin clout, thick-soled moccasins, a faded red headband, and nothing more. His coppery skin was sheened with a fine layer of sweat. The muscles in his arms and back rippled like water as he swung the axe through the air, slicing cleanly through the log at his feet.

Loralee had seldom seen a man without a shirt, never one without trousers, and she gazed in rapt fascination at the sight of so much exposed male flesh. The muscles in Zuniga's arms and legs were clearly defined as he hefted the heavy axe, and she noted with pleasure that he was strong, and beautiful to watch.

Zuniga felt a sudden heat suffuse him, a heat that was caused, not by the sun, but by Loralee's gaze wandering over his flesh. He had been instantly aware of her presence. The mere sight of her, the fact that she was so obviously admiring what she saw, filled him with elation, and desire.

Loralee's cheeks burned with embarrassment when she realized she was staring at Zuniga in a very unladylike way, and that Zuniga was no longer chopping wood but watching her as well, a bemused expression on his swarthy face. He did not seem the least bit ashamed by the fact that he was very nearly naked.

"Good . . . good afternoon," Loralee stammered.

Zuniga nodded in reply, and then he grinned faintly. She would be shocked indeed if she happened to glance in the direction of his loincloth again and see the very real evidence of his desire for her stirring to life.

"I . . . I was just out . . . out riding."

Zuniga nodded again, his dark eyes alight with amusement at her obvious discomfort. She made a lovely picture, sitting primly astride the dainty black mare. Her riding habit was of dark blue velvet and showed off her full breasts and trim waist to full advantage. Her cheeks were flushed with color, her brown eyes luminous. She wore her hair coiled in a neat knot at the nape of her neck. There were black leather riding gloves on her hands, smart black kid boots on her feet. She looked every inch a lady, cool and collected, save for the high color in her cheeks, and the single drop of perspiration that trickled down her neck and disappeared inside the collar of her blouse.

Zuniga followed the tiny drop of sweat with his eyes, swallowing hard as it vanished from sight into the cleft between her breasts.

Tearing his eyes away, he drew a ragged breath. It was disconcerting, the effect she had on him. A look, a smile, her very presence filled him with such longing it was almost painful. Why, of all the women he had known, did it have to be a white woman who fired his blood? A woman who was forbidden. Untouchable. But so desirable.

The silence stretched between them, loud and awkward. Zuniga mopped the sweat from his brow with the back of his hand. Bending, he picked up the wood he had cut and tossed it on the pile stacked a few feet away.

Loralee watched his every move, awed by the play of muscles beneath his taut skin, by the easy strength in his arms and shoulders and back. She knew she should leave immediately. She had no business staring at a man who was nearly naked, no business being in the hills alone with a man of Zuniga's reputation. But she made no move to leave.

She swallowed hard as Zuniga dropped the axe and walked toward her. His long legs covered the distance between them in four easy strides. She licked her lips nervously as he laid one hand on Lady's neck. His face, damp with sweat, was only inches from Loralee's. Her heart beat wildly as his eyes met hers.

"You should not be out here alone," he said, stroking Lady's neck. "It is not safe."

Loralee nodded. How odd, she thought, that he would say the very thing she had been thinking only moments earlier.

"There are wild animals in the woods," Zuniga went on. His voice was strong and deep, washing over her like an invisible caress. "Bears, wolves, mountain lions."

Indians, Loralee thought. Unable to draw her eyes away from his, she nodded again, wondering why it was so difficult to speak. She was aware of his hand, big and brown, still stroking the mare's neck. Almost, she could feel that hand stroking her skin.

"Next time you feel like riding this far from the fort, take someone with you."

Loralee nodded a third time. She wondered fleetingly if she was being warned to stay away from Zuniga himself. She tried to think of some clever reply, but she couldn't concentrate, not when he was so near. His eyes were as black as ebony, deep and mysterious, filled with secrets she longed to discover.

"You had best head for home," Zuniga suggested. He gave the mare's neck a final pat, then took a step backward.

Loralee shook her head to clear it. What was happening to her? Why did this man have such a strange effect on all her senses, making her feel weak and warm and fluttery all over?

Confused, she turned the mare for home. It wasn't until she reached the bottom of the hill that she realized she hadn't said goodbye.

At home, she took a leisurely bubble bath, determined to put Shad Zuniga out of her thoughts once and for all. Instead, she would think about Sergeant Michael Schofield, who was taking her to a dance at the fort that evening. Mike was a wonderful man. He was kind, polite, considerate, ambitious, attentive, and civilized. And he loved her. He hadn't said so, but, womanlike, she knew how he felt better than he did.

Stepping from the tub, she toweled herself dry and dusted with powder before slipping into her undergarments.

She felt safe with Mike, she thought as she pulled on her stockings. He didn't fill her with strange emotions, didn't cause her heart to pound erratically, didn't make her mouth go dry or her palms sweat. She never wondered what it would be like to feel his hands on her flesh. . . .

Without quite knowing how it happened, Mike faded from her mind and she found herself thinking of Zuniga again, remembering how the sunlight had danced on his sweat-sheened flesh, how easily he had swung the heavy axe, how lightly he had stroked Lady's neck. She shivered convulsively as she imagined that big brown hand sliding over her thigh, felt the hot blood of shame wash into her cheeks at such a bold, unladylike thought.

Her hands were trembling as she stepped into a dress of light blue flowered silk. It was her favorite gown. The neck was tantalizingly low and square, the sleeves were short and puffy, edged with delicate white lace. A wide blue sash spanned her waist, tying in the back in a perky bow. The skirt was full and swished lightly when she walked. She threaded a matching blue ribbon through her hair.

She stared at her reflection as she applied a touch of color to her cheeks. Try as she might, she could not banish Shad Zuniga's image from her mind. He was wild and dangerous, more handsome than any man she had ever seen. Most disturbing of all was the way she responded to him. A look from his midnight eyes, the slightest touch of his hand, and she trembled with a primal emotion she dared not examine too closely.

Picking up her gloves, she gazed, unseeing, out the bedroom window. What would it be like to be held in Zuniga's arms? What would it be like to feel his lips on hers, to feel his hands stroking her back, to feel his fingers running through her hair?

She was glad when Mike arrived, interrupting her wayward thoughts.

The dance was in full swing when they arrived at the fort. Colored streamers and bright paper lanterns decorated the mess hall. Long tables covered with heavy damask cloths held large platters of meat and cheese and a variety of rolls and bread. An enormous crystal bowl was filled with red punch. At the far end of the hall, a half-dozen musicians filled the air with music.

Loralee smiled and shook hands with the post commander and his wife. She continued to smile as Mike introduced her to his friends and fellow officers, the names and faces blurring together after the first few introductions.

Glancing about, Loralee saw there were only four women present, including herself. The single men clustered around Loralee, eager to dance with her, to talk to her, or just to look at her. White women were scarce on the reservation and Loralee was the youngest, the prettiest, and the only woman not married. Mike was generous in letting her dance with the other men, but he was careful to keep several dances for himself, including the last one.

Loralee danced every dance. Most of her partners were young. A few were veteran soldiers with graying hair and service stripes that indicated more than twenty years in the Army. But young or old, they were all polite and well-mannered, and they all flirted with her outrageously, promising to marry her in a minute if she would only say the word. They exclaimed over the golden color of her hair, remarked on the flawless beauty of her face and figure, complimented her dancing.

Loralee had never enjoyed so much attention or received so much flattery in her life. It was a heady experience and she had to remind herself that it was all in fun and not to be taken seriously.

The men were anxious to please her and she was forced to accept several glasses of punch from men who were eager to wait upon her. To spare their feelings, she drank a considerable amount of punch before Mike mentioned that someone had emptied a bottle of whiskey into the punch bowl.

"Really?" Loralee exclaimed. "Well, it's certainly delicious!"

Mike laughed softly. "I think you may be just a little bit intoxicated," he mused.

"Do you think so?" Loralee asked. "I've never tasted whiskey before."

"Well, you'd better slow down," Mike warned good naturedly, "or you'll have a whale of a headache in the morning."

Later, during a lull in the dancing, the commander's wife took Loralee aside to "get better acquainted." Stella Freeman was a tall, angular woman with iron gray hair and sharp green eyes. Little went on at the fort or on the reservation that she was unaware of. She disliked the West and detested the Indians, but she made the best of it because it couldn't be helped. Her husband's life was here, and a woman's place was at her husband's side, giving him support. She could not abide people who complained about their lot in life. You played the cards you were dealt and hoped for a better hand in the future. She had learned to adjust to the West, to the climate, and to the rigors of life on an Army post. What couldn't be changed must be endured, and what could be changed, she changed. She insisted that her husband's officers behave impeccably. She tolerated no profanity in her presence, and insisted that the men smoke outside. Her home was as tastefully furnished as any home in the East, and she maintained a high standard of living.

Just now, she smiled as she took the new schoolteacher aside. Many women came West in hopes of finding a husband or a career. Most of them did not stay long. The West could be a hard, cruel place, even in these modern times.

"Mike tells me you're from the East," Stella Freeman remarked.

"Yes," Loralee replied. "Philadelphia."

"A lovely city. You're very brave to come out here to try and teach the savages to read and write, my dear. Why, it was only a few years ago that they were scalping people in their beds."

"I'm not brave at all," Loralee answered, bristling at the woman's use of the word "savage" to describe her students.

"Of course you are, my dear," Stella Freeman insisted. "We all are." She smiled benignly at the two women who had come to stand beside her, including them in the conversation.

The woman standing nearest Stella Freeman was a rather portly, middle-aged woman with russet-colored hair and washed-out gray eyes. She wore a high-necked dark brown silk dress that Loralee thought more appropriate for a funeral than a dance. The woman introduced herself as Martha Cogan, wife of Major Tom Cogan.

The other woman was hardly more than a girl, Loralee saw with surprise. She was quite tiny, with pale skin, ash blond hair, and mild blue eyes. She smiled shyly as she introduced herself as Sally Stockman, wife of Sergeant-Major Ken Stockman.

"People with weak hearts don't last very long in the West, I'm afraid," Stella Freeman declared, continuing her discourse. "I know.

76

I've been out here for years." She sighed dramatically. "More years than I care to recall. But Bradley wanted to campaign in the West, and he's done very well. Tell me, my dear, how is your little school coming along?"

"Quite well," Loralee answered, trying to hide her dislike for Stella Freeman. "I have sixteen children enrolled now and hope to have more very soon."

Stella Freeman patted Loralee's arm. "Of course you will. I don't mean to pry," she said in a serious tone of voice, "but one of the men told me you're tutoring that scoundrel, Shad Zuniga. Surely he was mistaken."

"It's quite true."

"Do you think that's wise?" Martha Cogan blurted. "The man's a savage!"

"I think it's very wise," Loralee responded firmly. "If it wasn't for Mr. Zuniga, none of the children would have come to school at all. He's been a tremendous help."

Stella Freeman rolled her eyes heavenward. "Zuniga, a help," she murmured. She placed one hand over her heart dramatically. "Lord, have mercy. The man is nothing but trouble. Why, he's got a gun hidden somewhere in the hills. He refuses to be counted on ration day, refuses to accept the food and clothing that are his due. Really, dear, the man is quite impossible. Fortunately, he seems content to spend most of his time up

77

in the hills with his grandfather. I don't know what would happen if he took it into his head to try and influence the others to rebel. For some reason, the young men all look up to him. I can't imagine why."

"Perhaps for the very reasons you disapprove of him," Loralee said. She could have bitten her tongue for speaking so hastily. Martha Cogan sent her a withering glance, and Sally Stockman blushed furiously. No one ever disputed the commander's wife. It was an unwritten law.

"Perhaps," Stella Freeman said stiffly. "You must come to our house one afternoon for tea so we can get better acquainted. Ah, here comes your young man to claim you. He's quite handsome, our Sergeant Schofield. Don't you think so?"

Loralee flushed under Stella Freeman's probing gaze, nodded quickly before taking Mike's arm. She could feel Stella Freeman's disapproval as she walked away. Why had she defended Shad Zuniga when the commander's wife so heartily disapproved of him? What had she hoped to gain?

It was quite late when Mike escorted Loralee back to her house. They stood together at the door, reluctant to see the evening end. Loralee did not resist when Mike took her in his arms. His mouth was warm when he kissed her, firm upon her own as she kissed him back. It was pleasant, kissing Mike, but there were no fireworks, no bells, none of the wondrous excitement the novels described in vivid detail when the hero took the girl in his arms.

"Good night, Loralee," Mike said huskily. "I had a great time."

"Me, too. Thanks, Mike."

He bent and kissed her once more. "Sleep well."

Loralee stood outside, watching Mike ride away. Then, with a little sigh, she went inside to get ready for bed. But sleep wouldn't come. She was too keyed up from the music and the dancing and the unfamiliar effects of the whiskey.

Dressed in her nightgown and a bulky robe, she wandered outside to walk in the yard. The night was dark, the sky like black velvet decorated with stars and a cold silver moon. In the distance, a coyote yapped a melancholy tune.

How different things must have been just a few short years ago, Loralee mused. She would not have dared to wander outside alone and unarmed then. People had been afraid to sleep at night, fearful of being killed in their beds by prowling Apache warriors. Men had carried rifles wherever they went, even while plowing their fields. Women had been afraid to venture out of the safety of their homes. How frightening it must have been, never knowing from one day to the next if the Apaches would strike, never knowing when you kissed your husband goodbye if he would return home that evening, or if his body would be found lying in the dirt in a pool of blood.

Loralee shivered. Drawing her robe more tightly around her, she laughed softly. She was letting her imagination get the best of her. Fortunately, those bloodthirsty days were gone. . . .

She gasped as a dark silouette emerged from the stand of trees at the south end of the house and came toward her.

Fear was a tight lump in her throat that made screaming impossible; a cold fist clamped tightly around her insides, leaving her too weak to flee for the safety of the house. Petrified, she stared at the rider coming toward her, his face as dark as the shadow of death.

As he rode out of the shadows, moonlight played over his face and shoulders, shining brightly on his copper-hued skin and midnight hair, enveloping him in a silvery haze.

Zuniga. Relief washed through Loralee like water through a sieve, leaving her weak and trembling. She watched, mesmerized, as he slid gracefully from the dun's bare back and walked toward her, his steps graceful, arrogant.

Loralee's mouth went dry as Zuniga came to a halt only a few inches away from her. He was so tall, so very big, he made her feel small, vulnerable, helpless. It was most disconcerting, and a little exciting.

She looked up at him, her lips slightly parted, her heart beating wildly in her breast. He smelled of leather and sweat, of woodsmoke and sage. His nearness, the sight and the scent of him, all filled her with a peculiar longing so that she swayed toward him, driven by an emotion she did not recognize. Did he know how his mere presence affected her?

Zuniga's eyes never left Loralee's face. Her skin was beautiful in the soft glow of the moonlight, her lips pink and slightly moist, her brown eyes as warm as the earth on a summer day.

He was tempted to draw her close, but he could not take her here. The chance of discovery was too great. And yet he could not keep from touching her. Slowly he lifted his hand. Gently he stroked the curve of her cheek. Her skin was smooth and soft and so inviting.

With an effort, he turned away and vaulted lightly onto the back of the dun.

Moments later, she was standing alone in the moonlight, wondering if it had all been a dream.

Loralee moved through the next day like a sleepwalker. As was her habit, she went to Sunday morning church with Mike, though she didn't hear one word of the sermon.

When she closed her eyes to pray, Shad Zuniga's dark image played across her mind, his face handsome and mysterious, strangely compelling. Their encounter the night before had been brief, silent, and yet something had happened between them, something she could not put a name to. Deep in her heart, she knew she would not have objected if he had taken her in his arms. In truth, she was disappointed that he had not tried to kiss her. The thought of his mouth touching hers sent shivers down her spine and filled her heart with guilt. Here she was, sitting in church, yearning for the kiss of a man who was virtually a stranger to her.

After church, Mike took Loralee to lunch at one of the restaurants in town. He was in a jovial mood. Loralee was lovely in a dress of soft pink muslin trimmed in yards and yards of white lace. A perky bonnet matched the dress. The more he saw of her, the more he loved her. Soon, he mused, soon he would propose to her. If all went well, she would accept his offer of marriage. If she refused, he would not give up. He would woo her and court her until he won her heart, no matter how long it took.

They went for a walk after lunch. Loralee listened as Mike outlined his plans for the future. She nodded and smiled and made all the proper replies, yet a part of her saw only a swarthy face and arresting black eyes that had the power to make her heart pound and her stomach behave queerly.

That evening they went to Colonel Freeman's house for dinner, and Loralee suffered through three hours of listening to Stella Freeman air her views about the Apaches, the West, the Army, and President Theodore Roosevelt, who had been elected to a second term of office.

Stella Freeman did not care for Mr. Roosevelt, possibly because everyone else did. Roosevelt was a man larger than life, Loralee thought, even though he was physically a rather dumpy man, heavily bespectacled. But he had enormous energy and a seemingly endless capacity for getting things done. It was rumored he drank his coffee with no less than seven lumps of sugar from a cup that was, according to one source, more in the nature of a bathtub. He was a soldier, a statesman, an adventurer, and the author of twenty-four books. Loralee's favorite bit of advice from Teddy was, "Do not hit at all if it can be avoided, but never hit softly."

Stella Freeman scowled when Loralee expressed her admiration for the President. "Some president," Stella remarked caustically. "Why, he acts more like a boy than a man. Playing baseball on the lawn of the White House! Imagine. And all those animals running around. Why, the man has everything from squirrels to bears living there. Is he running our country or a zoo? And the newspapers are forever writing about how he wrestles and has pillow fights with his children. I mean, it's all well and good for a father to play with his children, but I do think our President should display a little more reserve and dignity."

"I think he's charming," Loralee said. "He's certainly good for the country. Why, just look at the acres of forest land he has set aside to create national parks."

"Yes, that's all very interesting," Stella Freeman remarked with a wave of her hand, "but enough of Mr. Roosevelt's antics. Tell me, my dear, have you been successful in teaching Shad Zuniga to read and write?"

"Yes," Loralee answered. "Quite successful."

Stella Freeman smiled. "Imagine, teaching that savage to read. It's quite an accomplishment, my dear. Frankly, the colonel and I never thought you'd succeed with the school. Of course, we were hoping you would, but the Indians can be very stubborn, as you know."

"Yes." Loralee sent a pleading glance in Mike's direction, hoping he would come and rescue her from Stella Freeman. She felt a surge of relief when he correctly interpreted her look and came quickly toward her.

"I think it's time for us to say good night," Mike said, extending his hand to Loralee. "Are you ready to go?"

"Yes, Mike." Taking his hand, she rose gracefully to her feet. "Thank you for a lovely evening, Mrs. Freeman."

"You're welcome, my dear. Good night, Sergeant."

"Ma'am." Mike bowed over Stella Freeman's hand.

After taking their leave of the colonel, Mike and Loralee left the Freemans' home.

Mike smiled at Loralee as he helped her into the carriage he had rented from the livery stable. It was a smart rig, painted a shiny black, with yellow wheels and a fringed canopy.

"Old Ironsides give you a bad time?" Mike asked as he climbed in beside Loralee and took up the reins.

"Not really, but I get so tired of hearing her opinion on everything. Honestly, Mike, I don't think she likes anything or anyone. She never has a nice word to say about anything, except the colonel. And you."

Mike's eyebrows went up in surprise. "Me?"

"Yes. She thinks you're quite handsome."

"Does she now? And do you share her opinion?"

Loralee cocked her head to one side, her eyes moving over Mike's face as if she were making up her mind. "Yes, I think so," she said after a long pause.

"Anything you'd like to change?"

"No."

"Loralee." Mike's voice was no longer light and teasing, but husky with desire as he reined the team to a halt along the side of the road.

She did not resist when he took her in his arms, nor did she think to protest when his mouth closed on hers. Mike smelled of soap and cologne, nice civilized smells. His lips were cool against hers, his arms gentle around her waist as he gave her a squeeze.

"I'm crazy about you, Loralee," he murmured. "You know that, don't you?"

Loralee nodded, wondering how things had managed to get so serious so quickly.

"Is there any chance that you feel the same about me?"

"I like you very much, Mike. You know that."

Mike nodded as he drew away. Take your time, Schofield, he thought to himself. Don't rush her. But damn, it was hard to let her go, hard to wait, even though he was confident that, in time, he would win her love.

He kissed her again at her door.

"Good night, Mike," she whispered.

"Good night, Loralee. Sweet dreams."

Loralee remained outside, watching Mike ride away. She was about to go into the house when something, a sound, a smell, something, changed her mind. Drawing her cloak around her shoulders, she walked into the darkness toward the trees, her feet moving soundlessly over the sandy ground.

He was there, standing in the shadowy darkness, as she had known he would be. For a timeless moment, they stared at each other, unmoving. Then, drawn by a bond stronger than words, they moved toward each other until they were only a breath apart. Loralee's heart was singing as she lifted her face for his kiss. She closed her eyes as his mouth covered hers.

Sensation. Wave after wave of sensation flooding to every part of her body. Her blood was on fire, alive, humming. Her heart beat fast and wild, drumming loudly in her ears. Her legs grew weak so that she swayed against him for support. Her nostrils filled with the scent of him, and she breathed in the aroma of sage and woodsmoke, sweat and leather. His scent, earthy and wild, excited her the more.

Shad Zuniga wrapped his long arms around Loralee's trim waist, drawing her softly rounded body close to his own, letting her feel his rising desire. Her mouth was soft and yielding, her breasts warm against his chest. She smelled of lavender soap and perfume and an enticing woman-smell that was hers alone. He took a deep breath, memorizing her scent, so that he would be able to find her by smell alone in the dead of night. The blood pounded in his brain and in his loins, filling him with heat and a primal wanting that would have frightened Loralee had she known what he was thinking.

Drawing away, Zuniga removed the hairpins from her hair. Unbound, the silken mass fell to her waist in thick golden waves, tempting his touch.

Loralee shivered as Zuniga's fingers moved through her hair. She leaned against him, inviting his kiss, quivering with desire as his mouth slanted over hers a second time.

They kissed for a long moment. Then, still not speaking, they parted. Zuniga's eyes held hers as he reached out and gently stroked her cheek. And then he was swinging astride the stallion, his movements effortless, beautiful.

She stood where he had left her for a long time, listening to the sound of the stallion's hoofbeats grow fainter, fainter, until only silence surrounded her.

Zuniga rode hard for home, relishing the sting of the wind in his face, the cold air that cooled his fevered flesh. She was a white woman, forbidden fruit, and yet he wanted her as he had never wanted any of the women of his own tribe. He had not meant to go to her house again, had not meant to let her see him, but he had been driven by a deep hunger to hold her in his arms just once, to taste and to touch and to smell that which could never be his.

He rode as if pursued by devils, heading straight for home. Back where he belonged. No more would he attend the white man's school. No more would he see the woman who tempted him beyond his ability to resist.

At home, he turned the stud loose in the corral, shut the gate with a bang, and walked to his lodge. The sound of Nachi's soft snoring greeted him as he stepped inside.

The wickiup was dark. There were no windows; the doorway was nothing more than an opening covered with a deer hide. Two backrests made of willow were the only furniture the lodge contained. Two beds, made of old hides and blankets, were spread in the rear of the lodge.

Shad glanced fondly at the old man sleeping peacefully beneath a pile of robes. Shad had grown up on the old man's tales of white treachery. The white man was not to be trusted, Nachi said. The white man spoke with a double tongue and his promises were a lie. He would offer you peace with one hand while plotting how to steal your land with the other. Reservation living had not changed Nachi's opinion of the whites. Once, he had been a fearless warrior, as brave as a mountain lion, as fleet as a deer, as cunning as a fox. Now he was barely able to move, his body shrunken and withered like a dead leaf. But his eyes were still bright, and his spirit was still strong. The old man had outlived three wives, and sometimes, when the nights were long and cold, he threatened to find a young wife to warm his blankets.

Undressing quietly, Shad slipped naked under his blankets and closed his eyes. But sleep would not come. Instead, Loralee Warfield's face loomed in his mind, her warm red mouth curved in a shy smile, her deep brown eyes beckoning him. She was a beautiful woman, and he desired her as he had desired no other woman, red or white. But she was unattainable, as far from his grasp as the stars wheeling across the sky.

Still, he wanted her. And she wanted him. He knew it. Her desire had been plain in her eyes, in the way her lips opened to his, in the way her slim young body had swayed against his own.

She wanted him. The thought kept him awake the whole night long.

4

The following day, Loralee could think of little but Shad Zuniga's kiss, and her reaction to it. Impossible as it seemed, she could still feel the touch of his lips on hers, the strength of his arms around her waist, drawing her close, the heat of his body pressed next to her own.

Looking at her students, she tried to imagine what Zuniga had been like as a young boy. Had he been openly rebellious like Short Bear, or boldly curious like Star Gazer? She was preoccupied with thoughts of Zuniga all that day, so much so that the children sometimes had to ask a question twice before she heard them.

Questions. She had several of her own.

What had Zuniga been doing, prowling around her house after midnight? Had he been waiting for her? Or had their meeting been mere coincidence?

After school, she spent two hours at her desk, grading papers and preparing the lesson for the following day.

At home, she prepared dinner, tidied up the kitchen, fed the cat, all the while counting the hours until she would meet Shad Zuniga at the schoolhouse. She studied herself critically in the mirror before leaving for school. Her eyes sparkled, her cheeks were flushed, and she couldn't stop smiling. She was going to see Shad.

She waited at the school for over an hour, but he didn't come. It was with great disappointment that she left the schoolhouse and returned home. Why had he missed his lesson? Had she done something wrong? What could it have been? She spent a restless night wondering where he was, what he was doing, who he was with. . . . Sleep was a long time coming.

She was reading the poetry of Emily Dickinson to her class the following morning when Shad Zuniga stepped into the schoolroom. A murmur of excitement rippled through the children as they became aware of his presence, and there was much whispering and pointing in the visitor's direction. Short Bear frowned as his cousin took a place near the back door.

Loralee looked up, ready to scold the children for being so noisy. But then she saw Zuniga, and a smile quickly replaced the frown.

"Good morning, Mr. Zuniga," she said warmly.

He had never looked so handsome. He wore a shirt of bleached doeskin decorated with porcupine quills that had been dyed a deep blue. The whiteness of his shirt emphasized his dark hair and eyes. His trousers were buckskin, heavily fringed along the outer seam. His moccasins were decorated with quills dyed the same color as those on his shirt.

"Do you mind if I watch?" he asked.

"No. Please, sit down and be comfortable."

"I will stand here."

"Very well." It was difficult to go on with the lesson, with Zuniga so close. He leaned against the wall, his arms folded across his chest, his eyes watching her as she began to read aloud.

She found it impossible to concentrate on what she was reading while his eyes were on her, and she made several mistakes. She felt her cheeks grow warm as several of the children began to giggle. Miss Warfield *never* made mistakes.

Loralee finished the poem with a sigh of relief and quickly instructed the children to read quietly for a few minutes.

Zuniga watched Loralee with pride. She was a remarkable young woman. He could see that she genuinely liked the Apache children, that she believed what she was doing was worthwhile, important. Just as clearly, he could see that the children admired and respected Loralee. The younger ones especially responded to her innate warmth and affection.

Yes, Zuniga mused, she was a rare woman indeed. So many people had come to the reservation in the past, pretending they wanted to help the Apache, when all they really wanted was to take advantage of the Indians, to rob them of what little they had left.

He had not intended to see her again, knowing that nothing but trouble awaited them. The kisses they had shared had made him realize, if she did not, that they were on dangerous ground, and so he had stayed away from the schoolhouse the night before, determined to put an end to their relationship before it went too far. Determined never to see her again.

Yet here he stood, watching her, wanting her, unable to stay away.

He smiled as Loralee made her way toward him. She was looking very prim and proper today, with her golden hair in its customary knot at the nape of her neck. Her dress, a rich gold and brown stripe, highlighted the color of her hair and eyes. His gaze lingered on her mouth, remembering how it had opened to his like a flower unfolding to the sun.

"Can I help you with anything?" Loralee asked, coming to stand beside him.

"No. I only wanted to see how the children were doing. I think most of them would rather be somewhere else." Zuniga glanced at Short Bear. The boy was staring out the window. He refused to participate in the class, and Shad knew that his cousin would not be in school at all if it weren't for him. Perhaps he had been wrong to insist that Short Bear attend school. The boy had been moody and withdrawn ever since his father died the year before. Shad had hoped that going to school would give Short Bear something else to think about, would help him to get involved in something worthwhile, but the boy didn't seem to be learning anything.

"Perhaps they would," Loralee remarked, following Zuniga's gaze. "But they *are* learning. Once they begin to feel pride in what they're doing, they'll feel better about coming to school."

"Maybe," Zuniga agreed, but he did not sound convinced.

"I . . . I missed you last night," Loralee murmured, hoping he would explain his absence.

Shad nodded. "I am sorry I was not here. I will not fail to come again."

95

"Good." Loralee turned away so he would not see the relief in her eyes. Nothing was wrong. She had imagined the whole thing.

She turned her gaze toward the children. It was hard to be so close to Shad, hard to face him as though nothing out of the ordinary had happened between them. She longed to reach out, to touch him, to feel the hard length of his body pressed close to her own. She had responded to his kisses in a most unladylike way. She knew she should have slapped his face and walked away with her pride and dignity intact; instead, she had returned his kiss not once, but twice. And would gladly have asked for more.

It was almost a relief when Zuniga waved a cheerful farewell to the class and left the room.

The next three weeks were exciting ones for Loralee. She taught the children during the day, spent weekends with Mike, and continued to tutor Shad Zuniga five evenings a week. The lessons were supposed to last an hour, but they often stretched to an hour and a half or more. Some nights Zuniga did not want a lesson at all. Instead, they went for walks along the shallow stream that ran behind Loralee's house. Loralee spoke of her concern for Short Bear, of her hopes of reaching more of the Apache children, of her growing love for the West and the Indian people. In turn, Zuniga told her about Nachi, about his mother. He never mentioned his father, or made any reference to him beyond the fact that his father and Short Bear's father had been brothers, and Loralee did not ask.

As she grew to know Zuniga better, she realized he was a fascinating man, wise beyond his years. He knew the Indians had to change, but he was against it, for his people and for himself. He spoke often about the old days, and she knew he was sorry he had not been born years earlier, before the white man came and took over the land that had once belonged to the Indians.

And yet, Loralee mused, the Indians could not have ruled the West forever. There had been too many white people eager for land, for gold, for adventure. Too many people who had felt that the Indians were less than human.

She spent many hours with Zuniga, and she grew to admire his easy strength, his ability to hunt and track the deer and other game that populated the hills. She admired him because he was honest and straightforward, never saying one thing when he was thinking another, never sidestepping the truth, no matter how painful it might be.

She was thinking of Zuniga as she went through her cupboards one afternoon after school. She was out of sugar and flour and milk and butter and just about everything else. Jotting down a list, she stuffed it into her skirt pocket, saddled her horse, and rode to the fort.

At the sutler's store, she dismounted, tethered Lady to the hitch rail, and went inside. She wandered down the aisles, picking up whatever caught her eye as well as the items on her list: a sack of sugar, six apples, flour, a tin of coffee, yeast, a dozen eggs, potatoes, bacon, some canned peaches, a ribbon for her hair, a package of needles, a pair of stockings.

She paused at a long shelf stacked with Apache baskets. They came in a wide variety of sizes and shapes and were made of cottonwood, mulberry, willow, sumac, or squawberry. Some had intricate designs worked into them. After some consideration, she chose a small bowl-like basket called a *tsa*. The basket had a black star woven into the top and geometric designs on the sides. She also took a small water basket called a *tus*.

She was waiting for the clerk to add up her bill when she saw the camera on the shelf. Impulsively, she bought that, too. It would be fun to take pictures of her class, she told herself, but all the while she was thinking about Shad Zuniga.

The clerk was counting out her change when Zuniga entered the store. Loralee looked at him in surprise. Mike had said

Zuniga never came to the fort, or accepted anything from the whites.

She lingered at the counter, thumbing through a Sears mail order catalog, while she surreptitiously kept an eye on Zuniga. He selected only two items, a large can of coffee and a sack of sugar. She was stirred once again by how handsome he was. His hair, black and shiny as jet, hung to his waist. He wore a buckskin shirt, fringed along the sleeves and across the back, and a pair of snug buckskin pants. Traditional Apache moccasins hugged his feet. They were hardsoled, curving upward above the toe for protection against thorns and cactus. He was light on his feet, like a cat walking on eggs, she mused.

His eyes acknowledged her presence as he came toward the counter.

"Good afternoon, Mr. Zuniga," Loralee said politely.

Zuniga nodded as he placed his order on the counter top. "Miss Warfield."

She moved slowly out the door while he paid for his purchases, and smiled up at him when he fell in step beside her.

"Let me carry that for you," he offered, nodding at the bag in her hand.

"Thank you." She handed him the sack. "I didn't think you ever came to the fort."

"Every month or so," Zuniga replied with a shrug. "Whenever Nachi runs out of coffee or sugar."

"Where did you get the money to pay for it?"

Zuniga turned the full force of his gaze on her, one black brow arched upward in cynical amusement. "Do you really want to know?"

"I think so," Loralee replied uncertainly.

"I stole it."

"Stole it?" Loralee echoed, shocked. "From whom?"

Zuniga shrugged. "One of the soldiers. I didn't stop to ask his name."

"But how?"

"It is easy. I just wait for Saturday night. The soldiers drink too much, sometimes they pass out before they reach the barracks. It is easy to take a few dollars."

"That's terrible," Loralee said curtly.

"No more terrible than being forced to live on this reservation."

She had no answer for that. What did you say to a man who was a prisoner of the United States government?

"Thank you for carrying my groceries," she said.

Zuniga nodded. Setting the bag down, he lifted her onto the back of her horse and placed the sack inside the mesh carryall looped over the saddlehorn.

"I will see you at the school tonight," he reminded her.

Loralee nodded. "Thanks again."

She felt his eyes on her back as she rode away from the store.

The lesson was strained that night. Every time Loralee looked at Zuniga, she could almost feel the heat of his lips on hers. Was he also remembering? She thought of him living up in the hills with Nachi, stealing ammunition from the sutler's store, stealing money from the soldiers to buy sugar and coffee for the old man because he was too proud to take charity from the whites. She could not condone stealing, yet she understood why he did it and she could not condemn him. The Indians didn't believe it was stealing when the victim was the enemy.

She was hesitant to meet his eyes. Was she making too much of a few kisses stolen in the moonlight? He hadn't touched her since. Maybe he had been disappointed. Maybe he kissed every woman he met. Maybe he had just been curious to see how white women kissed, and now that he knew, he was no longer interested. And why should she care? He was nothing to her, only a student who was here to learn to read and write.

As the lesson drew to a close, Loralee met Zuniga's eyes, saw her own desire mirrored in the depths of his gaze. She knew then that he had not been disappointed in her response, and that he was still interested. Extremely interested. A sudden warmth enveloped her and she glanced away, feeling shy. Whatever was between them was not over yet.

The next day, Loralee took her camera to school. The Apache children were excited by the thought of being photographed once she explained what it meant. At first, she had planned to take a group picture, but the children were so anxious to see themselves that she took individual photos of each child. Only Short Bear refused to be photographed.

She took a picture of Zuniga, too. He was reluctant at first, but eventually he agreed to let Loralee take his picture.

The children were thrilled with the results. She dismissed the class early the day the pictures arrived. They were too excited to study, too eager to run home and show their families the photographs the magic box had taken.

Loralee was equally thrilled with the picture of Zuniga. She had photographed him astride the big dun stallion with the timbered foothills in the background. The horse had posed beautifully, head up, ears forward, eyes alert. Zuniga, dressed in his customary buckskin pants and sleeveless vest, his long black hair flowing down his back, looked every inch the warrior Apache.

Impulsively, Loralee pressed his picture

to her lips, then giggled self-consciously even though she was alone.

At home later that day, she placed Zuniga's photograph on her dressing table where she could see it first thing in the morning and last thing at night.

5

It was Friday evening and the lesson was half over. Loralee continued to be pleased with Zuniga's progress, and she began to wonder if he would consider going to college. She was certain he could obtain a degree in any field he desired and go on to make a success of his life. He could be a doctor perhaps, or a lawyer, and really do something for his people. She smiled as she envisioned him in a dark blue suit and tie, a briefcase under his arm.

She shook her thoughts away as he asked a question. Pausing at his shoulder, she bent down so she could see the book spread open on his desk. They were working on nouns and verbs, and though Zuniga thought such knowledge useless and foolish, he listened intently as she explained the difference.

Zuniga took a deep breath, inhaling Loralee's fragrance as she answered his question. She was so lovely, so close, it was all he could do not to draw her into his lap and ease his desire by claiming her lips. His eyes moved over her face and body, lingering on her mouth, her full breasts, the sweet curve of her hips.

Loralee glanced at Zuniga, and their eyes met and held. She saw the desire lurking behind his dark eyes, felt it in the heat of his gaze. Suddenly nervous, she licked her lower lip, then quickly turned away.

It was then she saw Mike standing in the doorway. She had not heard him come in, and she wondered how long he had been standing there, watching. Hot color suffused her cheeks as she moved away from Zuniga and ran a hand over her hair.

"Mike, is something wrong?"

Schofield glared at Zuniga. "No, nothing's wrong," he replied stiffly.

Zuniga stood up, his expression insolent as he returned Mike Schofield's stare.

Loralee glanced from Mike to Zuniga and then at Mike again. "If nothing's wrong, I'll see you tomorrow, Mike."

"I came to walk you home," Mike said.

Loralee slid a glance in Zuniga's direction. She could feel the anger building within him. She had promised Shadow they would meet alone, and now he must be thinking that she had broken that promise. He gave her one quick, accusing look and stalked out of the building.

"Zuniga, wait!"

"Let him go," Mike said. His hand closed over her forearm as she started toward the door.

Loralee whirled on him in a fury. "What are you doing here?" she demanded angrily. "I gave Shad Zuniga my word that no one would be here during his lessons, and now you've made a liar out of me."

"Loralee, I just wanted to—"

"If he doesn't come back, it will be all your fault. And if he stops coming, the children might stop coming to school, too, and if that happens, Mike Schofield, I'll never forgive you. Never!"

"I'm sorry," Mike apologized sullenly.

"He's such a proud man," Loralee remarked. "Can't you understand why he didn't want anyone to be here? He's a warrior, being taught by a woman. You've been here long enough to know how proud the Apaches are."

"I don't understand why he's here at all," Mike retorted. "I'd bet a month's pay he doesn't give a damn about learning to read or write or anything else."

"I think you're wrong," Loralee said

with conviction. "He's very bright, Mike. I hope I can encourage him to go on with his studies when I've taught him all I can."

Schofield laughed, shaking his head in wonder. Zuniga, go to college? It was the most ludicrous thing he had ever heard. Given the chance, the man would be riding the war trail, killing and scalping and raising hell from here to Mexico, and Loralee wanted him to go to college. Sometimes there was no understanding a woman's thinking.

"I don't see what's so funny," Loralee said irritably. "Shad Zuniga has a fine mind. The fact that he's an Indian doesn't change that."

"The man's a heathen savage, for God's sake," Mike said, annoyed by the way she defended Zuniga at every turn.

"I don't wish to discuss it," Loralee answered coldly. "If you'll excuse me, I'm going home."

"I'll walk you."

"No, thank you."

"Loralee, don't be a fool. I'll walk you home."

"Very well."

She extinguished the light, drew on her shawl, and locked the door. They walked in silence, Mike leading his horse.

"Thank you for seeing me home, Sergeant," Loralee said politely. "Good night."

"Loralee, I'm sorry for what I said about Zuniga. Let's not quarrel."

"All right." She smiled up at him. He was one of the few good friends she had, and she didn't want to argue with him.

"Good night," Mike said. He touched his hat brim with his fingertips.

"Good night." Loralee watched Mike mount his horse and ride away until he was swallowed up by the night, then she gazed up at the distant hills. Zuniga had been understandably angry. No doubt he thought she had arranged for Mike to meet her at the school. Had he been terribly embarrassed to have Mike see him sitting at a child's desk, being tutored by a woman? Would he refuse to return to school now? She rubbed her hand across the back of her neck. Should she ride up and talk to Zuniga tonight, or let things go until Monday and see what happened?

Undecided, she paced up and down in front of the house, wondering what to do. She owed Zuniga an apology, yet she was hesitant to ride up to his lodge after dark. She was about to go inside when she turned on her heel and headed for the corral to saddle Lady. She had to know where she stood, and she couldn't wait until Monday night to find out.

Loralee made her way slowly through the darkness, grateful there was a full moon to light her path. Lady snorted and shied at each sound and shadow, and Loralee kept a tight hold on the reins, fearing the mare might spook and bolt out from under her.

She had ridden about halfway up the hill to where Zuniga's lodge was located when a deep voice reached out to her.

"You should not be riding out here alone at night."

Loralee reined Lady to a halt and turned toward the sound of his voice. "I wanted to see you."

Zuniga guided his stallion out of the shadows. "Why?"

"To apologize for tonight. I didn't know Mike was going to come to the school. It wasn't my idea, and I wanted you to know it."

Zuniga grinned wryly. "Are you afraid I will stop coming to school?" he asked sardonically.

"Yes," Loralee answered honestly. "I think you have great potential, and I'd hate to see it go to waste because of a misunderstanding."

"No. You are afraid that if I do not come to school, the children will not come either."

"That's part of it," Loralee admitted, wishing he would not stare at her in such a probing way. She reached down and stroked Lady's neck, feeling her cheeks grow warm as Zuniga continued to stare at her. Why not tell him the real reason you don't want him to quit? an inner voice taunted. Why not tell him the whole truth? Why not admit that your insides turn to jelly and your heart pounds a mile a minute whenever he looks at you . . . that you want more than his kisses, much more?

Zuniga gazed at Loralee's bowed head. The moonlight danced in her hair, turning the gold to silver. He could see that her cheeks were flushed with color, and he wondered why. Was she embarrassed because she had come after him, or afraid he might read more into her little visit than she intended?

The stallion danced restlessly beneath him, sidling up against Loralee's mare, its nostrils flared as he breathed in the mare's scent. The stallion whickered softly as the mare's tail went up, signaling that she was in season and willing to accept a mate.

Zuniga grinned as he slapped the stallion on the neck. "Not now," he muttered to the horse. "Not for you, and not for me."

Loralee glanced up. "What?"

"Nothing. Do not worry. I will be there Monday night, just like always."

Loralee smiled up at him. Everything was not lost. He would keep coming to school. She would see him as before, talk to him, hear his voice. She admitted now that she had been afraid, not that he would stop his lessons, nor that the children would refuse to learn, but that Zuniga would go out of her life for good.

Shad drew a ragged breath. Loralee looked so beautiful sitting there in the moonlight, her eyes shining brightly, her smile dazzling. She wanted him. He knew it suddenly, surely, without question. But did she know it?

Throwing caution to the wind, Zuniga reached for her, his arm curling around her waist, dragging her from the back of her horse to his. His dark eyes burned with the memory of the kisses they had shared as his mouth closed over hers.

Loralee made no protest, nor did she think of resisting when his arms closed around her. She had been wanting him for days and now he was here, holding her, kissing her. Her arms went around his neck, drawing him closer.

"Loralee." He whispered her name as his hands removed the pins from her hair, allowing the golden mass to cascade down her back.

Loralee shuddered with pleasure as his fingers moved through her hair, then began to massage the back of her neck.

"Loralee?" His voice was deep and rich, husky with longing. She heard the question he did not ask, and she nodded, her eyes not quite meeting his.

He breathed her name yet again as he urged the stallion higher into the hills, and she settled back against the hard wall of his chest, content to be there. She did not ask where he was taking her, nor did she care. She wanted only to be forever in his arms, to feel the hard smoothness of his skin beneath her hand, to hear his heart beating beneath her cheek, feel his breath upon her face.

The hills were lovely in the moonlight. The stars were clear and bright, sparkling like early morning dewdrops against the indigo velvet of the night sky. The world was quiet save for the muffled thud of the stallion's hooves and the occasional cry of an owl or the lonesome wail of a coyote.

It was like a dream, Loralee mused as they traveled on through the darkness. Nothing seemed real, and yet reality had never seemed so sweet. She gave a little sigh as she snuggled closer to Zuniga, smiled as his arm tightened around her waist. She felt his lips move in her hair, and she hoped that she would not awaken to find herself alone in her narrow bed, cold and alone.

She turned a little so she could see his face, her hand reaching up to touch his cheek. It was not a dream after all. He was real. Content, she rested against his chest, a little smile of anticipation playing over her lips.

Higher and higher they climbed until they came to a small lake surrounded by timber. Moonlight turned the water to liquid silver, and Loralee gave a little gasp of pleasure. It was so beautiful, the lake and the trees and the star-studded night.

Zuniga reined the dun to a halt beside the shimmering pool, then stepped to the ground, still holding Loralee in his arms. Gently, he placed her on the ground, then stretched out beside her, his arms pulling her close. A thrill of exhilaration skipped down Loralee's spine as her body molded itself to his. He looked handsome and wild lying there beside her, his long black hair spilling over his shoulders, his dark eyes aglow with the warmth of his desire. His hands moved lazily over her body, the heat of his flesh burning through the fabric of her dress.

Slowly, his eyes never leaving her face, he began to unfasten the long row of tiny pearl buttons that started at the neckline and went all the way down to the hem.

Loralee sighed as he opened the bodice of her dress and began to unfasten her undergarments, gently fondling her breasts as the flimsy material parted beneath his questing fingertips. She shuddered with pleasure even as a little voice in the back of her mind warned her that she was letting him go too far. All her life she had been taught it was wrong to let a man kiss her intimately, or caress her in any way. It had been drummed into her head time and again that nice girls did not engage in any form of sexual activity before marriage. But, somehow, that no longer seemed important. Zuniga's hands were turning her flesh to flame, making her heart pound as though she had been running for miles. He lowered his head, his teeth nibbling at her neck, her breasts, her flat belly. Murmuring her name, he removed her dress and petticoats, sucked in a deep breath as his eyes wandered over her body. It was slim and beautiful, perfect in every detail.

Loralee blushed as Zuniga's eyes moved over her bare flesh. No man had ever seen her unclothed before, yet she was not ashamed, only a little nervous. What if he did not find her attractive? With some trepidation, she met his gaze and saw the admiration mirrored in his eyes.

And now it was her turn to explore. Biting on her lower lip, she began to undress him, marveling anew at the beauty of the man. His body was big, powerful, ridged with muscle. His neck was thick and strong, his shoulders broad, his chest wide and deep, his belly hard and flat. She hesitated only a moment before removing his buckskin trousers. He wore no underclothing and she felt her cheeks burn as she came face to face with the very visible proof of his desire.

Zuniga was grinning at her now, his fathomless black eyes alight with amusement as he reached out and drew her down beside him. Loralee gave a little cry of pleasure as her skin rubbed against his. Once, she had thought that nothing could feel better against her bare flesh than silk, but she knew now she had been wrong. There was nothing in all the world to compare with the heady sensation of flesh against flesh, nothing at all. Every nerve ending, every part of her body was vibrantly alive, tingling with anticipation, yearning for more as Zuniga rained kisses on her face and breasts, each caress making her hungry for more.

Her breath came faster and faster as his hands and mouth aroused her, drowning out the voice of her conscience that warned her she was going too far, too fast. And then Zuniga took her face in his hands, kissing her deeply, passionately, and all thought was blotted from her mind. She was caught in a whirlpool of sensation from which there was no escape. His manhood was a throbbing warmth against her thigh, making her yearn to discover once and for all the secrets that all women yearn to know.

And then he was rising over her. She knew a brief moment of fear, a twinge of discomfort, and then only pleasure as he began to move inside of her, their bodies merging with a knowledge that was as old as time, as ageless as the rocks and the mountains. He was man and she was woman, primitive, eternal.

She cried his name aloud, arching upward to meet him, wanting to be closer, wanting more and more of him inside her, certain she could never be close enough. She whispered his name as he began to move faster, the rhythm increasing until she was afraid she would shatter into a million pieces.

And then it was over. Zuniga shuddered to a halt, his face buried against her neck, his sweat-sheened flesh glued to her own. It had been wonderful, Loralee thought, and yet she felt as though she had missed something, though she did not know what.

Zuniga saw the question in her eyes later, when his breathing had returned to normal. He smiled at her, knowing that the first time was rarely satisfactory for a woman. The next time would be for her, he vowed.

They washed in the lake, and Loralee felt suddenly shy as Zuniga began to caress her again. It was a new experience, feeling his flesh against hers under water, kissing him, touching him. She had never felt so free, so alive. She was surprised and pleased when she saw that he wanted her again.

It was better the second time. Her arms drew him close, reveling in the strength of him. His mouth possessed hers, branding her lips with fire. She let her hands roam freely over his body, delighting in the touch of his heated flesh, in the taut muscles that quivered beneath her fingertips. She nibbled at his neck, at his ear lobe, and giggled with happiness when he groaned with pleasure. It was a heady sensation, knowing that her untutored hands and lips could arouse him as he had aroused her.

And then he was in command again, his body pressing hers down, his chest crushing her breasts as he parted her thighs.

She raised her hips to meet him, eager to have him possess her once more, and as he moved slowly within her, filling her, pleasing her, she discovered what she had missed before.

Later, blissfully content, she fell asleep in his arms, smiling happily because now she, too, knew the secret of being a woman and loving a man.

6

Loralee couldn't seem to stop smiling the next day. The children looked at her curiously, baffled by her strange behavior. She didn't scold them when they whispered during reading time, she didn't seem to mind when Short Bear pulled a small green snake from his pocket and let it slither around on the top of his desk, nor did she reprimand Little Man for not having finished his homework. Then, most surprising of all, she let them have an extra twenty minutes for recess, and then dismissed the class an hour early. It was most peculiar.

Loralee smiled happily as she put her books away for the day and left the schoolhouse. Her steps were light as she headed for home. Abruptly she turned off the trail and walked toward the stream where it formed a small shallow pool screened by trees and brush.

Sitting beside the pool, she removed the pins from her hair, letting it fall down her back. Then, impulsively, she removed her shoes and stockings and splashed her feet in the cool water, wishing she had the nerve to undress and go for a swim.

Lying back, her feet dangling in the water, her arms outstretched, she stared up at the sky. It was a beautiful shade of blue, bright and clear. Happiness bubbled up inside her and spilled out in a joyous burst of laughter. She laughed until her cheeks ached, amazed and amused by the wonder of it all. The world was beautiful, the sky was beautiful, the Apache children were beautiful, and all because of Shad Zuniga. It was incredible. It was impossible. But it was true nonetheless.

Loralee plucked a blade of grass and twirled it between her thumb and forefinger. All her life she had read romantic novels and dreamed of the day when she would fall in love with a tall, dark, handsome man who would sweep her off her feet and carry her away to his castle where they would live happily ever after.

Laughter welled in Loralee's throat again as she conjured up a mental image of Nachi's brush-covered lodge. Hardly a castle, she mused. And Zuniga was nothing at all like a prince in a fairy tale. He wasn't rich, he wasn't cultured, his family was not respected and well-known. Oh, but he was tall, dark, and handsome, and she would not have changed him into a prince if she could.

Tonight she would see him again, though how she would face him after the night before she did not know. She had never imagined anything could be so wonderful, so beautiful. She felt her heart race as she recalled her wanton response to his kisses. How could she concentrate on teaching him to read when she wanted nothing so much as to be in his arms, to feel his mouth on hers once more? What was she going to do? Was it possible she had fallen in love with a heathen Indian? Such a thing was unheard of. You could respect the Apache as a people, you could admire them, sympathize with them, feel compassion for them. But you did not fall in love with them. It simply wasn't done.

But she had fallen in love with Shad. It was a sobering thought.

She heard no sound to indicate that she was no longer alone, saw no movement to warn her that someone was creeping up on her, but she knew, suddenly, that she was not alone. One of the children, she thought, trying to scare me. Which one would it be? Prairie Flower, or Little Man? Certainly it would not be Short Bear. He was so sullen, so withdrawn, she was certain he was not the type to play pranks unless they involved dead insects or snakes.

A pair of hands dropped over her eyes, and she smiled with pleasure. It was Zuniga. She would recognize those strong brown hands anywhere.

She sat up, smiling shyly, when he removed his hands from her eyes. He was wearing buckskins, as usual. The pants were fringed along the sides and fit his long legs like a second skin, outlining the strong muscles in his calves and thighs. The shirt was open at the throat, revealing a broad expanse of coppery skin. A red headband held his long black hair away from his face. A single eagle feather was braided into his hair.

He looked very Indian. And very desirable.

"Are you playing hookey, teacher?" he asked, grinning at her.

"I guess so. It was too nice a day to stay cooped up inside, so I let the children go home early."

Zuniga nodded toward the pool. Sunlight danced on the flat surface, sparkling like tiny jewels. "Why do you not go for a swim?"

"Here? I couldn't. Someone might see."

"I know a place."

Loralee's heart thudded in her breast. "Do you?" she asked, knowing he was referring to the lake where they had made love the night before.

Zuniga nodded, his eyes on her face. She saw the question he did not ask, and she nodded slowly.

Moments later, they were on the dun, riding toward the hills. The stallion moved easily, apparently not bothered by his double load. Loralee wrapped her arms around Zuniga's waist, her cheek resting against his back, her eyes closed as the stallion carried them to their destination.

There, in a sheltered valley hardly bigger than Loralee's house, lay the quiet blue pool. She had not been able to appreciate the beauty of the place the night before. Now she glanced around in wonder. The blue pool was set in the grassy valley like a sapphire in a bed of emeralds. Tall pines stood like sentinels, their branches reaching toward the sun.

"It looks like something out of the Garden of Eden," Loralee murmured, enchanted by the pastoral beauty spread before her.

"Eden?" Zuniga prompted. Dismounting, he lifted Loralee from the back of the dun.

"Paradise," Loralee explained. "When God made the first man and the first woman, he placed them in a beautiful garden. It must have looked just like this, all green and peaceful."

"What happened to the man and the woman?" Zuniga asked, curious in spite of himself.

Loralee watched as he unsaddled the horse, thrilled by his easy strength and the way he moved, self-assured and confident. "They took something that wasn't theirs to take," she answered sadly, "and God made them leave the garden forever."

"The white man has not changed," Zuniga remarked with a twinge of bitterness. "He is still taking what is not his."

"Not today," Loralee said, smiling up at him. "Let's not talk about right or wrong. Let's just be happy."

"Shall we swim?"

"I . . . I don't have a bathing suit."

"Neither do I." He was stripping off his shirt and pants as he spoke. Motioning for her to follow, he waded into the pool and began to swim.

Loralee watched him for a few moments. He did everything well, she thought. He never seemed to be at a loss as to what to do or what to say. He knew who he was and what he was, and he was at peace within himself. She loved to watch him move, loved the latent strength that was reflected in the way he walked or rode, or glided through the water, the muscles in his arms and legs propelling him effortlessly through the water.

With a sigh, she stepped out of her dress and undergarments and ran for the cover of the water.

They swam for half an hour, content to

be together. Loralee felt freer than she had ever felt before, free and unrestrained by rules and restrictions and someone else's idea of what was right and what was wrong. The water felt wonderful against her bare skin, the sun was warm on her face, and her spirit felt light as a feather.

Zuniga left the water first. He stood on the bank, shaking the water from his long black hair, his skin glistening in the sunlight. How beautiful he was, Loralee mused, then blushed furiously when he turned around and saw her staring at him.

"Come on out," he called, reaching for her hand.

"I can't," Loralee wailed.

Zuniga frowned. "Why not? Are you hurt?"

Loralee shook her head in misery. How could she tell him she was embarrassed to let him see her naked in the full light of day? It sounded so silly after what they had shared the night before. But it had been dark then, and she been caught up in the throes of passion.

Zuniga's eyes filled with sudden understanding. She was shy, embarrassed to let him see her. Foolish woman, he thought indulgently, and turned his back toward her. Foolish, but oh, so beautiful.

Loralee had only pulled on her petticoat when she felt Shad's arms steal around her waist, felt his lips kissing the back of her neck and shoulders. She shivered with delight, her eyes closing with pleasure. What power his touch had over her. A few kisses, a caress, and her heart began to beat like a war drum while all the strength seemed to drain out of her limbs, leaving her weak and trembling like a newborn kitten.

She turned in his arms, and gave a little gasp when she realized he was still naked.

"Shad—"

He stilled her half-hearted protest with another kiss as his hands slowly removed her petticoat, sliding the garment over her hips and down her thighs until it rested in a heap around her ankles. Still holding her in his arms, he lowered her to the ground. Loralee's arms twined around his neck and she let him kiss and touch and explore to his heart's content, until she was lost, gloriously, wonderfully lost in the magic of his touch. . . .

They spent the day in the little valley, loving and sleeping and loving again. They took a walk around the pool, ate berries to take the edge off their hunger, watched a pair of determined red ants drag a dead beetle over a twig.

Later, lying side by side, they gazed up at the sky, watching as wisps of clouds floated lazily across the azure sky.

"I've always wanted to be a teacher," Loralee replied in answer to one of Zuniga's questions. "There's so much to learn, so much to know. If you studied your whole life, you could never learn it all."

Zuniga grinned at the note of excitement that crept into her voice whenever she talked about teaching.

"There are so many wonderful books to read. Homer and Shakespeare, Dickens and Brontë. There's poetry and history and theology, and—" Loralee laughed self-consciously. "I'm sorry. I didn't mean to bore you."

"You are not."

"There's so much your people could learn, Shad. If I could encourage just one child to become a teacher or a doctor or a lawyer, if I could just pique their interest in the world outside the reservation, I'll feel that I've accomplished something wonderful, something worthwhile."

"And do you think Short Bear could be a doctor or a lawyer?"

"Yes. He's bright enough, Shad, I know he is. If I could just break through that wall he's built around himself, I know he could be anything he wants to be."

"Anything?"

"Yes," she said firmly. "Anything."

"He wants to be a warrior," Zuniga said quietly. "Like his father, and his grandfather."

"He can still be a warrior in his heart," Loralee remarked soberly. "He can be honest and brave and true to himself and his beliefs. He doesn't have to give up like so many of your people have. You haven't."

"No?"

"No. You're as much a warrior as any Apache who ever lived."

"I wonder if Cochise and Mangas would agree with that," Zuniga muttered wryly.

"Times change," Loralee said. "People who want to survive learn to change with them. That's why education is so important to your people," she went on earnestly. "They need to know what's going on outside the reservation. They need to know what's available to them, about the opportunities that are waiting—"

Laughing softly, Zuniga placed his hand over Loralee's mouth. "School is out for today, teacher," he chided. "Remember?"

Loralee nodded, and for a moment they were silent. Loralee toyed with a strand of Zuniga's long black hair, curling it round and round her finger.

"Can I ask you something personal?" she asked after a while.

"You can ask," Zuniga replied, chuckling softly. "I cannot promise to answer."

"Have you made love to many women?"

"A few," he admitted, startled by the question.

She had expected just such an answer, but she had not expected the truth to hurt so much. She had wanted to be the first woman he had ever touched, as he had been the first man to touch her.

"I am sorry, Loralee," Zuniga said quietly. "I wish . . . oh, hell, you know what I mean."

Loralee nodded wistfully. "Who were they, the others? What were they like?"

Zuniga shrugged. "They were whores, mostly. Nameless women who did not mind taking a few dollars to sleep with an Indian." He thought briefly of Kelly. She had been the main outlet for his primal desires since he moved to the reservation. She was the only prostitute in town who didn't look down her nose at him because he was an Apache.

"Why haven't you ever married?"

Zuniga grinned. When Loralee decided to get personal, she got personal! "I don't know," he replied honestly. "I have thought about it a few times. I guess I never met the right woman, if there is such a thing."

His eyes lingered on Loralee's face. He had never met a woman he wanted to spend his whole life with, until now. He wondered what it would be like to be married to Loralee Warfield, to have her waiting for him at the end of each day, to see her smile just for him. It gave him an odd feeling in the pit of his stomach, just thinking about it.

Loralee's cheeks grew pink under Zuniga's continued gaze. What was he thinking?

"Why aren't you married?" Zuniga

asked at last. "Why aren't you teaching your own children to read and write?"

"I guess the right man hasn't asked me yet," Loralee answered, very softly, and it was suddenly hard to speak, or think. His eyes, as dark as midnight, burned with an intense inner fire. She knew with sudden certainty what he was thinking, and she uttered a little sigh of contentment as he took her in his arms once more, his mouth slanting over hers in a kiss that drove every other thought, hope, or desire from her mind.

It was late when Zuniga saddled the dun and helped Loralee mount.

"I hate to see the day end," she remarked.

"There will be other days," Zuniga said gravely. And he knew it was true. He had never meant to become seriously involved with Loralee Warfield. He had thought only to woo her and win her and abandon her when he tired of her. She was only a white woman, after all. If and when he decided to marry, he had thought to take an Apache woman for his wife. But no more. The few hours he had spent with Loralee had sealed his fate. For him, there would be no other woman.

Zuniga was waiting for Loralee after school the following day. Her horse stood beside the dun, saddled and ready.

"Where are we going?" Loralee asked, smiling up at Zuniga.

"I want you to meet my grandfather."

"I'd like that."

They rode most of the way in silence, with Shad occasionally remarking on a point of interest or directing her gaze toward a clump of bright purple flowers or a deer grazing on the short yellow grass.

The wickiup looked the same as before. The yellow dog wagged its tail as Zuniga dismounted. Loralee was suddenly ill at ease as Zuniga lifted her from her horse. She had heard tales of Nachi from Mike Schofield. The old man had been a redoubtable warrior in his time. No doubt he had killed many a white woman and taken many a scalp. Her heart was pounding wildly as she followed Zuniga into the brush-covered lodge.

It was dark inside, with only the light of a small fire for illumination. There were no windows, no furniture of any kind save for two crude backrests made of woven willow branches and covered with hides. An old man sat cross-legged beside the fire, his chin resting on his chest, a blanket draped across his shoulders.

"Grandfather," Shad said, his voice low and filled with respect. "I have brought someone to meet you."

The old man glanced up, his sharp black eyes as bright and inquisitive as a child's. "The school woman," he said with a nod.

Zuniga grinned. "Yes, the school woman. Her name is Loralee Warfield. Loralee, this is Nachi."

Loralee smiled uncertainly. Should she offer to shake the old man's hand? Did Indians shake hands?

Nachi grinned as he patted the ground beside him. "Come, sit," he invited.

"Thank you." Loralee sat down beside the old man. The floor of the lodge was hard and cold.

Zuniga remained standing near the doorway. The old man smiled up at his grandson. "You have a good eye for a woman," he observed candidly.

Loralee smiled, pleased by the compliment. She liked the old man, she decided. His eyes were honest and direct, his smile sincere.

She listened quietly as Shad told his grandfather about the school, and what Loralee was trying to teach the children, and then Nachi began to talk of the old days, of Geronimo. Geronimo had never truly been a chief, Nachi said, shaking his head, not like Cochise or Mangas. Nor was Geronimo a Chiricahua, as many thought, but a Bedonkohe Apache. He was the fourth child in a family of four boys and four girls. Geronimo firmly believed in destiny, and in the magic of the number four. He had four wives that were full-blooded Bedonkohe Apache, and four that were part Bedonkohe.

Four of his children had been killed by Mexicans, and four were held in bondage by the United States. Yes, Nachi said, nodding sagely, the sacred number four was evident in Geronimo's life.

Loralee nodded as the old man paused. She knew a great deal about Geronimo herself. He had surrendered for the last time on September 4 (four again, she thought), 1886. A few days later, he had been put on board a train and sent to Florida along with other Apache warriors, where they were put to work sawing logs. They were kept at hard labor for nearly two years. Sometime later, they were sent to Alabama, where they remained for several years until they were transferred to Fort Sill, Oklahoma. And that was where the old warrior lived now.

Loralee smiled faintly as Nachi broke into another war story. Geronimo was a fighter no longer. He had joined the Dutch Reformed Church and had been a Sunday school teacher, of all things! He had quickly learned the value of a white man's dollar and he spent hours promoting himself, hawking photographs or bows and arrows at fairs and expositions. But, for all his popularity, he was still a prisoner of war.

Loralee's attention turned to Nachi. He had stopped talking of war and was talking about Usen, the Apache God, and the various Apache tribes. Usen had created a special place on the earth for each tribe, Nachi remarked. The Indian was tied to the land, to his birthplace. Take him away from his homeland and he withered and died.

"It is true, even today," Nachi said with conviction. "My people do not prosper when they are taken away from the land of their birth."

Loralee nodded in agreement. It was true. The Apaches who had been taken to Fort Sill and other faraway places had not done well. Many had sickened and died, just as Nachi said. Today, their numbers were few.

Nachi spoke of General "Three Stars" Crook and how he had been respected by the Apache. He spoke of life in the high mountains, of the days when Usen had smiled on his red children.

After about forty minutes, Nachi sighed heavily. His head lolled forward, and Loralee assumed that he had fallen asleep. She glanced at Zuniga, who was squatting on his heels near the doorway.

"I miss my girl," Nachi said. He lifted his head and stared hard at Loralee. "My lodge is empty without her."

Loralee glanced at Zuniga again. Girl? What girl?

A flicker of sadness surfaced in Zuniga's dark eyes and was quickly gone. "He means my mother," Shad explained quietly.

"You would have liked my Nadina," Nachi said, smiling at Loralee. "She was a good daugther, always thinking of her family. It was a sad day when she married Nakai. He was much older than she was. He was no good." Nachi spat into the firepit. "Shad will tell you the same thing."

"I wish I could have known your daughter," Loralee said sincerely. "She must have been a very special woman."

Nachi nodded as he bestowed another warm smile on Loralee. "She would have liked you. Always, she wanted a daughter, but I think it was better she had no children after Shad. Nakai was not a good father. He drank too much, and when he was drunk, he beat Shad and my Nadina. Our wickiup was a happier place when he was not in it."

Zuniga stood up abruptly. "It is time for us to go, grandfather. I must take Miss Warfield back to the reservation."

Nachi nodded, then grinned with pleasure as Loralee placed a kiss on his withered cheek. "Come again," he said. "My lodge is yours."

"Thank you," Loralee replied. "I will."

Zuniga laid a hand on his grandfather's shoulder, then followed Loralee out of the lodge.

"I hope he did not bore you with his stories," Zuniga muttered.

"No, it was wonderful. Why did we leave so suddenly?"

"He was in a talkative mood. Pretty soon he would have started telling you things that are better left unsaid."

"Like what?"

Zuniga stared into the distance, a muscle working in his jaw. He was obviously upset, Loralee mused, but why?

"What is it?" she asked.

"Forget it, Loralee."

She nodded as she followed him toward the corral, willing to let the subject drop. For the moment.

"He's a dear man," Loralee remarked. "Not at all what I expected."

"What did you expect?" Zuniga asked dryly. "War paint, feathers, and fresh scalps hanging from the ceiling?"

"Of course not," Loralee retorted with a toss of her head.

"Sure you did," Zuniga insisted. "But just to set the record straight, my people rarely took scalps."

"I didn't know that."

"I thought you knew all about us."

"Not everything," Loralee admitted with a shy smile.

"Did you know scalping was introduced to the Indians by the whites?"

"Yes. And I also know the Mexicans used to pay a hundred-dollar bounty for Apache scalps."

Zuniga nodded, his eyes dark and fierce. "The bounty was supposed to be for the scalps of fighting men only, but hair is hair, and there's no way to tell if it belonged to a man or a woman, or a child, once you hack it off."

It had been a shameful practice, Loralee thought, but it had happened. She glanced at Zuniga out of the corner of her eye. He was leaning against the corral, staring into the distance toward the setting sun. What deep, dark secret was he hiding, she wondered. What had he been afraid Nachi might say?

"My grandfather was a brave warrior in his day," Shad mused. "I wish I had lived then."

"Not me," Loralee said with a shudder. "All that fighting and killing. Never knowing what was coming from one day to the next. Never feeling safe, even in your own home. No, I like it better now."

"My people were better off a hundred years ago. Now, most of them are lost. They cannot change their ways of life to live in a white world."

"They will, in time."

Zuniga shook his head. "No. The Indians do not think like the whites. Our values are not the same. The white man has a need to own things, especially land. The Indians never thought of the land as theirs. You cannot own the earth. It belongs to the Great Spirit. There was enough room for everybody, but the white man could not share the land with the Indian. He had to fence it and fight for it. In the old days, an Apache warrior never owned anything but his horse and his weapons. The lodge and everything in it belonged to his woman."

137

Zuniga laughed bitterly. "But the white man's ways are catching on fast. Our women want to live in square houses and cook on stoves. They want cotton dresses and wash-tubs and tables and chairs. They are no longer content to cook and live in the old way."

"Why should they be? Why not take advantage of things that make life easier? Why cook over an open fire when you can cook on a stove? Why sit on the floor when you can sit in a chair and be more comfort-able? Why spend days cleaning and tanning a smelly old hide when you can buy a bolt of ready-made cloth and have a new dress in only a few hours?"

"Why?" Shad demanded angrily. "Why? We are Apaches, not white men. Why should we try to become like the whites? I will never be a white man! We are living on the white man's charity, and look what it has done to us. My people have lost their pride, their identity, their reason to live. Even if we were to eat, dress, live, and talk like the whites, we would never be white. We are Indian! No matter how hard we try to be like your people, they will never accept us as equals. It would have been better for us if we had all been killed rather than surrender."

Loralee was taken aback by his sudden burst of anger. She took a step back, keenly aware of the differences between them. "Do you really feel that way?"

"Yes."

"Then why did you come to school? If you don't want to change, if you don't want your people to change, why did you come?"

Zuniga closed the distance between them, his black eyes looking steadfastly into hers. "To be near you," he answered quietly.

"Oh."

Loralee's cheeks flushed with pleasure and she felt suddenly shy. Would he make love to her again? He was still watching her intently, and she began to fidget with the collar of her dress. His nearness made her senses come alive, and she was suddenly nervous without knowing why.

"I'm sorry you're against changes for your people," she said, not liking the heavy silence between them. "I think things are better now than in the old days. It might have been a lot of fun for the men, always out hunting and fighting and having a good time, but what about the women?" She was babbling in an effort to keep him away, not certain if she wanted him to know how much she needed him. "I'm glad I have a laundry tub to wash my clothes in so I don't have to haul them down to the river and pound them on a rock. I like having a sewing machine and a stove and all the other things that make my life easier, and I know most of the Indian women would feel the same if given half a chance."

"Maybe," Zuniga allowed. "All I know is

that something is missing from my life. I do not know what it is, but sometimes I feel like I do not belong anywhere." He stared past her, the fire gone from his eyes as he gazed at the distant mountains.

Loralee felt a twinge of disappointment. She had expected him to take her in his arms. Why had she rambled on about washtubs? What had she been afraid of?

They were silent for several minutes. Loralee's thoughts returned to their visit with Nachi. Zuniga was hiding something from her. What could it be?

"What was Nachi going to say that you didn't want me to hear?" she blurted at last, her curiosity overcoming her manners.

"I said forget it."

"It was about your father, wasn't it?"

"Loralee—"

She ignored the warning in his voice. "Did he beat you often?"

"I do not want to talk about it," Zuniga answered brusquely. "Some things are best left in the past and forgotten."

"But you haven't forgotten it," Loralee exclaimed. "I can see it in your eyes, hear it in your voice. Whatever it is, it's eating you up inside."

"You are right. I have not forgotten it." Zuniga laughed softly, bitterly. "Nachi was right. Our wickiup was a happier place when Nakai was not there. My mother would sing when we were alone. Sometimes she would dance the old dances with Nachi. My mother loved to laugh, but she never laughed when Nakai was home. No one did. I don't know why she loved the bastard. He never brought her anything but grief."

"You can't pick and choose the people you love," Loralee remarked wistfully. "It just happens."

"Maybe. I do not know. All I know is that my mother should never have married Nakai. He was twisted inside, never happy unless he was hitting something. And that something was usually me. He beat me when I tried to protect my mother from his cruelty, he beat me when I refused to steal whiskey for him, and sometimes he beat me just for the hell of it. Is that what you wanted to hear?"

"No." She chewed on her lower lip, saddened by what she had heard. Mike had told her that Zuniga had killed his father.

As if reading her mind, Zuniga turned to face her, his eyes seeking hers. "You have probably heard many rumors about me," he said flatly. "The people at the Agency do not like me. They think I am a thief and a liar. Most of their stories are lies, but the big one is true. I killed my father, and I want you to know it."

Loralee shook her head, not wanting to hear any more.

"Yes. He was drunk that night, but then, he was always drunk. And he was a mean

141

drunk. I do not know what set him off that night, but it did not take much to arouse his temper. I was not at our lodge when it began, but I could hear my mother screaming for help when I rode up.

"I ran into the lodge and almost fell over Nachi, who was lying unconscious on the floor across the doorway. I learned later that he had tried to defend my mother, and Nakai had hit him over the head with a beer bottle. My father was beating my mother, hitting her in the face and throat with his fists. She was bleeding from her nose and mouth when I dragged him away from her."

Zuniga's face grew dark and his eyes were terrible to see as he relived the incident in his mind. He could see it all clearly: his father, short and stocky, strong as an ox, his face flushed with drink, his black eyes wild with irrational anger as he hit Nadina with his fists; Nachi, lying on the floor, his gray hair matted with blood; Nadina's face, swollen and bleeding, her eyes damp with tears.

"My father swung at me and missed," Zuniga said, resuming his story. He laughed softly. "That really made Nakai mad. With a scream of rage, he grabbed his knife and came after me. We fought for what seemed like a long time. Finally, he managed to cut my forearm and I guess I went a little crazy. I shouted the Apache death cry and lunged at him. I knocked him off his feet and he dropped the knife. I killed him with my bare hands."

Loralee shuddered. She could see it all so clearly in her mind: Nadina sobbing as her husband and her son struggled on the floor, the hate in Shad's eyes as he fought to defend his mother against Nakai's drunken attack, the grandfather he loved lying on the floor, unconscious.

"Surely that was self-defense, not murder," Loralee whispered.

"No. I did not have to kill him. My mother died in my arms a few minutes later. The next morning, early, I dumped my father's body in a ravine and covered it with dirt and rocks."

"Did it happen here, on the reservation?"

"No. In the Dragoon Mountains."

"How old were you?"

"Sixteen."

"How awful that must have been for you."

Zuniga shrugged. "I am not sorry I killed him. I would do it again."

Loralee looked at him, her eyes filling with compassion. What could she say? He had done a terrible thing, yet she could understand why he had done it.

"Come," Zuniga said. "I'll take you home."

7

Loralee arrived at the schoolhouse early the next night, wondering if he would come, wondering if she would feel the same now that she had heard his story. She paced the floor in front of her desk, thinking about what Zuniga had told her. No matter how Zuniga had felt about his father, no matter what his reason for killing him might have been, it must be an awful burden to bear.

She whirled around when she heard the door swing open, felt her heart leap with gladness when he entered the room and closed the door behind him.

Wordlessly, he took his customary seat, opened his McGuffey's Reader to the page she specified, and began to read:

"Charles was an honest boy, but his neighbor, Jack Pilfer, was a thief. Charles would not take anything which did not belong to him; but Jack would take whatever he could get.

"Early one summer's morning, as Charles was going to school, he met a man who had oranges to sell. The man wished to stop and get his breakfast, and asked Charles if he would hold his horse while he went into the house. . . ."

Loralee listened as Zuniga read. His voice was deep, resonant, pleasing to the ear as he read the story of Jack and Charles.

She looked up askance as Zuniga broke off in mid-sentence.

"This is a foolish story for a grown man to read," he declared, and closed the book with a resounding bang.

"I'm sorry you feel that way. Maybe I can find you something more thought-provoking."

"I have learned to read, and I have learned to write. It is enough."

"What do you want to do, then?"

Zuniga rose to his feet. He towered over her, making her feel small and helpless, vulnerable in a way that was both frightening and titillating.

"I want to make love to you," Zuniga replied evenly.

Loralee swallowed hard. Seven little words, yet they affected her whole body. Her heart began to beat faster, her cheeks grew hot, her knees grew weak as a sudden warmth started within her and heated her whole body.

"What did you say?" she stammered.

"I want to make love to you," Zuniga repeated. "Here. Now."

"Here?" Her voice was weak.

He nodded, his eyes watching her face. What he saw reflected there pleased him. Going to the lamp, he extinguished the flame, then gathered Loralee into his arms and kissed her, his mouth crushing hers as he claimed the kiss he had hungered for since he entered the schoolhouse that night. She yielded without a struggle, her eyelids fluttering down as her mouth opened to the invasion of his tongue. Her arms twined around his shoulders for support, her fingers digging into his back as she drew him closer still. She was hardly aware of it when he lowered her to the floor behind her desk. The planks were cool against her flesh as he expertly removed her clothing and then his own before he stretched out beside her. His body was warm, hard, eager, and she urged him on, wanting him to make love to her, to enter her and make her whole. Her hands moved restlessly over his broad back and shoulders as she wrapped her legs around his waist, moaning softly as he thrust into her again and again until, at the last, she cried his name.

Seconds later, Zuniga shuddered to a halt. With a sigh of satisfaction, he rolled onto his side, drawing Loralee with him so they lay face to face, arms and legs entwined. He kissed her cheek and neck as he whispered her name, and Loralee closed her eyes, utterly content, utterly happy.

She was dozing off when she heard a knock at the door. With a gasp, she started to sit up, but Zuniga held her down, motioning for her to be silent.

"Loralee?" It was Mike's voice.

Panic made Loralee's heart pound in her breast as she heard the door swing open, heard Mike call her name a second time. Tears of shame welled in her eyes. What would Mike think of her if he found her lying on the floor in Shad Zuniga's arms? How could she ever explain? What could she possibly say?

She held her breath, grateful for the darkness. Then an overwhelming sense of relief came over her when she heard the door close.

She was suddenly aware of Zuniga beside her. His arm was like iron beneath her neck, his whole body was taut with anger as he stood up and pulled on his pants.

"What's the matter?" she asked in a small voice.

"You were ashamed, were you not? Ashamed to think he might find you with an Indian."

Loralee scrambled to her feet, wanting to make him understand, but it was too late. He was already gone.

Loralee stared at Zuniga's shirt and moccasins piled beside her dress and shoes, and she began to laugh. He had been so anxious to get away from her, he had not even taken the time to finish dressing.

She laughed and laughed and it was only when she felt the wetness on her cheeks that she realized her laughter had turned to tears.

8

"I stopped by your house last night," Mike was saying, "but you weren't there, so I went over to the schoolhouse. You weren't there either." He looked at her expectantly, waiting for an answer. "Where were you?" he asked when Loralee offered no explanation.

Loralee looked down at her hands. "We finished the lesson early and I went for a walk."

"A walk? At night? Alone?"

"Yes. I . . . I needed some time by myself. To think."

"About what?"

"Different things. Teaching, mostly. I . . . I'm having trouble with Short Bear in class. He's causing trouble, and I don't know how to handle it."

"Tell him to leave."

"No, I don't want to do that. He's a very bright boy. I know he could learn if he would just apply himself."

Mike nodded slowly. Loralee seemed sincere, yet her words did not quite ring true. "Is Zuniga still coming to school?"

"Yes. No."

"Well, which is it? Yes or no?"

"I'm not sure. He . . . he said he's tired of reading children's books. I don't think he'll be coming back for any more lessons."

"Good." Mike smiled at Loralee, wondering why she looked so pale. "If you fix a nice lunch, I'll take you on a picnic tomorrow morning."

"All right."

"Loralee, is anything troubling you? Besides Short Bear, I mean? You're not mad at me for coming by the school last night, are you?"

"No. Everything's fine."

"You'd tell me if something was wrong?"

"Of course. I'm fine, Mike, really."

"Good." Taking her hands in his, he drew her close and kissed her. His moustache tickled her upper lip, his mouth was warm and firm, insistent. Loralee kissed him back eagerly, almost desperately, wanting to love this kind, gentle man, wanting to feel the same passion she felt when Zuniga took her in his arms. She was disappointed when nothing happened.

"Loralee, you're driving me crazy," Mike said huskily. "I think about you all the time." He kissed her again, his mouth demanding a response she could not give.

Mike groaned low in his throat as he released her. "I love you, Loralee. How would you feel about being an Army wife?"

Loralee stared up at him, flustered by his unexpected proposal. Marry Mike? The idea had occurred to her, of course, but that had been before she met Shad Zuniga. She had been attracted to Zuniga the first moment she saw him stepping from his lodge —deeply attracted even though he was an Indian and could not be for her. But she could not deny her feelings. His nearness had aroused her in a way that was different from anything she had ever experienced. No other man had ever affected her in such a way.

She studied Mike. He was young and handsome, with a brilliant career ahead of him. He was sweet and gentle, thoughtful, the type of man every girl dreamed of. Why couldn't she return his love? Why did she feel nothing more than friendly affection for him?

"Loralee?" His hand stroked her cheek as he waited for her answer.

"I . . . I don't know."

"Think about it, will you?"

"I will. I promise."

"Good. Don't forget about the picnic. I'll pick you up about ten and we'll make a day of it."

Loralee smiled and waved as he swung into the saddle and rode toward the fort.

Mike arrived promptly at ten Saturday morning, a bouquet of flowers in one hand, a bottle of wine in the other.

"Ready?" he asked.

Loralee nodded. Picking up a large wicker basket, she followed Mike outside, and smiled as he lifted her into the shiny black buggy he had borrowed for the day.

They chatted about the weather and the people at the fort as they rode toward a shady spot beside the stream. Mike helped Loralee from the buggy and tethered the horse to an overhanging tree branch while Loralee spread a blanket on the ground.

"It's pretty here, isn't it?" Mike mused.

"Yes, lovely."

"Shall we take a walk before lunch?"

"If you like."

Hand in hand, they walked along the stream, stopping now and then to admire a wildflower or plant. Mike couldn't keep his eyes off the woman beside him. She was an enchanting creature, as charmed by the antics of a prairie dog as any young child. She stopped at an ant hill to watch dozens of red ants scurry back and forth in search of food, and smiled with pleasure when a tiny yellow butterfly perched on her shoulder.

Back at the blanket, she removed her shoes and stockings and dangled her feet in the water.

"How long have you been stationed out here, Mike?" she asked.

"Two years."

"Did you request a Western post?"

"Yes. The fastest promotions still come to those who serve on the frontier."

Loralee laughed softly. "I didn't think there were any frontiers left."

"It's still pretty uncivilized out here," Mike remarked. He plucked a long blade of grass and twirled it between his thumb and forefinger. "It wasn't all that long ago that Geronimo was running wild in these parts, you know."

"That's true. Why did you join the Army?"

"Just following in my father's footsteps, I guess," Mike answered with a grin. "I was born at Fort Lincoln while my father was off campaigning against Crazy Horse and Sitting Bull at the Little Big Horn."

"Your father rode with Custer?"

"Yes. My old man said it was a hell of a fight."

"But all the men who rode with Custer were killed."

"They were," Mike said, his face grave.

"But Custer split his forces into three groups, you know. My father was with Reno's platoon."

Loralee nodded. General George Armstrong Custer had been a brash, arrogant, headstrong man. His men had called him "Hard Ass" behind his back. It was rumored that he had abandoned Major Joel Elliott and nineteen men on the banks of the Washita River back in 1868 while campaigning against the Cheyenne Indians. Some said it was an error in judgment, and some said it was an act of cowardice.

Custer had made another error in judgment the day he rode into the valley of the Little Big Horn. He had refused to believe his own scouts when they warned him there were many Indians camped in the valley. He had refused to wait for Terry and Gibbon, who were to be part of a three-pronged attack against the Sioux and Cheyenne. Ignoring his orders, Custer had split his forces and attacked the Indians two days early. His men, badly outnumbered, had been slaughtered.

Captain Frederick Benteen and Major Marcus Reno, the two officers left in charge of Custer's remaining men, had also engaged in heavy fighting that fateful day, suffering heavy losses. The Sioux and Cheyenne had ridden against the soldiers with a vengeance, evening out old scores, avenging the men, women, and children who had been massacred at Sand Creek and the Washita.

Custer's defeat at the battle of the Little Big Horn was still talked about whenever Army men got together. Few battles in American history had been fought and refought so many times. The Custer family had lost five men that day. In addition to the general, his two brothers, Boston Custer and Tom Custer, had been killed, as had the general's favorite nephew, Henry Armstrong Reed, affectionately known as Autie, and Custer's brother-in-law, Lieutenant James Calhoun. The sole survivor of Custer's battalion had been Captain Myles Keogh's horse, Comanche. The horse died in 1891, fifteen years after the battle.

Loralee shivered as she imagined the battle at Little Big Horn, the Seventh Cavalry fighting valiantly against overwhelming odds, the war cries of the Sioux and Cheyenne, the dust churned up by the hooves of hundreds of Indian ponies, the screams of pain as feathered arrows pierced human flesh, the smell of blood and fear as the ground turned red with blood. Thank God those days were gone.

"Loralee? Are you all right?"

"What? Oh, yes. I was just thinking how awful the battle must have been."

"Yes. My father said it was the worst two days of his life. He said they fully expected to die on the ridge where they had holed up. The Indians had a big celebration that night. My father said they could see the Indian campfires and hear their victory shouts. The soldiers spent the night digging trenches while the Indians danced and sang. In the morning, the Indians attacked their position for a short time and then, for no apparent reason, they broke away and left the valley. One of the scouts said the Indians just got tired of fighting and called the whole thing off."

"Do you like the Army?"

"Most of the time. Now and then I get a little tired of taking orders, but if everything goes as planned, I'll soon be giving them instead."

"A promotion, Mike? That's wonderful."

"I can sure use the money that goes with it," Mike remarked, "what with the prices going up the way they are. Last time I got a haircut in town, it cost me two bits."

Loralee nodded. Prices were going up at an alarming rate. Beef was ten cents a pound, potatoes were two cents each, and a man's suit cost five dollars.

"You'll make a wonderful officer, Mike," Loralee said.

"I hope so. Of course, it isn't definite yet. But Colonel Freeman likes me, and he thinks I'm doing a good job. Heaven knows I've put in enough extra hours and licked his boots enough times to earn those lieutenant's bars."

"Mike!"

"Well, it's true. Sometimes I'd like to bury my fist in Freeman's face. The man is a stickler for rules and regulations, all spit and polish and playing by the book." Mike laughed. "Hey, I brought you out here to have a good time, not listen to a bunch of complaints."

"I am having a good time. Where are your folks, Mike? They must be proud of you."

"They live in Virginia," Mike grinned at Loralee, his blue eyes twinkling with mischief. "I'm twenty-nine years old," he said, executing a snappy salute. "My father raises thoroughbred horses. My mother is an excellent cook and housekeeper, and raises the most beautiful roses in the world. I have three older brothers, all gainfully employed and happily married, and a younger sister who dreams of being an actress, much to the consternation of my parents. I don't smoke, and I only drink at parties."

Loralee laughed merrily. "How did you know I was going to ask all those things?"

"Male intuition," Mike answered, grinning hugely. "Now, what about you?"

"I'm twenty-three," Loralee said in the same businesslike tone of voice that Mike had used. "I'm an only child, though I have several cousins back in Philadelphia. My parents were killed when I was thirteen. I don't sing or dance, but I can play 'Silent Night' on the piano. I'm in excellent health and have all my own teeth."

Mike roared with laughter. "You're hired," he declared, still laughing. "How's your cooking?"

For an answer, Loralee opened the picnic basket and served him a lunch of cold fried chicken, potato salad, cole slaw, freshly baked buttermilk biscuits spread with homemade jam, and chocolate cake for dessert.

Mike sighed with contentment as he polished off a second slice of cake. "I didn't think anybody in this world could make a better cake than Mom's," he remarked, "until now."

"Why, thank you," Loralee said, smiling. "That's high praise indeed."

They were packing the leftovers into the basket when Loralee glanced up. Her heart skipped a beat when she saw Zuniga in the distance. He was mounted on the big dun stallion, riding toward the hills. He was naked save for clout and moccasins, and as she looked at him, she imagined that was how he must have looked while riding to war, his hair flowing down his back, his handsome face streaked with paint.

"What is it?" Mike asked, noticing her intense gaze. "Oh. Zuniga. Damn! I knew he had a rifle."

Loralee nodded absently. She could see

the sunlight glinting off the barrel of the Winchester that Shad held in his right hand.

"I'd give a month's pay to know where he hides that rifle," Mike muttered.

"I don't understand what difference it makes if he has a rifle or not. He only uses it for hunting."

"It's not the rifle," Mike explained. "He isn't supposed to have a gun, and as long as he does, it's like a slap in the face. He's always putting himself outside the reservation laws. He comes and goes pretty much as he pleases. I know he's slipped off the reservation several times in the past six months, and someday, by damn, I'll catch him."

"And then what?"

"I'll throw him in jail, that's what."

Loralee nodded, her eyes still on Zuniga. She watched him until he was out of sight, her heart beating fast with the memory of the night they had shared.

Later, at home, Loralee wandered aimlessly through her small house, her mind skipping back and forth between Mike and Zuniga. Both men were still in her thoughts when she finally went to sleep.

On Sunday she went to church with Mike as usual, but all through the day she was counting the hours until Monday, wondering if Zuniga would come to the school to see her. Hoping with all her heart that he would give her a chance to explain.

161

But he did not show up at the schoolhouse on Monday night, or any other night.

The next few days passed slowly. At first, Loralee continued to wait anxiously at the schoolhouse each evening, certain he would come back, certain he could not just walk out of her life after what they had shared, but Zuniga never came to the school. She walked around the grounds at night, hoping he might seek her out, but he never did.

She cried copious tears, berating herself for her stupidity. Of course he would not come back. He had taken what he wanted and now he was through with her. But in her heart she knew that was a lie. She had offended his pride, and that was why he was no longer interested in her. If only she could have made him stay and listen. Yet what could she possibly have said? She had been ashamed; ashamed of the compromising position she had been in, ashamed of being in Zuniga's arms when she had no right to be there. She had been ashamed, not of Shad, but of her own weakness.

But now that he was gone, she no longer cared what people would think or what was right. But it was too late. She had lost him.

She threw herself into her teaching, spent long hours poring over books and stories to make learning more interesting. She taught her students more than just reading and writing, she encouraged them to think, to paint, to sing, to dance, to let their imaginations run wild. And because she was genuinely interested in the Apache children, and truly fond of them, they began to respond. Yellow Basket had a flair for poetry. Young Deer had a talent for painting. Star Gazer could sing like a nightingale, while Little Hawk could tell the most amazing stories.

As the weeks went by, three of the older boys began to attend class. They came grudgingly, openly resentful of her because she was white, and a woman. Many times she was tempted to throw up her hands in exasperation and expel them from the class, but she stubbornly refused to admit defeat, and with patience and affection, she gradually won them to her side. When they complained about reading the same books as the younger children, she brought them newspapers and novels to read, and when she discovered how bright and intelligent the boys were, she demanded more of them.

Mike complained that she was always preoccupied with teaching, but he could not deny the results. The children were learning, and liking it.

The days for Loralee took care of themselves, but the nights . . . oh, the nights when she was in bed, alone and unable to sleep. That was when she missed Zuniga the most. It was then that her body began to torment her, every fiber yearning for the touch of Zuniga's lips, for the sweet magic of his hands on her too willing flesh, for the wondrous ecstasy that had filled her heart and soul as they became one.

Night after night she cried herself to sleep, hating him because he had deserted her, hating herself for wounding his fierce masculine pride, hating her body because it hungered for the pleasure of his caress.

One night when she could not sleep, she buried her face in the shirt Zuniga had left at the schoolhouse in his haste to be away from her. Closing her eyes, she took a deep breath. The shirt smelled faintly of tobacco smoke and sweat and of Zuniga himself. His voice, angry and accusing, echoed in her mind.

"You were ashamed, were you not, ashamed to think he might find you with an Indian?"

"Damn you, Shad Zuniga," she murmured brokenly. "Why can't I forget you?"

Time and again she saddled her horse and started toward his lodge, only to turn back. She could not go to him. What could she say? What would she do if she humbled herself enough to beg his forgiveness and he laughed in her face? She had to hold onto her pride at all costs. It was all she had left.

She spent more time at the fort and at the Agency office, hoping to hear news of him, but all she heard were the same old rumors, the same tired tales. Funny, she thought, the soldiers never seemed to grow weary of speculating about Zuniga, or about the number of weapons he was rumored to have secreted in Nachi's lodge. To listen to some of the men, Zuniga had enough rifles and ammunition stashed away to arm every man, woman, and child on the reservation. One wag even claimed that Zuniga had an old Army howitzer cached away in the hills somewhere. Loralee would have laughed if she hadn't been so miserably unhappy.

She rode to the Agency on ration day, hoping to catch sight of him, hoping he might show up just once for the beef or blankets that were his due. But he never did.

She took long rides in the hills, careful not to stray too near his lodge, but always hoping she might accidentally run into him on the trail. She wandered through hills and valleys, down cutbank arroyos and dry river-beds, until she knew every tree and rock and path, until she was certain she had ridden over every inch of the reservation, but she never saw him.

Anger followed on the heels of despair. Who did he think he was, to purposefully avoid her? She had willingly given him her most priceless possession, the most precious token of her love, and now he had no further use for her. Damn him! She would hate and despise him until the day she died. He was exactly what everyone said he was, and she had been foolish not to listen. He was nothing but a heathen savage, after all, and she was well rid of him! She had simply fooled herself when she had thought that she loved him. It had just been infatuation and lust, nothing more . . .

Shad Zuniga sat on his horse atop a hill, screened from Loralee's sight by a tangled mass of shrubs and cactus as he watched her follow a narrow deer trail up into the foothills. He had seen her several times, always from a distance, always careful to stay out of sight. He had been a fool to think she had learned to care for him. She had wanted him in the way a woman wants a man, but she did not love him, he saw that now. She had been ashamed of him, ashamed of her desire for an Indian. Zuniga laughed bitterly. Perhaps it had been the fact that he was an Apache, and therefore forbidden, that had sparked her desire for him in the first place.

He swore a vile oath. He would never forget the look on her face that night in the schoolhouse when she thought they were going to be discovered. She had been ashamed, not because they were almost caught, but because she had almost been caught with him. It had cut his heart like a knife, wounding his fierce male pride, killing the love he had felt for her. And perhaps it was better so. He had always known she could never truly be his. Perhaps it was better that it had ended now, before it had really begun, before it became impossible to let her go.

With a rueful grin, he admitted he still desired her. For all that she had never known a man before, she had quickly learned how to please him, to arouse and excite him, to satisfy him as no other woman ever had.

As he watched from the hilltop, his eyes lingered over the swell of Loralee's breasts and the feminine contours of her hips. She sat her horse well, moving with the animal, not sitting stiff and tense in the saddle the way most whites rode. The sun made her hair glow like a golden halo, and he remembered how soft it had felt in his hands and against his face and chest.

Damn! He was sorely tempted to ride after her, to make love to her one more time, but he did not follow her, only sat there watching her until she was lost from sight. Then he turned for home.

Loralee looked at the stack of papers on her desk, but she was not in the mood to grade exams. It was a Saturday afternoon, bright and clear and beautiful. Much too nice a day to sit inside.

Shoving the papers into her desk, she went outside and saddled Lady and rode up into the hills. As always, her thoughts turned to Zuniga. Where was he? What was he doing? Did he ever think of her?

Lost in thought, Loralee almost rode

past the boy lying in the shallow ravine. But for his faint moan of pain, she would have ridden on by, unaware of his presence.

At the cry, she reined Lady to a halt, her head cocked to one side. Was she imagining things? But no, there it was again, a hoarse sob.

Determining the location of the faint cry, she dismounted and picked her way to the edge of the ravine, her heart pounding with anxiety. Was the cry human, or that of a wounded and therefore potentially dangerous beast?

Peering over the side of the ravine, she gave a gasp of recognition as she saw Short Bear huddled on the ground below.

Loralee called his name as she started down the side of the ravine, leading her horse.

Short Bear glanced up, his handsome young face a mask of pain. For a moment, he felt a surge of gratitude that help had arrived at last. Then recognizing Loralee, he grimaced with displeasure.

Loralee knelt beside the boy, frowning. "Where are you hurt?"

"My leg," Short Bear replied stiffly. "It's broken."

She could see that now. His right leg was twisted and swollen, a grotesque shape beneath his buckskin trousers.

"Can you stand up if I help you?" Loralee asked.

"I don't need your help."

Loralee was about to argue, then thought better of it. "Very well." She stood up, waiting for him to get up on his own.

Short Bear took a deep breath, then tried to stand up. He gasped with pain as he accidentally put pressure on his broken leg. Sweat popped out on his forehead and he felt suddenly sick to his stomach. That would be the final humiliation, he thought in anguish, to vomit before a woman.

Without a word, Loralee stepped forward and took Short Bear's arm to give him support. A cry of pain escaped his lips as he struggled to his feet, and he flushed with embarrassment. An Apache warrior did not show pain, especially in front of one who was not of the People. It was galling, having to rely on a woman for help. What would his cousin say when he found out? The other boys would tease him unmercifully when they learned that Miss Warfield had found him lying helpless in a ravine.

With Loralee's help, Short Bear managed to climb into the saddle. He was perspiring heavily by then, his face pale, his breathing labored.

"Hang on," Loralee said encouragingly. Taking Lady's reins, she started up the ravine.

It was slow going. The dirt was soft, and Loralee slipped several times, her steps hampered by her long riding skirt. Thankfully, the mare had no trouble navigating the steep slope. Once, glancing over her shoulder, Loralee saw that Short Bear's eyes were tightly closed. His hands were white as they gripped the saddle horn, and she knew that each step the mare took was causing the boy intense pain.

At the top of the ravine, Loralee paused to catch her breath and get her bearings. The reservation was some distance away, but Nachi's lodge was just over the next rise. Still, she hesitated. How could she go there? How could she face Zuniga?

A muffled whimper of pain dissolved her doubts. Short Bear was hurting. He needed help, and he needed it now. Her own personal feelings were of no importance at the moment.

It took almost three-quarters of an hour to reach Nachi's lodge. Tying Lady's reins to a bush near the wickiup, Loralee rapped on the lodgeflap, praying that the old man was at home and Zuniga was not.

The lodgeflap lifted immediately and Zuniga stepped into the sunlight. He was naked save for a brief clout and knee-high moccasins, and for a moment Loralee could only stare at him, the reason for her presence at his lodge forgotten. Here was the man she dreamed of at night, the man whose touch she longed for. Her eyes drank in the sight of his broad shoulders and lean flanks, even as her nostrils filled with the scent of tobacco and leather and man. Her stomach fluttered wildly.

"What do you want?" His curt greeting was like a slap in the face, but it served its purpose, quickly reminding Loralee why she was there.

"Short Bear broke his leg. I brought him to you for help."

Zuniga's dark eyes swept past her to where Short Bear sat slumped in the saddle. The boy's eyes were closed, his body rigid with pain.

Mouthing a vague obscenity, Zuniga went to Short Bear's side. With ease, he lifted the boy from the saddle.

"A snake spooked my horse," Short Bear muttered.

"Later," Zuniga admonished. "You can tell me what happened later."

"It was a big snake. Sun Dancer bucked and shied and I fell over his neck and down the hill." Short Bear gritted his teeth as pain knifed through his leg. "Stupid horse bolted for home."

Zuniga nodded as he carried Short Bear into the lodge and carefully placed him on Nachi's sleeping robes. The old man had gone down to the reservation to visit a friend and would not be back for several hours.

"Water," Short Bear husked.

Zuniga held a clay bowl to the boy's lips. "Only a little," he warned.

Short Bear drank greedily in spite of

Zuniga's advice, then fell back, his face sheened with sweat.

"Just lie still," Zuniga said. Drawing his knife, he slit the boy's trousers along the seam, exposing the injured leg. It was badly swollen and discolored around the break.

Loralee lingered outside the lodge, irritated by Zuniga's brusque attitude. He hadn't even bothered to thank her for bringing Short Bear to him, she mused sourly, but then, what could you expect from such a man? She wished she had the nerve to march into the lodge and tell him what she thought of him. Instead, she took up Lady's reins and prepared to mount.

"I need your help," Zuniga's voice called to her from within the lodge.

Loralee's eyebrows went up in surprise. Needed her help, did he? Well, he could whistle for help for all she cared, she thought in a huff, but then she thought of Short Bear. She couldn't just ride off if the boy needed her.

With a sigh of resignation, she ducked inside the gloomy wickiup. "What do you want?" she asked, hoping her voice sounded as curt and unfriendly as his had been.

"I need you to hold him down while I splint his leg. Can you do it?"

"Of course." Loralee knelt beside Short Bear. His eyes were glazed with pain. She saw the fear lingering behind his eyes, fear of the pain that was to come. For all his brave front, he was still just a boy. She sent him an encouraging smile as she placed her hands on his shoulders.

"Keep him as still as you can," Zuniga instructed.

Loralee nodded. She felt Short Bear grow tense as Zuniga took hold of his broken leg, and she leaned across the boy's body, blocking his view as she held him down.

The boy gave a hoarse cry of agony, then went mercifully limp as Shad pulled the bone into place.

Sitting back on her heels, Loralee watched as Zuniga quickly and expertly splinted the boy's leg.

Seeing there was nothing more for her to do, she stood up, anxious to be away. There was so much she wanted to say to him, so much to explain, yet the words would not come. With a curt nod, she left the lodge and swung into the saddle.

"Thanks."

He had followed her out of the lodge. She could feel his presence behind her, could feel his eyes on her back.

Loralee nodded, afraid to speak, afraid to look at him for fear she would dissolve into tears.

She did not go riding in the hills any more after that. Seeing Shad was too painful. She could tell herself she hated him until she was blue in the face, but in truth, she loved him desperately. Would always love him.

But she never wanted to see him again.

9

Short Bear frowned at his cousin. "How much longer do I have to lie here?" he asked sullenly.

"Another two weeks," Zuniga answered matter-of-factly.

Short Bear groaned. Two more weeks of lying on his back, doing nothing, or sitting out in the sun, or hobbling around on the crutch Zuniga had improvised. Two more weeks of inactivity, when he longed to be out with the other boys, or riding the hills on that wretched horse that had thrown him.

"Red Crow stopped by with your school work while you were asleep," Zuniga remarked.

Short Bear groaned again. Miss Warfield

made certain that one of the boys brought him his homework every day. Often she sent him encouraging notes, commending him for a paper that was exceptionally well done, or she penned a few words to say she hoped he was feeling better. Once she had sent him a box of oatmeal cookies. Another time she had sent a get well card that had been signed by the whole class. Zuniga seemed amused by it all, but Short Bear was confused. Only a few months ago, he had been trying to drive the new schoolmarm away, and now she was sending him homemade cookies and get well cards.

With a sigh, he looked at the book Zuniga handed him, then dropped it onto the ground. "I don't feel like studying," he declared. "Tell me about the time you were in jail in Mexico."

"It was a bad time," Zuniga replied, frowning at the memory. "Why do you want to hear about it?"

"Because you were so brave," Short Bear answered.

"You are the brave one," Zuniga countered. "You did not cry when I set your leg, and you have not complained once about the pain. You would have made a fine warrior."

Short Bear's face glowed at his cousin's praise. To be a warrior was all he had ever wanted, all he cared about.

"Tell me about California, then," Short Bear prompted.

"California," Zuniga drawled, smiling. "A pretty place. Forests and valleys and mountains. And that beautiful blue ocean."

"Murdock," Short Bear stated impatiently. "Tell me about Murdock."

John Murdock was a wealthy rancher who owned a large cattle ranch that covered thousands of acres.

"I was just passing through," Zuniga began, his mind going back in time. "It was shortly after I escaped from prison, and I had the urge to travel. It was about noon on a hot day in July. I was crossing Murdock's land when I heard a scream for help. I started toward the sound and saw a small boy in the middle of a lake. His shirt was caught on a snag and he could not get free. He was tiring fast, and he went under the water as I rode up. I swam out and got him and he asked me to take him home.

"I thought Murdock was going to shoot me on sight," Zuniga said, grinning, "but then he saw the boy sitting behind me, and he came running down the porch stairs.

"'What the hell happened?' Murdock demanded, and the boy began to explain how he had gone for a swim and got hung up. Murdock grabbed my hand and pumped it up and down, thanking me all the while for saving his grandson's life.

"He insisted I stay on for a couple of days, and I took him up on his offer." Zuniga shook his head in wonder. "I never lived so good in my whole life. Three good meals a day, every day. And if I wanted something special to eat, all I had to do was ask. Murdock even offered me a job bustin' broncs, but I turned him down. Nice as his place was, it was not home, and I was just passing through."

"But he said you could have the job any time you wanted it," Short Bear said.

"Yeah. And he gave me the dun as a going away present," Zuniga finished.

"Do you think you'll ever go back to California?" Short Bear asked.

Zuniga shook his head. "No reason to go back."

Short Bear studied his cousin intently for a moment, then blurted, "Why aren't you courting Miss Warfield anymore?"

"I never courted her," Zuniga answered tersely.

"It looked like courting," Short Bear said candidly. "Everyone on the reservation thought you would marry her."

Zuniga stared at the boy, speechless. How did such rumors get started? Marriage, indeed!

"I think perhaps you speak of that which you know nothing about," Zuniga said curtly.

"I know more than you think. I saw the two of you together at Shadow Lake one day."

"Have you taken to spying on me?" Zuniga demanded angrily.

"I was not spying," Short Bear answered with dignity. "I was hunting. I did not stay to watch what happened after you kissed her, but I know what goes on between a man and a woman."

"Do you?" Zuniga asked, his anger momentarily forgotten.

"Yes." Short Bear's face flushed guiltily.

"And who taught you how to be a man?"

Short Bear shrugged. "No one. A girl in town. A street girl."

Zuniga grinned, amused by his cousin's unexpected revelation.

"You are not going to marry the white woman?" Short Bear's query was more like a plea than a question.

"No," Zuniga answered tonelessly. "I am not going to marry her."

"But you would like to?"

"Have you always been so full of questions? Go on, do your school work and stop pestering me."

The sound of hoofbeats roused Zuniga from a restless sleep. Visions of Loralee responding to Mike Schofield's caresses faded into nothingness as he rose quietly to his feet, his hand automatically reaching for the hunting knife at his bedside. He glanced quickly at Nachi and Short Bear, still sleeping soundly, then slipped outside.

The morning was cold, the sky overcast and dreary. He turned sharply to the right, his eyes narrowing in anger as he saw Sergeant Schofield and a dozen other soldiers surround the lodge.

Schofield glared at Zuniga. The Apache was clad in a brief deerskin clout, nothing more, and Schofield thought derisively that he looked more like a wild animal than a human being. He had a fleeting image of Loralee bending over Zuniga's shoulder as she explained the difference between a noun and a verb.

Anger washed through Schofield as he remembered the way Zuniga's eyes had moved over Loralee's face and body, lingering on the swell of her breasts and the curve of her hips. His hand caressed the butt of his service revolver. It would be so easy to unleather the weapon and place a bullet between Zuniga's eyes. So easy . . . revulsion welled within Schofield as he realized what he was thinking. He was not a man normally given to violence. How could he even contemplate killing a man in cold blood, even Zuniga?

Schofield's hand dropped stiffly to his side, and he stared intently at the knife in Zuniga's hand. "I'll take that weapon," he said curtly. Dismounting, he held out his hand.

Zuniga shook his head. "No."

"I said I'll take that knife."

"And I said no."

A muscle worked in Schofield's jaw. He

had no right to take the knife, but he couldn't back down now. Not in front of his men. Not in front of Zuniga.

"Hobart!"

"Sir!"

"Disarm him."

"Yes, sir!"

In a move that had obviously been executed before, three men dismounted and moved toward Zuniga, their sidearms drawn and cocked, their faces determined. They were all young men, well disciplined and eager to prove themselves capable of handling any situation.

Corporal Hobart stopped directly in front of Zuniga and held out his left hand.

Zuniga ignored the corporal and the two men standing behind him. His eyes never left Schofield's face as, with lightning speed, he reversed the knife in his hand and, with a flick of his wrist, sent the blade sailing through the air to land in the dirt between Mike Schofield's feet.

Startled, Schofield cursed loudly as he took a hasty step backward, and he felt his neck burn as a few of the older men snickered. A stern look silenced the laughter.

With as much dignity as he could muster, Schofield bent down and plucked the knife from the dirt. It was a deadly-looking weapon, the blade long and straight, sharp as a razor. The handle was made of bone, wrapped with hide.

"Hobart, Ryan, search the lodge," Mike ordered brusquely. "The rest of you, scout around out here."

Without a word, Zuniga turned on his heel and followed the two soldiers into the lodge. Short Bear and Nachi were awake now. Short Bear was standing at the rear of the lodge, the crutch under one arm. He threw Zuniga a worried look.

"It is all right," Zuniga said, his eyes warning the boy not to do anything foolish.

Nachi sat cross-legged on his blankets, his aged face impassive, his black eyes smoldering with fury as the enemy prowled around his lodge making crude jokes. Stupid pinda-lick-o-ye, he mused. Stupid white men. They never learned. Many times in the past they had come to his lodge searching for Zuniga's weapons, but they never found anything. When would they give up? When would they realize that his grandson was too smart to hide the forbidden weapons inside the lodge where they would be easily discovered?

Closing his eyes, the old man let his mind wander back in time, back to the old days when he had ridden the war trails, when his arrows had sliced into the white man's flesh. Ah, those had been the good times, the shining times. With a little sigh, he fell asleep, his chin dropping to his chest. In his dreams, he was a young man again, full of strength and vigor.

Zuniga stood near the doorway, his arms crossed over his chest, while the two white men searched the lodge, poking into jars and pots, peering under his bedroll, rifling through Nachi's meager belongings as they made derisive comments about the Indians and their primitive way of life.

"There's nothing here," Hobart muttered as he lifted a pile of robes. "You'd think the sergeant would give up."

"Yeah," Ryan agreed. "Let's get out of here. This place stinks."

A low rumble of anger welled in Short Bear's throat. How could Zuniga stand there and say nothing while the white men rummaged through their belongings and made tasteless jokes about their home, their women? He met his cousin's eyes, silently pleading for Zuniga to do something, but Zuniga only shook his head.

"Shit, let's go," Hobart growled. "If I have to stay in here much longer, I'm gonna puke."

The two white men ducked outside, and Zuniga followed them, first warning Short Bear to stay inside.

"Well?" Schofield asked impatiently. "Did you find anything?"

Ryan shook his head. "Clean as a whistle."

Zuniga met Schofield's accusing glance with an insolent grin. The soldiers had searched Nachi's lodge more than a dozen

183

times in the past six months, but they never found a thing. His rifle and his handgun were safely buried in the middle of the horse corral, safely wrapped in an oilskin together with several boxes of ammunition. His bow and arrows were hung in a tree, virtually invisible unless you knew where to look.

Mike Schofield held Zuniga's gaze. Damn the man! He was nothing but trouble. Everyone knew he was a liar and a thief, yet no one could catch him in anything the least bit underhanded. But he would, Mike vowed. By damn, one day he'd catch the bastard red-handed, and then they'd see who had the last laugh!

Face grim, Schofield swung into the saddle. "Mount up," he ordered tersely. Back stiff as a ramrod, he gigged his big bay horse into a trot and rode away from the old man's lodge.

10

The first inkling Loralee had that something was sorely amiss came on a cool morning in late November when she vomited her breakfast. She passed it off as an upset stomach caused by overeating at the weekly dance at the fort the night before and thought no more about it, until it happened again the next morning. And the next. Stricken, she realized that she had not had her monthly flow since the first of October. Over six weeks ago.

She flew to her mirror, shook her head in disbelief as she studied her reflection in the glass. Her breasts seemed larger, tender to the touch. Her belly was gently rounded instead of flat. Or was it merely her imagination?

"No!" She shook her head, refusing to believe what she knew to be true. She was pregnant.

Guilt and remorse dropped over her like a dark shadow. What a fool she had been to think she could flaunt the laws of God and man and not have to pay the price. Still, it had never occurred to her that she might get pregnant. That was something that happened to other people.

She spent a sleepless night pacing the floor, wondering what to do. She was pregnant, and Shad Zuniga was the father. She would never be able to live down the scandal. She would lose her job, her good name, everything she had worked so hard to achieve. And all because she had been unable to control her desire for a man who did not want her.

She wept bitter tears, her fists pounding the pillow in frustration. What would people say? What would Mike say? She would have to leave the reservation before anyone found out. She could not bear the shame.

The tears came harder as she thought of leaving the children. She had grown to love them dearly. Why did this have to happen now, when she was finally making real progress, when they were beginning to enjoy the knowledge she was imparting? Oh, it wasn't fair!

Mike watched her closely for several days, wondering what was bothering her. At first, he attributed her long silences to some problem she was having at school, but when her melancholy mood lasted more than a week, he began to worry.

"What is it, Loralee?" he asked one night as they were walking in the moonlight. "What's troubling you?"

"Nothing, Mike." She hated to lie to him, but how could she tell him the truth?

"Loralee, look at me."

"I'm fine, Mike. Really."

"Like hell!" He grabbed her arm and forced her to stop walking and look at him. "What is it?"

His voice was soft and caring. His eyes were kind, sympathetic. How could she tell him what she had done? How could she bear to see the affection in his face turn to disgust?

"Loralee?"

"Oh, Mike," she whispered, and burst into tears.

"Loralee, honey, what is it?" He took her in his arms, and felt her body tremble with the force of her sobs.

Loralee cried for several minutes, unleashing all the unhappiness of the past few days in a torrent of cleansing tears. She didn't want to tell Mike what was troubling her, but she didn't want to move out of the circle of his arms either. It felt so good to be held, to know that he loved her even though she couldn't love him in return.

When her tears subsided, she took a deep breath, then drew away from him. "I'm pregnant, Mike," she said flatly.

Mike stared at Loralee, wondering if he had heard right. "Pregnant?"

She nodded.

"How?" he asked. "Who?"

"Zuniga."

Mike's face went white with rage. "That bastard!" he hissed. "I'll kill him."

"I'm as much to blame as he is." They were the hardest words she had ever spoken.

Mike shook his head, not wanting to believe her.

Two large tears of shame rolled down Loralee's cheeks. "I'm sorry, Mike. Good night."

Turning on her heel, she lifted her skirts and ran home as fast as her legs would carry her. Tears blurred her vision, and she stumbled in the darkness, skinning her knee as she tripped over a large rock.

She sat where she had fallen, the tears falling faster and faster. She had lost Zuniga, and now she had lost Mike, and there was no one to blame but herself.

"Loralee," Mike's voice called to her out of the darkness, and then she felt his hand on her arm. Gently he helped her to her feet.

"Leave me alone, Mike. Please, just go away and leave me alone."

"Does Zuniga know about the baby?"

"No."

"Why haven't you told him?"

"He hates me."

"Why?"

"He just does. Oh, Mike, what am I going to do? I don't want to leave the reservation. The children need me, and they're learning so much now—" She broke off as another wave of tears washed down her cheeks.

"Loralee, don't cry. Please don't cry." She sounded so unhappy and looked so forlorn that his heart went out to her. Whatever had happened, he was certain it hadn't been her fault.

"I've made such a mess of everything."

"Are you in love with Zuniga?"

"No."

"No?"

"No," Loralee repeated firmly.

"Okay, I believe you." But he didn't, not really.

With a sigh, Mike took Loralee by the arm and escorted her back to her house. Inside, he brewed her a cup of tea, wiped the blood from her skinned knee, and bandaged the shallow cut. And all the while a thought took root in the back of his mind.

Loralee sipped the tea slowly, her eyes on Mike's face. What was he thinking?

With the air of a man who had just made up his mind, Mike sat down at the table across from Loralee and took her hand in his.

"Marry me, Loralee."

"Marry you?"

Mike nodded. "You need a husband right away," he said, keeping his voice light, "and I need a wife. We were made for each other."

"But I don't love you."

Mike shrugged. "It doesn't matter," he said, serious once more. "I love you, and I'll try to be a good father to your baby. What do you say?"

"I don't know what to say."

"Say yes, and I'll get started on the paper work tomorrow morning."

It sounded so simple. Marry Mike, and all her problems would be solved. She would have a name for her baby. She could keep teaching the Indian children. Her reputation would be saved. She would have someone to take care of her.

"It can be a marriage in name only, if that's how you want it," Mike offered. "And who knows, maybe one day you'll learn to love me, too, and we'll have a real marriage."

"But, Mike, it seems so unfair to you."

"Not really. I'll be getting a live-in cook and housekeeper and family all in one."

It sounded so easy.

"Say yes, Loralee," he coaxed, squeezing her hand. "You won't be sorry."

She lowered her head for a long moment, and when she raised it her eyes were still wet.

"All right, Mike, I'll marry you if you're sure it's what you want."

"I'm sure. No more tears now." Rising, he came around the table, bent and kissed her cheek. "I'll talk to the colonel and the chaplain first thing in the morning. Don't you worry, I'll handle everything. You go on to bed and get some rest. You look all done in."

"I am. Thank you, Mike."

He gave her a warm smile. "Dream of me, will you?"

"I'll try."

With a nod, he picked up his hat and left the house, whistling softly.

Loralee stared after him. What had she gotten herself into? How could she marry a man she didn't love? And yet, what else could she do? Mike was kind and good and sweet, and she did care for him. Perhaps everything would work out for the best after all.

11

Zuniga passed the sacred pipe to Nachi, who took four puffs and passed it on to Red Dog, the chief of the tribe. A small fire burned in a deep pit. Branches had been laid over the surface of the pit to disperse the smoke.

The men smoked in silence. Zuniga glanced from face to face. Did his own countenance reflect the same hopeless expression as those he saw? Six Bears raised the pipe toward heaven. He was the paper chief of the tribe, the one who had been appointed by the Agency. He had no power over the people, but he was respected because he had once been a great warrior in his own right. There were five other men gathered around the firepit. They were the men who policed the tribe, who settled disputes and listened to the problems, complaints, and concerns of the People.

Zuniga grinned into the darkness. He was the only man present under the age of fifty, and he was here because he refused to bend to the white man's rule. The young men of the tribe looked up to him. He was their leader, their spokesman. The soldiers and the Indian Agent would have been surprised to discover that Zuniga knew as much about what went on within the bounds of the reservation as they did, and even more surprised to learn that what he said and thought was listened to with interest and respect.

This night the head men of the tribe were discussing Crow Dog's youngest daughter. She had reached the age of puberty and desired to participate in the ancient puberty ceremony. It was a good thing, when a girl became a woman. The puberty ceremony, or Sunrise Ceremony, would be held in two days. It was decided to hold the ceremony at night, when there was little chance of interference by the whites.

The men discussed a few other tribal matters, then the fire was extinguished and the men disappeared into the darkness.

Zuniga and Nachi stayed where they were. Nachi brought out his old clay pipe and lighted it with a coal from the ashes. He took several deep puffs, then passed the pipe to his grandson.

"What has become of the white woman?" the old man asked after a lengthy silence.

"Nothing."

"Why do you no longer meet with her at the schoolhouse?"

"I have learned to read and write. It is enough."

The old man nodded thoughtfully. "Something is not right between you."

Zuniga glanced at Nachi with affection. "Do you now read my mind, Grandfather, that I can have no secrets from you?"

Nachi laughed. "I have known you since the day you were born. I know when you are troubled."

Zuniga nodded. He was troubled. Troubled and lonesome.

"Was it not good between you?"

"Grandfather?"

"Did she not please you when you made love to her?"

"She pleased me well enough."

"But?"

"She was ashamed of what we had done. Ashamed because she had let an Indian defile her. I will not have a woman who feels shame when I touch her."

"Perhaps she was only ashamed because the two of you were not married."

"What?"

"An Apache woman feels shame when she lies with a warrior outside of marriage, even if she is deeply in love with the man. Perhaps the white woman felt the same."

Zuniga stared at Nachi. It had never occurred to him that Loralee might feel that way. The Apache did not credit the whites with modesty or honor. It was well known that the whites had slept with their slaves before the Civil War, and that they had violated Indian women without a qualm. He had supposed that white women were of a similar nature. Was it possible that Loralee had valued her chastity? If so, he had wronged her terribly.

It was a thought that bothered him deeply.

"Come on," Mike coaxed. "There's nothing to be afraid of."

"I feel like we're trespassing on something sacred," Loralee answered as she followed Mike onto the reservation.

"We're not trespassing. I have every right to be here."

Side by side, they stood in the shadows, watching as the tribe gathered around a particular lodge. Soon a young girl exited the wickiup and all the young people began to chase her. The girl ran northward for perhaps a hundred yards, then she turned and ran southeast, then east, and then north again, running the same distance in each direction.

When she returned to her own lodge, sacred pollen was sprinkled over her head. At the same time, a prayer was offered to the gods, asking for their ever-protecting care and guidance in the young girl's life. A new blanket was spread on the ground and the girl danced on the blanket while the people sang to her.

Loralee watched, fascinated, as the dancing went on for over an hour. She knew that the ceremony had once lasted for four days, but would now only last the night.

After the girl finished her dance, the Gans began to dance. These dancers represented the mountain spirits. They wore grotesque costumes and masks and carried wooden swords.

Later, the girl sat on a blanket with her eyes closed. For this brief time, she represented White Painted Lady and was thought to possess special powers. The girl was dressed in a buckskin dress that had been made especially for this occasion. It was covered with yellow ocher and decorated with suns and moons and stars. A small eagle feather was attached to each shoulder to enable the girl to run as light as a feather. A single white eagle feather was tied in her hair in the hope that she would live until her hair turned the same color as the feather.

It was a lovely ceremony, Loralee mused as the girl rose from her blanket and her parents and relatives began serving food to the guests. The Western Apache believed there was a time when White Painted Lady, also known as Changing Woman, lived all alone. After many years, she desired to have children, so she slept with the Sun, and soon after that she gave birth to Slayer of Monsters. Four days later, Changing Woman became pregnant by Water and gave birth to Born of Water, or Child of the Water. As the half-brothers matured, Changing Woman instructed them in how they should live and then they left home and, following their mother's advice, they cleansed the world of most of its evil.

Changing Woman never grew old. When she got to be a certain age, she walked toward the east, and after a time she saw herself in the distance walking toward her. When the two came together, only one remained, the younger one. Then she was like a young girl all over again. One of the blessings of the Sunrise Ceremony provided a young girl with longevity and the capability to remain forever young.

"It's fascinating, isn't it, Mike?" Loralee asked, touched by the beauty of the ceremony, and by the poise and serenity of the young Apache woman.

"Yeah, I guess so, if you believe all that nonsense."

"It isn't nonsense," Loralee argued. "I

don't think their beliefs are any more peculiar than some of ours, not when you understand them."

Mike laughed shortly. "How can you possibly begin to understand all that superstitious hocus-pocus? Mountain spirits, indeed! It's all a lot of hogwash."

"Well, I think it's lovely," Loralee said stubbornly.

"Okay, okay," Mike said goodnaturedly. "It's lovely. Let's go. I've got to be back at the post by ten."

Zuniga stood in the shadows, watching the ceremony. He rarely participated in any of the reservation events, preferring to stay out of sight of the soldiers and the reservation police.

He was about to head for home when he saw Loralee walking with Mike Schofield. They were laughing softly, their heads close together, their hands entwined.

Zuniga felt his anger begin to grow as they went on their way, oblivious to his presence. He did not like the way Loralee smiled into the white man's face, or the possessive way the white man put his arm around her shoulders.

Silent as a stalking puma, Zuniga followed the couple, his hand straying to the knife sheathed on his belt. It would be so easy to drive the narrow blade into the white man's back. So easy, but it would only cause trouble for his people if the man's body should be found. And his people had trouble enough.

He paused, silent as the night, as Mike handed Loralee into the buggy and took a place beside her. Lifting the reins, Mike clucked to the horse and they drove away.

Zuniga stood in the darkness, undecided, and then he began to run, his moccasined feet making no sound as he ran after the buggy.

He came to a halt as Mike drew rein at Loralee's house, and watched through narrowed eyes as the white man lifted Loralee to the ground and walked with her to the front door. They stood close together, then Mike bent his head and kissed Loralee. Jealousy, more painful than the cut of a knife, more deadly than the poison of a rattler, surged through Zuniga's veins as Loralee's arms went around the white man's neck. They kissed for a long time before Mike let Loralee go.

"Good night, Mike," Loralee murmured, her voice soft and dreamy. "Thanks for taking me to the ceremony. I enjoyed it."

"Any time, honey. See you tomorrow?"

Loralee nodded, lifting her face for one last kiss.

She was humming softly when she opened the door and stepped into the parlor. Lighting the lamp on the table beside the sofa, she dropped her shawl across the back of the couch. Her hand flew to her throat when she saw Zuniga standing in front of the fireplace.

"You!" she exclaimed. "What are you doing here? How did you get in?"

"Did you go to the reservation tonight to make light of our ways?" His voice was angry and accusing. He had intended to apologize to her for violating her virginity. He had thought he might offer to marry her. But that had been before he saw her in the white man's arms, before he saw her kiss Mike Schofield with such fervor. "Did you?"

"Of course not."

"I heard you laughing and making jokes."

"We weren't laughing at your people, Shad."

"Weren't you?"

"You know how much I like and respect your people," Loralee argued quietly. "I would not make fun of their religion, and you know it."

He did know it, but he could not admit it now, could not think clearly with Loralee standing so close. She was wearing a new dress. It was light blue in color with a pattern of tiny dark blue flowers and green leaves. The neck was square, the sleeves were short and puffy, edged with lace. The skirt flared over her hips. Her hair was pulled away from her face with a dark blue grosgrain ribbon. She looked very young, and very beautiful. He remembered the night they had shared at Shadow Lake and his heart began to pound. He had thought of her for weeks, missing her, wanting her, dreaming of her lying in his arms, her body pressed against his, her lips whispering his name as he possessed her.

And then he remembered the way Mike Schofield had held Loralee, the possessive look in the white man's eyes as he kissed her, and anger exploded through Zuniga, crushing his tender feelings with a jealousy so intense, so violent, it was like a physical pain in his heart.

"You spend a lot of time with Schofield." He hurled the words at her.

"Yes." Loralee was suddenly confused. One minute he was accusing her of belittling the beliefs of his people, and the next he was questioning her relationship with Mike. What did he really want?

"Why?"

"Why?" She felt herself growing angry. What right did Shad Zuniga have to come to her house in the middle of the night and cross-examine her? He had not seen her in weeks, and now he came here as if he had every right to badger her with questions that were none of his business.

"I'll tell you why I spend so much time with Mike," Loralee said with sugary sweetness. "He's a very nice man, a gentleman, if you will. I enjoy being with him, and I intend to marry him. Does that answer all your questions, Mr. Zuniga?"

Loralee's gaze lingered on Shad's face as she waited for him to say something. For weeks she had professed to hate him, but she knew now that it wasn't true, had never been true. She longed to tell him that she loved him, loved him and was pregnant with his child.

She might have swallowed her pride and said the words if Zuniga had not been looking at her as if he hated her.

She felt the tears start and she closed her eyes, not wanting him to see her cry. If only he would take her in his arms. If only he would say he cared, she would pour out her heart and tell him everything.

But still he did not speak, and when she opened her eyes, she saw that she was alone in the house.

Zuniga ran through the quiet night, his powerful legs carrying him effortlessly over the miles. Like all Apache males, he had been trained from childhood to run mile after mile without food or water. In the old days, it was not uncommon for a warrior to outrun a horse.

He ran through the night with no destination in mind. It felt good, to have the wind in his face, to feel the earth beneath his feet, to fill his lungs with the cool desert air. He ran steadily, and his feet pounded out the words that echoed and re-echoed in his mind: She's going to marry the white man, she's going to marry the white man, she's going to marry . . . The image of Loralee standing in Schofield's arms was burned into his brain. She was going to marry the white man . . .

He ran until his legs felt like rubber and his lungs were on fire, but he could not outrun his anger, or his jealousy.

The holidays came, and Loralee experienced a twinge of homesickness as she thought of the Christmases she had known in the East, of the good times she had shared with her family. Christmas had been a special time of love and giving, of pies and cookies and treats for everyone, a time of secrets and sharing. After her parents died, Christmas had lost some of its glow. Usually, she had spent Christmas with the servants in whatever house she was working for at the time. This year she would share it with Mike. The thought did not cheer her as it should have.

The week before Christmas, Loralee made a batch of gingerbread men for her Indian students. The younger children were charmed by the gingerbread men, oohing and aahing with pleasure as they bit into the spicy cookies. One young girl refused to eat her cookie man, declaring that the little brown figure looked like an Apache boy. The older boys pretended indifference, but they, too, were pleased with the unusual treat. Even Short Bear took one.

The Indians didn't celebrate Christmas, but Loralee could not resist telling them the story of Mary and Joseph and the infant Jesus. She told them of the shepherds and the Wise Men, and of the wicked king, Herod, who ordered all the babies killed.

"Just like Chivington," muttered Short Bear.

Loralee frowned. John Chivington had been a Methodist minister from Ohio. He was an imposing man, six and a half feet tall, weighing 250 pounds. He started life as a peaceful man, and was a presiding elder of the Rocky Mountain Methodist District. He had organized a Sunday school and did some circuit preaching through mining towns. When Colorado raised a cavalry troop during the Civil War, Chivington had been offered a chaplain's commission, but he had refused, demanding a fighting commission rather than a "praying" one. In November 1864, Colonel John Chivington and the Third Colorado Volunteers rode through a small village of peaceful Cheyenne, callously butchering five hundred Indian men, women, and children. Chivington and his men rode into Denver with more than one hundred scalps.

"Yes," Loralee said slowly. "Just like Chivington. Throughout history there have been men who gloried in bloodshed. But let's not talk of that now," she said, eager to change the subject. "Let's open our reading books to page forty, shall we?"

Christmas was a peaceful day. Mike took Loralee to church in the morning, and then they went back to Loralee's house for a big breakfast of ham and eggs and fried potatoes with biscuits and gravy.

After breakfast, they exchanged gifts. Mike gave Loralee a lovely gold heart on a dainty gold chain.

"Oh," Loralee breathed as she lifted the heart out of its velvet-lined box. "It's beautiful, Mike, but it must have cost half a month's pay."

Mike grinned. "Not half a lieutenant's month's pay," he said.

"Oh, Mike! You've been promoted!"

"Yes, the colonel gave me a Christmas promotion."

Mike fastened the chain around Loralee's slender neck. "It's to remind you that my heart will always be yours," Mike murmured, brushing the back of her neck with a kiss.

Loralee's eyes filled with tears. She longed to say she felt the same, that her heart was his, but she could not lie to him. He deserved better than that. For a moment, she closed her eyes and Shad Zuniga's swarthy countenance danced before her, a mocking grin on his handsome face.

Shaking his image from her mind, Loralee handed Mike a gaily wrapped package. "Merry Christmas, Mike."

Mike whistled softly, appreciatively, as he opened the small square box and withdrew an intricately carved silver pocketwatch.

"It was my father's," Loralee said. "I hope you like it. I noticed you don't have a watch."

"It's a great gift, honey," Mike said, kissing her cheek. "Are you sure you want to give it away?"

"Yes." Loralee smiled. "Besides, I'm not really giving it away. After all, it will still be in the family once we're married."

Mike smiled. "That's true!" he exclaimed, catching Loralee in his arms and hugging her close. "I'll make you happy, Lorie, I promise."

"I know you will," she replied. She placed her arms around Mike's neck, closing her eyes as he kissed her cheeks and forehead and nose, slowly working his way to her mouth. She returned his kiss fervently, wanting to love him, wanting to respond to his touch with the same desire she had felt for Shad Zuniga. But no matter how she tried, she could not feel anything remotely like passion, only a pleasant sensation kindled with warm affection.

Later that afternoon they went to dinner at Colonel Freeman's house. Stella Freeman set a lavish table, complete with sparkling crystal, gleaming silverware, and flickering candles. The colonel's striker served an elaborate dinner that had been prepared by the Army cook who proved that, with the proper ingredients and the right incentive, he could create a culinary delight to rival that of a French chef.

After dinner, there was sherry for the ladies, brandy and cigars for the gentlemen.

"I hear you're soon to be a bride," Stella Freeman remarked when the ladies were alone."

"Yes," Loralee replied, forcing a smile. "Mike has kindly asked me to marry him, and I have accepted."

"It's rather sudden, isn't it, my dear?" Stella Freeman asked. "You've only known each other a short time."

"That's true, but Mike doesn't want to wait."

"I see. Have you set the date yet?"

"No. We're still waiting for the paperwork to come through."

Stella Freeman made a gesture of despair. "That could take months, my dear," she lamented. "You know how slowly the Army moves."

"Yes." Loralee sighed. If the paperwork didn't arrive soon, everyone on the reservation would know why they were getting married in such a hurry.

For a while, the ladies discussed weddings they had been invited to, the current styles, wedding dresses and veils, and the rising prices at the general store.

Loralee only half listened to what was being said. She felt Stella Freeman eying her speculatively several times, and she was glad when the gentlemen finished their cigars and came back inside.

It was late when Mike took Loralee home. He lingered at her front door. It was hard to be close to her and not touch her, hard to believe that a girl as sweet and as gently reared as Loralee could be in love with a damned Indian. Still, soon she would be his wife. He would woo her tenderly, patiently, tell her daily that he adored her, until he had won her love for himself.

It was her wedding day. Loralee stood before the mirror, carefully studying her reflection. She looked like a bride, she mused, but she did not feel like one. Brides were happy, excited, laughing creatures with eyes that sparkled and skin that glowed. There were dark shadows under her eyes caused by many sleepless nights; her heart was heavy, her expression resigned. How could she marry Mike when she was three months pregnant with Shad Zuniga's child? How could she not?

She ran her hand along the smooth satin of her skirt. Her dress was lovely. The bodice was fitted, the neck modest, the sleeves long, the skirt full enough to hide her expanding girth. She had not wanted to wear white, but Mike had insisted. Now, surveying her image in the looking glass, she felt like a fraud. She didn't deserve to wear white. White stood for purity, modesty, chastity. By rights, she should be wearing black, she mused bitterly, or maybe scarlet.

Mike had wanted to be married in the post chapel, but she had adamantly refused, and Stella Freeman had graciously offered her home for the ceremony.

With a little sigh of resignation, Loralee picked up the long white veil and pinned it in place.

A short time later, there was a knock at the door and the colonel's wife stepped into the room. She was clad in a dress of light blue silk, a single strand of pearls at her throat.

"We're ready, dear," the older woman said.

"Thank you."

"Smile, my dear," Stella Freeman chided. "This is supposed to be a happy occasion."

"I'm just a little nervous, I guess. I've never been a bride before."

"Well, you look lovely, just lovely. Hurry now. Everyone is waiting."

Loralee nodded. With a last glance in the mirror, she left the room. Mike was waiting for her in the Freemans' spacious parlor, standing beside the post chaplain. Mike looked quite handsome in his dress uniform, his hair carefully combed, his boots and brass shined to perfection. He gave her a wink and a smile as she walked toward him.

Loralee saw Sally Stockman standing near the front, a happy smile on her face. Sally nodded at her, as if to say everything would be all right.

Loralee tried to return Sally's smile, but failed. This was her wedding day. She should be happy, elated. Instead, she felt like crying. In minutes, she would be Mrs. Michael Schofield. Somehow it didn't seem real.

Like a sleepwalker, she stood beside Mike, her hand in his as she repeated the brief vows that made her his wife. His kiss was tender, filled with hope and promise.

The rest of the day passed in a haze. There were numerous toasts to the bride and groom. There was a barbecue in the Freemans' backyard. There were good wishes and presents. Somehow Loralee managed to say and do all the right things, but it was as if she were watching it all through someone else's eyes.

And then, too soon, she was alone with Mike. And she knew she had made a terrible mistake.

12

Zuniga stared at the glass in his hand for a long moment before he tossed off the contents and poured another drink. He had been sitting in the back of the saloon for over an hour, methodically working his way through a bottle of bonded bourbon in an effort to forget that Loralee had married Lieutenant Michael Schofield the week before.

He had seen her as she left the Freemans' house on the day of the wedding, her face flushed with happiness, Schofield beaming at her side. She had been a vision of loveliness in a gown of white satin. The knowledge that she belonged to another man slammed into him like a fist, making him feel sick to his stomach.

Torn by anger and jealousy, he had vowed to forget her, but it was useless. He spent hours prowling the hills. He cut more wood than they would ever need, working until he was exhausted so that he could sleep at night, but even in sleep she came to haunt him.

And now, lastly, he had turned to whiskey, hoping to drown her memory in a haze of alcohol. But even that failed him, the bourbon having no more effect than water.

Occasionally he wandered through the reservation, studying the girls who were of marriageable age. Perhaps he would take a wife. One woman was the same as another, after all, but none of the women he saw appealed to him. Some were beautiful, some were sensuous, more than a few would willingly share his lodge, with or without marriage, but none of them had hair like gold silk or skin like fine cream.

"Hello, Indian," purred a husky female voice at his elbow. "Long time no see."

Zuniga nodded. "Kelly."

"Mind if I sit down?"

"Do whatever you want."

"What is it?" Kelly asked, laying her hand over his forearm. "You look like hell."

He nodded morosely. "I feel like hell."

"Can I help?"

Zuniga looked at her for the first time.

She wasn't a bad-looking woman, he thought absently. Her figure was firm and round and he had spent many a lonely night in her bed. Looking at her now, he wondered how he had ever touched her, then he swore under his breath. Loralee had spoiled him for all other women, he thought irritably. Damn her! He clenched his fist and banged it on the table, causing the whiskey in his glass to slosh over the rim and onto the green baize table top.

"Hey," Kelly said softly. "Are you all right?"

"Fine," he growled. "Just fine."

"I could make you better," Kelly murmured. She leaned across the table, giving him a clear view of her ample breasts. "No charge."

"Thanks," Zuniga said, rising. "Maybe some other time."

Grabbing the bottle, he left the saloon.

13

Loralee stood in the doorway, waving to Mike as he left for work. She stood staring after him until he was out of sight, a pensive expression on her face. They had been married for two weeks, and Loralee was doing her best to make the marriage a success even though she knew it was doomed to fail.

Closing the door, she went into the kitchen and began washing the breakfast dishes. Her honeymoon had been a disaster. Following the reception at the Freemans' house, they had gone to Mike's place. Her belongings and furniture looked out of place in his quarters. As out of place as she felt. Alone, they were strained and awkward with

217

each other. Mike had poured himself a drink, but left it untouched.

In the bedroom, Loralee had hesitated before undressing for bed. Sensing her shyness, Mike had left the room. She was in bed when he returned, the sheets pulled up to her chin, her eyes wary.

"Go to sleep," Mike had said, his voice husky. He gave her a lopsided smile. "I'm a patient man. When you're ready, you let me know."

She had stayed awake a long time, staring bleakly at the ceiling. Marrying Mike had seemed like the perfect solution to her problem, but now she knew it had been wrong, very wrong.

She washed the last dish and began to dry them. Life with Mike wasn't all bad. She had never been so pampered or cared for in her life. He refused to let her do anything remotely strenuous, and even scrubbed the floors himself so she wouldn't have to. They shared many common interests like reading and walking and playing cards. Loralee felt she could tell Mike anything and he would understand. In turn, she offered a listening ear at the end of each day when he came home needing to let off steam about how Captain Rodgers was harassing the new recruits, or how Private Cooper drank on duty

With a sigh, she put the last of the dishes in the cupboard and began to wipe the counter off.

If only she could love Mike as he loved her. If only she could feel more than just friendly affection for the man who was her husband. She tried to respond when Mike kissed her, tried to feel some stirring of desire, but always in vain.

The only happiness she found was in teaching. Her class had grown and she now had twenty-six children enrolled. Short Bear had stopped coming to school soon after Christmas, and she missed him. He had been her only link to Shad.

When she wasn't teaching, she filled every spare minute with work. She dusted and swept and ironed and mended until her back ached and her hands were red and sore. She baked bread and pies and cakes until Mike complained that none of his uniforms fit properly anymore. She waxed the furniture until it fairly glowed, washed the windows, made new curtains. She planted a small vegetable garden, and when that was thriving, she planted flowers.

They attended all the social functions at the fort, and Loralee learned to endure Stella Freeman's patronizing airs.

It was at one such affair that Loralee heard Zuniga's name mentioned.

"I'm sure it was him," one of the sergeants was saying. "I'd just come out of the saloon and I was feeling pretty good, if you know what I mean. Not drunk, mind you," he added hastily for the colonel's benefit, "just feeling good. I was on my way to the barracks when someone came up behind me and whacked me across the side of the head. When I woke up, my pockets were empty."

Colonel Freeman's face was grave. "How can you be certain it was Zuniga? Did you see his face?"

"Not exactly."

"What do you mean, not exactly? Either you did or you didn't."

"I just got a glimpse of long black hair and buckskin pants," the sergeant admitted, "but you know he's got a reputation for being a thief. He's always got money to spend. Where the hell does he get it?"

"I'm sure you're right," Colonel Freeman remarked, "but I can't very well arrest the man without any evidence other than your suspicions. And there are a number of men with long black hair and buckskin pants." The colonel turned to Mike. "Are you still keeping an eye on his lodge?"

"Yes, sir," Mike answered. "We've checked the place out twice in the last week, but we haven't turned up anything. No weapons, no cash, nothing."

Loralee moved away, remembering a conversation she had had with Zuniga in town. She had asked him where he got the money to pay for the coffee and sugar he had bought, and he had answered that he stole it from the soldiers who drank too much on

Saturday nights. She had thought that such a thing was shameful, but she knew that the Indians didn't consider stealing from the enemy to be stealing. It had been a way of life for hundreds of years. A warrior bragged about the horses and women and goods he took from the enemy, but he never stole from a friend or a member of the tribe. To do so would result in banishment from the tribe, as well as a loss of honor.

That night, it seemed as though everyone was talking about Zuniga. It was more than Loralee could stand, and she went outside in search of a little peace and quiet.

Mike sought her out in the colonel's garden. "You okay?" he asked.

"Yes, fine. I just needed a little fresh air."

"Do you want to be alone?"

"No, not really."

"Did I tell you how beautiful you look tonight?" Mike asked lightly.

"Yes," Loralee answered, grinning. "About six times, I think."

Mike laughed self-consciously. "I can't help it. You *are* beautiful."

He was going to kiss her. She saw it in his eyes even before he took her in his arms. She closed her eyes, letting him draw her to him, feeling the rapid beat of his heart against the palm of her hand as his mouth closed on hers. He kissed her for a long time, his hunger for her evident in the way his hands caressed her back and thighs, the heat of his hands penetrating her skirts.

He was breathing hard when he drew away. "Loralee, don't make me wait any longer. Please, honey, I want you, need you, so much that it hurts."

"Mike—"

"I know, I know. I promised not to push you." He drew a ragged breath, his hands clenched at his sides. "You go on back inside. I'll be along in a minute."

He was unusually quiet when they returned home that night, and Loralee felt a rush of pity for him. What was she saving herself for anyway? Zuniga was forever lost to her.

Undressing, she climbed into bed. Mike joined her a few minutes later. She could feel the tension in him and she thought how difficult it must be for him, lying beside her night after night, wanting her. She stared into the darkness. Maybe it wouldn't be so bad, letting Mike make love to her. She longed to be held, to be loved. Zuniga had awakened the passion within her, and she yearned to feel the touch of a man's arms, to experience the pleasure that came from a man's touch.

Slowly she reached out and placed her hand on Mike's arm, her fingertips stroking his skin. Perhaps she could find the same fulfillment in Mike's arms that she had found in Zuniga's.

Mike groaned low in his throat as Loralee touched him. His whole body ached with wanting her.

"Loralee," he murmured hoarsely. "Are you sure?"

"Yes." She whispered the word, knowing it was a lie.

Mike uttered a soft cry of joy as he rolled over and pulled her into his arms, covering her face with kisses as his hands reached under her gown to stroke her soft flesh.

Loralee squeezed her eyes tight shut as Mike caressed her, his hands gentle yet urgent as he whispered that he loved her. He lifted her nightgown a little higher, his hands seeking her breasts, his manhood hard and warm against her leg.

Loralee bit down on her lip, stifling the urge to scream. Mike was her husband. He had every right to make love to her. Indeed, he had been patience itself as he waited for her to let him do what he had every right to do.

With a cry of despair, she twisted out of his arms. "I can't, Mike. I'm sorry. I just can't."

"It's all right," Mike said hoarsely. He sat up, his head cradled in his hands as he listened to Loralee weeping softly into her pillow. He longed to hold her and comfort her, to tell her that it didn't matter, but he dared not touch her. He was a man, after all, not a saint. He had promised he would wait until she was ready. At least she was trying. Maybe next time would be better. He hoped he wouldn't have to wait too long to find out.

14

February 1906

Zuniga sat outside Wild Eagle's lodge, listening to the soft beat of the medicine drum, listening to the shaman's soft chant.

"Go away, sick," Crooked Leg sang in a voice weak with age. "Go away, sick. Go away, sick."

There was a pause in the singing, and Zuniga knew that the aged medicine man was spitting into the fire, sprinkling sacred cattail pollen over Wild Eagle's ailing wife.

"Go away, sick. Go away, sick." The shaman's voice drifted out of the lodge.

Zuniga gazed into the darkness. The singing and the praying would go on all night.

Rising, he walked through the lodges of

his people, nodding to some, stopping to say a few words here and there. Wherever he went, he heard people talking about the schoolteacher and how she had married one of the bluecoats.

Abruptly changing direction, Zuniga left the lodges. Swinging aboard his dun stallion, he rode across the dark land until, without conscious thought, he found himself at the schoolhouse.

Reining his horse to a halt, he stared at the darkened building, remembering how patiently Loralee had taught him to read, how pleased she had been with each new accomplishment. He had never admitted it to her, but after his first token show of resistance, he had enjoyed learning to read and write and cipher.

Closing his eyes, he recalled each detail of her face: the clear brown eyes, the full red mouth, the finely shaped nose, her stubborn chin, the skin smooth and unblemished. The image of her body came to haunt him, and he felt the heat rise in his loins. He had made love to other women, nameless street girls who sold their body for the price of a cheap bottle of booze, but none had ever satisfied him the way Loralee had. He had used the others and forgot them as soon as his desire had been quenched. But Loralee had been in his thoughts day and night since the first time he had seen her.

Riding on, he wondered what it would

have been like to marry Loralee and settle down somewhere, and then he laughed. He was not cut out to be a husband. He was a man who had always lived alone, keeping his thoughts and fears to himself. Even with Nachi, he was alone, always a man apart from others. He had few friends, though many would have been his friend if he would let them. But he did not like to be close to people, did not find it easy to share himself with others.

He had what he needed. A few close friends, a cousin whose company he enjoyed, Nachi. And there was Kelly. Once he had sought her company on a regular basis, but he had not shared her bed since he met Loralee.

He reined the stallion to a halt beside Shadow Lake and stared at the man reflected in the dark water, a man too proud and stubborn to admit he had lost the only thing he ever wanted.

Muttering an oath, he touched his heels to the stallion's flanks and headed for home. Loralee was Schofield's wife now, and the sooner he stopped thinking about her, the better.

It was late when Zuniga reached home. At the corral, he dismounted, opened the gate, removed the horse's saddle and bridle, and turned the animal loose in the rough enclosure. Closing the gate, he started toward the wickiup.

He paused at the doorway. A coldness seemed to reach out to him, surrounding him so that he shivered convulsively, the ancient fear rising up within him.

He knew that the old man was dead before he entered the lodge.

Nachi had died peacefully in his sleep. His face, as lined and rough as aged saddle leather, was at peace.

Zuniga gazed at his grandfather for a long time, remembering the many good times they had shared: the hunts, the battles, the laughter. Nachi had always been there, solid as the mountains, dependable as the sunrise. And now he was gone.

Zuniga smiled faintly. He recalled the last fight they had been in, and how Nachi had been in the thick of it, his eyes bright, his voice raised in the shrill Apache war cry. During a brief lull in the battle, they had stood together and Nachi had raised his gun above his head. "Ah, grandson," he had shouted enthusiastically, "it is a good day to die!"

Stepping out of the lodge, Zuniga lifted his voice to the night, his lament carried aloft by the rising wind. From the distant hills, a lone coyote howled in reply, its melancholy wail an echo of Zuniga's grief.

He sat outside the lodge until the sun began to climb over the mountains. His cheeks were still damp with tears as he watched the rising sun brighten the horizon, the colors changing from pale gray to gold to fiery shades of orange and crimson.

He sat there a moment longer; then, resolutely, he rose to his feet and went to the corral where he saddled the dun and threw a bridle over Nachi's bay gelding.

Returning to the lodge, he dressed Nachi in his finest buckskin trousers and fringed war shirt. Tenderly he brushed the old man's hair. As an afterthought, he placed an eagle feather behind Nachi's right ear. That done, he wrapped the body in a blanket and carried it outside.

The dun shied and snorted nervously when Zuniga placed the body across its back. A soft word calmed the stallion, and Zuniga swung up behind the blanket-wrapped body, took up the bay gelding's reins, and rode away from the lodge, leading the bay.

He rode high into the hills until he came to a sunlit patch of ground surrounded by tall trees. Dismounting, he dug a grave, gently placed the frail body in its final resting place, and covered it with earth. That done, he sprinkled ashes and pollen around the grave, beginning at the southwest corner in the belief that this would help Nachi's soul enter O'zho, heaven. Following ancient traditions, he left a small bag of provisions at the gravesite so that Nachi might have food on his journey to the land of spirits. Lastly, his face void of emotion, he placed a bullet between the bay gelding's eyes so that Nachi might enter heaven in comfort.

That done, he stood at the burial site for a long moment, his head bowed. An owl hooted, making a lonely sound. According to the beliefs of his people, owls called for the dead after they were buried and took their spirits into the air.

With a sigh, he left the grave. Only rarely would he speak his grandfather's name, lest Nachi's spirit be called back to earth.

The ride back to the wickiup seemed long and lonely. Removing his clothing from the lodge, he set fire to the brush-covered structure.

He sat a safe distance from the blaze, his face impassive, as he watched his grandfather's lodge and belongings burn to the ground.

Loralee took a deep breath as she turned Lady toward the schoolhouse. She had left several papers there that needed to be graded before Monday, and she looked forward to the short ride. Mike had tried to persuade her not to ride in her condition, but she had insisted that she felt fine. Lady was a reliable mount, surefooted as a mountain goat and not easily spooked.

Loralee let out a long sigh as she thought of Mike. He was a good man. If only she could love him. Certainly he deserved more out of their relationship than he was getting, but he never complained, never indicated that he regretted his decision to marry her.

She shook her head sadly. After all this time, she still longed for the touch of Zuniga's hands in her hair, for the taste of his lips, the warmth of his flesh against her own. Often her dreams were haunted with his image. In her dreams, he came to her, his copper-hued body a study in male perfection, his black eyes warm and adoring as he swept her into his embrace and made love to her hour after hour. She woke from such dreams feeling flushed and guilty, as though she had been physically unfaithful to Mike.

Loralee was halfway between the fort and the schoolhouse when she saw the smoke. Without thinking, she reined Lady toward the hills, urging the mare to go faster, faster, until they topped the rise where Zuniga's lodge stood.

She gasped aloud at what she saw. The brush-covered wickiup was gone, and in its place stood a few blackened poles and a pile of smoldering ashes. Horrified, she wondered if Shad and his grandfather had been inside.

Relief, sweeter than honey, washed through her when she saw Zuniga materialize through the blue-gray haze. He walked toward her, his face void of expression. Blood dripped from several cuts on his forearms, and she knew then that Nachi was dead, for it was the Apache way to vent their grief by self-inflicted wounds.

Now that she knew Zuniga was safe, Loralee was eager to be gone, but Zuniga reached out and grasped Lady's bridle.

For a moment, they studied each other. Then, without a word, Zuniga lifted Loralee from her horse. His hands slid along her rib cage as he lowered her to the ground, then came around to rest on her belly. His breath caught in his throat as he felt the swell of her abdomen beneath his hands. He had heard she was pregnant, and he had assumed the child was Schofield's. But now he knew otherwise.

He took a closer look at Loralee. Her breasts were fuller, her hands were swollen. Birth and death were not mysteries to the Apache. He had seen enough pregnant women to know that Loralee was too far along for the child to be Schofield's. Unless . . .

His eyes, dark and accusing, locked on hers.

Loralee glared back at him, her cheeks growing hot under his probing gaze. Why had she come here?

Unable to hold his gaze any longer, she lowered her head, and now her eyes rested on Zuniga's hands. The long brown fingers were spread across her abdomen, and her mouth went dry as she remembered how those same fingers had stroked and explored every inch of her body.

"Look at me," Zuniga demanded, and when she refused, he captured her chin between his thumb and forefinger and forced her head up.

"You are with child," Zuniga said, each word cracking like a pistol shot.

"Yes." There was no point in denying it.

Zuniga's eyes narrowed. "You have only been married for eight weeks."

"So?" She knew suddenly what he was getting at, and her heart began to beat faster.

"You are more than eight weeks pregnant."

"Really?" Loralee replied sarcastically. "And when did you get to be such an expert on women in the family way?"

"Is the child mine?"

"No."

"No? Then you were sleeping with the white man while you were sleeping with me." A surge of white hot anger enveloped him at the thought of another man touching her, caressing her.

Loralee opened her mouth to deny Zuniga's accusation. How could he even think such a thing? The words of protest died in her throat. If she said she hadn't slept with Mike, Shad would know without a doubt that the child was his. And she did not want Zuniga to know he had fathered her child. Not now. Not ever.

"Well?" Zuniga prompted. His hands fell away from her face and balled into tight fists as he waited for her answer.

Loralee lifted her head proudly, her brown eyes flashing defiantly. "I'm only eight weeks pregnant," she lied boldly. "I've just been eating too much and"—she shrugged nonchalantly, praying that Zuniga would believe her—"I've gained a lot of weight, that's all. It's perfectly normal."

It was possible, Zuniga thought skeptically, and yet he knew, deep in his heart, that the child was his. Why wouldn't she admit it?

"I do not believe you," he said stubbornly.

Loralee took a deep breath. "Well, it's true whether you believe it or not."

Zuniga continued to stare at her intently. She was lying through her teeth and he knew it. But why? Was she ashamed to admit that an Indian had fathered her child? Or had she been sleeping with Schofield before they were married? Rage boiled through Zuniga. If Schofield had dared touch Loralee before they were married, he would die for it.

Zuniga swallowed his fury, and as he did so, a new thought occurred to him. Perhaps he had misjudged Loralee all along. Perhaps she was not the sweet innocent he had thought her to be. Perhaps she slept with every man she met and didn't know who the father was. Yet even as the idea crossed his mind, he knew it wasn't possible. Loralee had been a virgin when he took her the first time, and he was certain she had been with no other men but himself and Schofield.

Loralee licked her lips nervously. "I don't care what you believe," she retorted. "The child is Mike's, not yours, and there's nothing you can do about it."

Zuniga took a step closer, his dark eyes ablaze with jealousy. "Does the white man please you as I did?"

Loralee gasped, outraged that he would dare ask such a thing. Hot color rushed to her cheeks, and she turned away, refusing to answer him, refusing even to look at him.

"Do you call his name and claw his back as you once did mine?" Zuniga demanded. He took her chin in his hand and forced her to look at him. His eyes were like liquid ebony, deep and dark and angry. "Do you?"

"Shut up," Loralee hissed. She tried to pull out of his grasp, but his hand was like an iron vise, holding her immobile.

"Do you whimper softly when he strokes your sweet thighs, Loralee?" Zuniga taunted angrily. "Does he know the hills and valleys of your body as well as I do?"

"Shut your filthy mouth!" she shrieked. Tears welled in her eyes and she dashed them away with her fists. What right did he have to humiliate her in such a fashion, to make what they had shared seem cheap and degrading?

She gasped as Zuniga released his hold on her chin and grabbed a handful of her hair. Jerking her up against him, he pressed his mouth over hers, his lips grinding painfully against her own. Furious at his unwarranted assault, she bit down on his lower lip as hard as she could, and felt her stomach churn with revulsion as his blood filled her mouth.

With a wordless cry, she twisted out of his embrace. Arms wrapped around her swollen belly, she vomited until her stomach was empty and sore.

Face grim, Shad handed her the strip of cloth he used as a headband. Loralee accepted it grudgingly, embarrassed that she had disgraced herself before a man who only moments before had accused her of being no better than a harlot.

"Loralee." His voice was soft, all trace of anger and accusation gone.

"Leave me alone." She wiped her mouth with the cloth.

"Here. Drink this."

She took the gourd of water he offered her, and rinsed her mouth before taking a drink. The water was cool and sweet, but she refused to thank him for it.

"Loralee?"

Reluctantly she met his eyes. For a fraction of a second, she was sure that she saw love reflected in his gaze, but the expression was so quickly gone that she thought she must have imagined it. The desire in his eyes was easier to read. Too late, she realized that he meant to kiss her again. She did not struggle this time; instead, she stood in his arms, stiff and unmoving as a slab of stone, determined to accept his kiss passively until he released her, and then she would leave. Hopefully, she would never see him again.

Zuniga grinned, well aware of her tactics. Gently, his mouth moved over hers, light as the wings of a butterfly as he endeavored to arouse her. His hands played over her back and buttocks, pulling her against him so that she could feel his body and thighs and the hard bulge of his desire.

Loralee squeezed her eyes tight shut, trying to think of Mike, of the cruel things Zuniga had accused her of, of how much she hated him. But his lips were warm, persuasive, reminding her of past pleasures, of present desires. His body was hard, exciting, demanding. Slowly, hardly aware that she was doing so, she began to kiss him back. Her eyelids fluttered down as she surrendered to his kiss, reveling in the warmth that swelled within her being. Her blood was hot and sweet, singing in her veins, humming in her ears. She swayed against him, wanting to be closer to his masculine strength, certain she could never be close enough to satisfy the longing he had aroused in her. This was what she wanted. This was what she had yearned for.

She felt bereft when he released her.

"Let's go," Zuniga said gruffly.

Loralee looked at him blankly. "Go?"

"I am leaving the reservation." He gestured toward the pile of ashes that had been Nachi's wickiup. "I have no reason to stay now, and I am taking you with me."

Loralee stared at Zuniga. She shook her head as he began to reach for her. "No."

"Do not argue with me," he warned.

Loralee backed away, still shaking her head. She couldn't go with Zuniga, no matter how tempting the thought was. She was married to Mike now. He had given her his name, saved her from a life of shame, saved her child from the awful stigma of being born a bastard. If she lived to be a hundred, she could never repay Mike Schofield for his kindness. She could not shame him by running away with Zuniga.

With ease, Zuniga caught Loralee by the waist and lifted her onto the back of her horse. Then he swung aboard the dun.

"Follow me." He started down the hill, glancing over his shoulder to make sure that Loralee was following.

She urged her horse after Zuniga, pretending to be willing to do as he said. Gradually she let him get farther and farther ahead, and when the path leveled out, she swiftly reined Lady around and drummed her heels into the mare's flanks. The horse broke into a gallop, running hard for home.

Loralee felt her insides grow cold as a wild cry split the air. Zuniga was after her! She kicked Lady hard, begging the little mare for more speed, but her horse was no match for Zuniga's dun stallion. Tears of frustration stung Loralee's eyes as Zuniga pulled up alongside her. Leaning from his horse, he grabbed the reins from her hand and slowed her horse to a walk.

"Do not do that again!"

"Why are you doing this?" Loralee demanded.

"Because of the child. I will see for myself if it is mine."

Loralee glared at Zuniga. "What are you saying?"

"I am going to keep you with me until the child is born. If it is mine, I intend to keep it and raise it to be Apache."

"And if it isn't yours?"

Zuniga's face grew ugly. "Schofield dies."

"How will you know if the baby is yours? It might look like me."

"I will know."

"And what are your plans for me once the child is born?"

"If it is mine, I will keep the child and send you back to your husband." The last word was spoken with a sneer. "If the child is Schofield's, you may keep the child. But Schofield dies."

"You must be out of your mind,"

Loralee murmured, truly frightened now. "Don't you think Mike will come looking for me when I don't come home tonight? He'll kill you for this."

"He can try."

"You can't fight the whole Army," Loralee declared, exasperated. "Anyway, the baby isn't due for months."

Zuniga shrugged. "Apaches are known for their patience."

Stunned, Loralee didn't resist when Zuniga began to lead her horse southward. What was she going to do? If she admitted that the child was Shad's, he would keep her until the child was born and then send her back to Mike, keeping the child for himself. If he decided that the child wasn't his, Mike's life was in danger.

And then there was Mike to consider. What would he do when she didn't come home? How long would he wait before he began searching for her? Mike was a good soldier, and he had several young Apache scouts, but they had not been trained as Zuniga had been trained. In her heart, she was afraid that Mike would not be able to find her. Zuniga was Indian through and through. He could cover his tracks with ease. He could live off the land as his ancestors had, surviving on the food that nature provided. He knew where the waterholes were, where the rivers were.

She was equally afraid that Mike might

find her. In his present state of mind, Zuniga might well try to kill her husband.

Loralee glared at Zuniga, riding ahead of her. He rode easily, his body moving in rhythm with the stallion's, his long legs dangling loosely at the horse's sides. His back was straight and broad, his shoulders wide. He wore no shirt, only the familiar sleeveless vest, buckskin pants, and moccasins. His arms were the color of dark copper, ridged with muscle. His hair, long and black, fell past his shoulders. He had beautiful hair, she thought absently.

Her thoughts turned to Mike. He was tall and handsome, yet he did not kindle her desire, only a warm affection and a feeling of friendship. Still, she was married to him. He had given her a home and security and a name for her child, things Zuniga could never provide. Things he had never offered to give.

Loralee shook her head. She had been raised to be a proper lady all her life. Happiness came from doing what was right. Those who defied the laws of civilization and morality were shunned by decent society. Never, before Zuniga, had she found the courage to fly in the face of convention. Always she had done what was expected of her, behaved as a lady was expected to behave.

She had never been sorry. Until now. For the first time in her life she was ready to defy the laws of decency and morality and follow her heart. Only Zuniga didn't love her. All he wanted was the child who had been conceived out of their lust for each other. And when he had the child, he would send her back to Mike.

Loralee laughed a silent, humorless laugh. Mike would not want her after she had spent five months living in the wilds with an Apache warrior. No decent man would want her.

A single tear rolled down her cheek as she thought of the child growing under her heart. For the first time, she thought of it as a living being and not just a problem that needed solving. How could she let Zuniga take her child? It would be like losing a part of herself, a precious part of her heart and soul that could never be replaced no matter how many other children she might have.

Lost in thought, she did not notice the passing of the hours, or pay any attention to the direction they were taking. It wasn't until Zuniga came to a halt that she realized the sun was setting.

Glancing around, she saw they were in a box canyon. A thick stand of timber screened the entrance.

Zuniga dismounted. Paying no attention to Loralee, he removed the bridle from the dun and turned the horse loose to graze on the sparse yellow grass growing beside a small seep. Opening his war bag, he removed a side of bacon, some biscuits, a coffee pot and a sack of coffee, a tin cup, a frying pan, and matches.

That done, he lifted Loralee from the back of her horse, then nodded at the supplies spread on the ground.

"Fix dinner," he said curtly.

Loralee cast a grim look at the bacon and biscuits. "Is that all there is?"

"That's it."

With a distasteful sigh, Loralee began to slice the bacon into the skillet while Zuniga laid a small fire, then unsaddled and hobbled Loralee's horse. Bacon, biscuits, and coffee were better than nothing, Loralee mused irritably, but not much. The bacon was old, the biscuits were stale and hard, and there was neither milk nor sugar to sweeten the coffee. Still, she ate all he gave her, refusing to thank him. She wasn't here as his guest, after all.

It was full dark by the time they finished eating and cleaning up. Loralee watched apprehensively as Zuniga spread his blankets by the fire.

He glanced up, grinning, and Loralee felt her stomach flutter nervously. He had made only one bed. Obviously, he meant for her to share it with him.

Turning on her heel, she stalked into the darkness, seeking a place to relieve herself.

"Watch for snakes," Zuniga called, and laughed softly at her horrified gasp.

Eyes darting warily from side to side, Loralee squatted behind a clump of gray-green chaparral, cursing the day she had left the East. Her friends had been right, she thought dourly, she should have stayed home where she belonged. Then she wouldn't be relieving herself in the dirt like a wild animal. She wouldn't be pregnant by a man who was more savage than civilized. She wouldn't be married to a man she didn't love.

Zuniga was sitting on the blankets staring into the fire when she returned to camp. He glanced up, his eyes thoughtful, when he heard her footsteps.

Loralee remained standing, not wanting to sit beside him.

"Get some sleep," Zuniga said. "We're going to get an early start in the morning."

Loralee glanced pointedly at the blankets, and then at Zuniga.

With a wry grin, he stood up and handed her one of the blankets. Loralee felt a moment of disappointment when he didn't insist on sharing her bed. Then, admonishing herself for even considering such a thing, she curled up in the blanket and closed her eyes.

It seemed as if only moments had passed before Zuniga was shaking her awake. Wordlessly he handed her a cup of hot coffee, then began saddling her horse.

His stallion stood a few feet away, bridled and ready to go.

Loralee drank the bitter coffee, and then threw the grounds on the ashes of last night's fire. Rolling her blanket into a tight cylinder, she packed the skillet, coffee pot, and cup into Zuniga's war bag. Going to the seep, she rinsed her hands and face in the cold water. She wished fleetingly for a comb and a bar of soap.

By the time she had finished her crude toilet, Zuniga had the blankets strapped behind her saddle, his war bag over the horn.

Without a word, he helped her into the saddle, vaulted lightly onto the dun's bare back, and rode out of the canyon, heading southwest.

15

Mike was late getting home that night and he wasn't surprised to see that the house was dark. Loralee's pregnancy was making her more tired than usual and she often went to bed early.

Unsaddling his mount, he turned the horse loose inside the corral behind the house, forked the animal some hay, then stepped inside the house.

Moving quietly, he went into the kitchen and warmed up a pot of coffee. Sitting in the dark, he removed his sidearm and boots, unbuttoned his shirt, and sat back in the chair, his eyes closed. Married life agreed with him, he mused, even though he was living more like a monk than a bridegroom.

His love for Loralee grew with each passing day, and he was certain that she was beginning to care for him. Though he hadn't made further attempts to make love to her, they shared the same bed, and he enjoyed seeing her lovely face first thing in the morning and last thing at night. There were times when it took every ounce of will power he possessed to keep from taking her by force, times when her very nearness was the worst kind of torture. Her pregnancy helped keep his desires in check, but in a few months, the baby would be born. He hoped by then that Loralee would have grown to love him as he loved her.

Thinking of her, wanting her, made his blood run hot, and he stood up abruptly, poured himself a cup of coffee, and gulped down the contents in three long swallows.

"Patience," he murmured. "Just have patience."

Placing his cup in the sink, he went into the bedroom.

The bed was empty, the covers neatly in place.

Frowning, he lit the lamp beside the bed and looked around the room. Everything was in its place. He checked the closest and the dresser; all her clothes were there, and he breathed a sigh of relief. She hadn't left him, as he had at first feared.

Moving into the parlor, he lit another lamp and looked around for a note. There was none. It occurred to him that her horse had been missing from the corral. Perhaps she had ridden over to the schoolhouse, though he couldn't imagine what she would be doing there at such a late hour. Nevertheless, he pulled on his boots, saddled his horse, and rode to the school. There was no one there.

He rode to her former house, but that too was empty and dark. Truly worried now, he rode back to the fort and checked with Stella Freeman and the other women, but no one had seen Loralee since early that afternoon.

Back at home, he unsaddled his horse, then went into the house, his steps heavy, his mind in turmoil. There was nothing to do now but wait until morning.

He paced the parlor for an hour before he went to bed, but sleep would not come. Where could she be? Please, God, let her be all right, he prayed.

Rising, he wandered through the house until the eastern sky began to turn gray. Downing a quick cup of coffee, he saddled his weary horse and rode to the Agency office. Summoning his Indian scouts, he quickly explained that his wife was missing, and they rode back to Mike's house to look for signs.

Mike watched impatiently as the chief scout dismounted and checked the ground. If only one of the older warriors would agree to scout for him, he mused ruefully. These young Apaches were good, but they lacked the finely honed tracking skills that seemed to come as second nature to the older warriors.

Mike was about to give up hope that the scout would find the trail when the Apache gave a little cry of triumph. Mounting his horse, he turned toward the hills.

Mike felt his nerves grow taut as he realized that they were heading straight toward Shad Zuniga's lodge. He shook his head, not wanting to believe the thought forming in his mind. It couldn't be true.

When they reached the lodge, they found it burned to the ground. The chief scout pointed out that while they had followed a clear set of single tracks up the hill to the lodge, two sets of tracks led away.

Despair tore at Mike's heart. Always he had harbored a secret fear that Loralee would go to Zuniga, and now it had happened.

Thanking the Indians for their help, he sent them back to the reservation.

Mike sat there for a long time. Too numb to think, he stared off into the distance, his heart filled with pain. After a while, anger washed through him. Little bitch, he thought, the hell with her. Let her run off with that damn savage and have her bastard in the hills like a damn squaw! He had given her his name, offered her his love, saved her reputation from ruin, and this was how she repaid him, by running off with that damn Apache buck!

Then despair came again, smothering his anger. How would he live without her? She had become the most important thing in his life.

And then a new thought occurred to him. Maybe she hadn't gone with Zuniga willingly. Maybe the bastard had kidnapped her.

The thought died as soon as it crossed his mind. Loralee had gone to Zuniga's lodge of her own free will. The tracks proved that. She had gone to him, and left with him, so anxious to be with her Indian lover that she hadn't even taken the time to pack.

Muttering an oath, Mike Schofield wheeled his horse around and rode back to the fort.

16

"Where are you taking me?" Loralee demanded. It was dark, and they had been
traveling for over eight hours. Her back
ached, her thighs felt raw, and she was
weary, so weary.

"The mountains," Zuniga replied curtly. They were taking the long way there,
backtracking now and then in case they were
being followed.

"Mountains? What mountains?"

"To the south."

Loralee was not familiar with the country once they left the reservation. She knew
that Tucson lay somewhere to the south, and
she thought she might try to find her way
there if she could escape from Zuniga. If she
could get to Tucson, she could send a wire to

Mike, and he would come and take her home.

She shivered as a chill wind blew across the prairie. Were they going to ride forever without stopping? Her eyelids were heavy, and her eyes gritty with the need for sleep.

The moon was fading when Zuniga called a halt. Too tired to care where they were, Loralee slid off her horse. Her legs refused to support her and she sank to the ground, falling asleep as soon as she closed her eyes.

When she woke, it was the gray hour just before dawn. Zuniga slept beside her, and she glanced around. They were in a shallow draw. Their horses were hobbled a few yards away, heads hanging, noses almost touching the ground. She thought briefly of trying to slip out from under the blanket and running for her horse, but even as the idea formed in her mind, Zuniga was moving. He came instantly awake, his eyes meeting hers. He grinned wryly, and Loralee wondered if it was possible for him to read her mind.

"Fix breakfast," he ordered curtly, and rose smoothly to his feet.

Sullen-faced, Loralee rummaged through his warbag for the coffee pot. There was only a little bacon and one biscuit apiece for breakfast, but Loralee ate without complaining. Her whole body ached from spending the night on the ground.

Too soon, they were riding again, crossing a wild, unsettled stretch of ground. Loralee saw squirrels and porcupines, prairie dogs and gophers. An eagle soared on the air currents. Once she saw a rattlesnake coiled in the shade of a rock. In the distance, she saw several vultures fighting over the carcass of some dead animal.

Zuniga rode without speaking, and she wondered what he was thinking, why he was so eager to have her child. He did not seem like the type of man who yearned to be a father. He did not seem to care for her any longer. What did he intend to do with the child?

Zuniga drew to a halt late in the afternoon. Wordlessly he lifted her from her horse, and before she quite realized what he meant to do, he had tied her to a young oak tree. When she opened her mouth to protest, he jammed his headband into her mouth, then tied a kerchief around her mouth to keep the gag in place.

She watched through frightened eyes as he tethered her mare to another tree, then swung onto the back of the dun and rode away.

Days of doubt and worry erupted in a flood of tears, rolling down her cheeks and neck, making her eyes itch and her throat ache. Where had he gone? Was he coming back?

Hours passed. She fretted over an itch she could not scratch. Her arms and legs grew weary, and her mouth was dryer than the Sonora desert in summer. Inwardly she cursed the day she had met Shad Zuniga. He had brought her nothing but misery, she lamented, nothing but pain and heartache . . . and hours of passion. She closed her eyes, remembering how eagerly she had surrendered to his touch, how she had thrilled to the taste of his lips, the press of his flesh against her own, the masculine scent of him that had aroused her primal senses. She had loved him with all her heart, she thought sadly. And she still loved him. That was the worst part, because he didn't seem to have any feeling left for her at all.

Zuniga rode quietly through the hills, headed for a ranch house located a few miles to the north. They needed food, and money too, if he could find some.

He rode warily, eyes and ears alert for any sign of man or beast, his thoughts on Loralee. He desired her with every fiber of his being, but he had hardened his heart against her. She had lied to him about the baby. Obviously, she did not love him. Probably she was ashamed to be carrying an Apache child. Why else would she have lied to him? Why else would she have married the white man? If she had cared for him, she would have come to him and told him about the baby. He would have married her in the white man's way if that had been her desire.

Now it was too late. He could not live with a woman who was ashamed of him, ashamed of his heritage. But he meant to have the child. His child. A faint smile softened the harsh lines of his face as he thought of the child.

It was near dusk when he reached the outskirts of the ranch. Dismounting, he tethered the stallion to a low-hanging tree limb, then padded toward the house. Taking a place behind a clump of mesquite, he hunkered down on his heels to wait.

He sat there for an hour, unmoving, his eyes fixed on the house. He remembered the long hours he had spent with Nachi, learning to become a warrior. Being a novice warrior was no easy task, and not one to be taken lightly. A boy had to participate in four expeditions against the enemy. He had to be reliable and obedient. He had to be brave and truthful. He must not eat too much between raids lest he become a glutton. There were many restrictions placed on a boy on his first four raids. He was not to speak to any warrior except to answer a question. He was to speak respectfully to all men and not talk obscenely in front of women. He was to show courage and endure all hardships without complaint. It was up to the novice to fetch wood and water and do all the heavy work around the camp. He rose early in the morning and lit the cookfires, cared for the horses, did the cooking, stood guard duty. Novice warriors could work, but they could not fight.

There were ceremonial words that were used during a boy's first four raids, replacing ordinary forms of speech. After the fourth trip out with the warriors, a novice was permitted to enter the ranks of the men as long as none of the warriors objected.

Zuniga smiled into the darkness. It had been good to become a warrior. No longer did he have to stay home with the women and children. He was free to do as he pleased, to express his own ideas in council. He could smoke, he could marry, he could participate in war dances.

So much to learn, Zuniga mused, and so little time to practice all he had been taught. It seemed like such a short time that he was able to practice the skills he had learned, and then his people had been defeated, and there was little need anymore in knowing how to track or fight. A man did not need to be proficient in the skills necessary to be a warrior to live on a reservation. The men no longer had a reason to live, and so they drank too much, losing themselves in the white man's whiskey. They had no hope, no desire to live, no desire for anything but the whiskey that made them forget what they had become.

Zuniga rose smoothly to his feet as the lights went out inside the ranch house. Noiselessly he padded across the barren ground, using every bit of cover he could find.

Again, he waited, listening. After thirty minutes, he jimmied open a window and climbed inside the house. Slowly, carefully, he moved through the place until he came to the kitchen.

He found an empty burlap bag on the counter and began to fill it with nonperishable food from the pantry: canned goods, coffee, sugar, salt, onions, potatoes, carrots, a sack of flour. He took a frying pan, several boxes of matches, a package of cigarettes, a handful of cookies he found in a jar, three loaves of freshly baked bread. Moving through the house, he picked up two blankets, a poncho for Loralee, a heavy buckskin jacket for himself. He found a wad of greenbacks inside a tin box.

In the barn, he took a lantern and a sack of oats. Pleased with his booty, he returned to his horse, the burlap bag slung over his shoulder.

Fear settled on Loralee as darkness covered the land. Zuniga had been gone for several hours now, and with the passing of each moment, a new fear flooded her mind. He had been hurt. He had been killed. He had decided he didn't want the baby after all and he was never coming back.

A coyote yapped in the distance, and Loralee shivered with apprehension. Soon the predators would be running across the prairie in search of food. There were all manner of wild beasts in the area—wolves and coyotes, black bears and wild hogs.

Her fear intensified as the moon climbed in the sky, goading her into a fresh attempt to escape the bonds that held her, and she began to pull against the rope. The rough hemp cut into her tender flesh, but she ignored the pain and the blood trickling down her hands. Tears of frustration welled in her eyes.

Her struggles ceased as the cry of a wolf sounded a few yards to her right. Fool, she lamented. Writhing against the ropes had drawn blood. And the blood scent had drawn the wolf.

Her heart began to pound wildly as she heard the wolf move through the under-brush, and then it was only a few feet away, its eyes shining in the darkness. It was a big wolf, black in color, with hungry yellow eyes and sharp yellow fangs.

Loralee pressed back against the tree, shaking her head in terror as she sent a silent prayer to heaven. "Oh, God, please help me. Please, please, help me."

The wolf lifted its head, nostrils testing the air. The scent of fresh blood was strong, but the human scent was stronger. Unde-cided, the wolf whined low in its throat as it stared at Loralee, its tongue lolling out the side of its mouth.

Mesmerized, Loralee stared at the animal, too frightened by its nearness to hear the muffled sound of hoofbeats coming toward her. There were no reliable accounts of a wolf ever attacking a man, she told herself, but there was always a first time. Perhaps this wolf didn't know that its species didn't attack people. Perhaps it was too hungry to care. Perhaps she was mistaken, and wolves attacked and ate everything they encountered.

She couldn't take her eyes off the animal. Was it going to attack? Time lost all meaning as she waited for the beast to pounce on her and rend her flesh.

She jumped as the sound of a gunshot rent the stillness of the night, sending the wolf scurrying into the darkness. Fear melted into overwhelming relief when she saw Zuniga walking toward her.

Without a word, he removed the gag from her mouth and the rope from her wrists. He frowned when he saw the blood oozing down her arms, and the pain and fear mirrored in her eyes.

Taking her by the hand, he led her to where his horse was tethered. There was a blanket spread beneath a tree and he motioned for her to sit down.

Too weary to ask questions, Loralee did as bidden.

Zuniga's face was grim as he took a pot of bear grease from his war bag. Kneeling at

261

Loralee's side, he stared at the blood on her arms, as bright and red as the guilt in his heart. He had not meant to cause her harm. The last thing he wanted to do was hurt her, but it had been necessary to tie her up. He could not trust her to stay until he returned, could not take a chance of her running back to Schofield.

Thoughts of Schofield ignited Zuniga's anger, and his hands were rough as he began to smear the grease over the abrasions in Loralee's wrists. She winced at his touch, and Zuniga swore under his breath as his conscience stabbed him again. The lacerations were not deep, but he knew they were painful, knew it was his fault she was hurting.

When he finished, he picked up the burlap bag and dropped it at Loralee's feet. "Fix dinner," he said tersely.

Heaving a sigh, Loralee rummaged around inside the bag, and in a short time, dinner was cooking.

They ate in silence. Loralee longed to tell Shad she loved him, longed to wipe the anger from his face, to see his eyes light with love and desire. But she could not form the words. He had treated her abominably, frightened her half to death. Had he said even one word to indicate he was sorry, she would have flown into his arms. But he remained aloof, untouchable. His face was expressionless, his eyes unfathomable.

Loralee sighed heavily. How had the love they once shared turned so quickly to hatred?

Several days passed, each one taking Loralee farther from Mike, farther from civilization. They were fast approaching the mountains, and Loralee was becoming resigned to the fact that she was going to spend the next five months living with Shad Zuniga whether she liked it or not. Once, the thought of going away with him would have filled her with happiness. Once, she would have been glad to spend her whole life with him. But not now, not when he had become a stranger to her. She dreaded the days ahead, dreaded the thought of living in the mountains away from everything that had become familiar to her. Worst of all was the thought of having her baby alone in the mountains with no woman to encourage her, and no doctor available to help her if something went wrong. She was not afraid to have the child, not really. Childbirth was a perfectly normal, natural process, but she could not help being concerned about what they would do if something went wrong. Complications could happen, and as knowledgeable as Zuniga seemed about most things, he was not a doctor.

But far more troubling than having her baby alone was the thought that Zuniga meant to take the child from her. How could she bear to be parted from her first-born child? Zuniga's child. How could she make him change his mind?

She was thinking of that now as she washed and dried the dinner dishes. Zuniga remained cool and aloof, rarely speaking to her except to order her about as though she were his personal slave. His arrogance, his smug self-assurance, nettled her. She longed to strike out at him, to hurt him as she had been hurt, but she was at a loss as to how to go about it. He was impervious to her insults, seemingly oblivious to her tears. If only she had a weapon! For a moment she fantasized that she had a gun and that Zuniga was *her* prisoner. How she would like to order him about. Oh, but she would make him crawl, and enjoy every minute.

Loralee laughed silently, mirthlessly. Even if she had a gun, Zuniga would still be in control. He would know she lacked the courage to use it, and that knowledge would make the gun useless in her hands.

She slid a glance in his direction. He was hunkered down across the fire from her. The flames cast dancing shadows across the hard planes of his face, making him look wild and primitive and beautiful. If only she could tell him what was in her heart. If only he would listen.

She was pouring herself a cup of lukewarm coffee when four men dressed in denim pants, dark shirts, and heavy jackets rode into camp. Zuniga rose smoothly to his feet, his hand curling around the butt of the gun shoved into the waistband of his trousers.

A smile of welcome crossed Loralee's face as she glimpsed the badge pinned to the shirt of the man in the lead. They were Arizona Rangers, and she felt a flicker of hope ignite within her breast. Perhaps her salvation was at hand.

Zuniga studied the four men. The Arizona Rangers had been organized in 1901 by Governor Nathan Murphy, mainly to take action against smugglers and rustlers. The newspapers loved the Rangers, Zuniga recalled scornfully. Loralee had let him read several newspapers from various Arizona towns while she was tutoring him. The pages had been filled with the heroic exploits of the Rangers, describing in glowing terms their bravery, loyalty and ability to get the job done.

"Smelled your coffee, ma'am," the leader of the riders remarked, touching his hat brim respectfully. "Could you spare a little for four thirsty men?"

"Of course," Loralee answered, ignoring the warning look that Zuniga slanted in her direction. "Please, step down and join us."

The four lawmen dismounted. Pulling tin cups from their saddlebags, they hunkered down around the fire. Loralee filled their coffee cups, smiling and chatting amiably as the men introduced themselves.

The leader was Captain Colin Webster. His men, all in their early thirties, were Sergeant Jody Powell, Private Seth Parker, and Private Tom Davidson.

"Where are you folks headed?" Webster asked. He spoke to Loralee, but his eyes were on Zuniga. What the hell was a white woman doing way out here with an Indian?

"We're headed for New Mexico," Zuniga answered. The lie rolled easily off his tongue. There was no shame in lying to the enemy. "My wife has family there."

Colin Webster nodded, but his eyes were doubtful. He had been a lawman for over twenty years, and his instincts told him something wasn't right. He turned his gaze on Loralee, noting the ring on her finger, the slight swell of her belly, and the way she avoided looking directly at the Indian. The tension between the white woman and the Apache was almost visible. Something was definitely amiss, Webster thought. He'd gamble his reputation on it.

"Are you searching for an escaped felon, Captain?" Loralee asked.

"No, ma'am. Just scouting around. I have three hundred and fifty miles to cover each month." He smiled affably. "It's all routine, but it takes a heap of time." Webster slid a casual glance in the Indian's direction again. Was it possible he was the woman's husband? It didn't seem likely. The woman was obviously a lady of quality and good breeding. Such women didn't marry Apache bucks.

"I see." Loralee felt a twinge of dismay. She had hoped that the lawmen were searching for her. "More coffee?"

"Half a cup, thanks," Webster said, holding out his cup. "Then we'd best be on our way."

"So soon?"

Colin Webster quickly caught the note of panic in Loralee's voice. His expression did not change as he rose smoothly to his feet. Casually he shifted his coffee cup to his left hand, his right hand moving toward his hip so that his gun was only inches from his grasp.

It was a move that did not go unnoticed by Zuniga. Or by Webster's deputies. One by one, the three lawmen rose to their feet, acutely aware of the tension building around the campfire.

Colin Webster sipped his coffee slowly, his eyes on Loralee's face. Just give me a sign, lady, he mused, and I'll drop the redskin where he stands.

Zuniga glanced at Loralee, and then his eyes moved over the four lawmen. It was up to Loralee now, he thought. Colin Webster was suspicious, but you couldn't arrest a man because of what you thought.

Loralee chewed on the inside of her

lower lip, suddenly uncertain as to what she should do. If she asked the Rangers for help, there was sure to be trouble. She knew that Zuniga would not surrender without a fight, and it was highly unlikely that he could outgun four trained lawmen. More likely he would be captured, perhaps killed. She could not bear the thought of his death, nor could she abide the thought of seeing him sent to prison, his wild spirit caged behind cold iron bars.

Webster was watching her intently, waiting for her to make the first move.

Pasting a stiff smile on her face, Loralee went to stand beside Zuniga. Her arm slid around his waist and she gazed up at him, hoping she looked like an adoring wife.

"I guess we shouldn't keep you any longer, Captain," Loralee said with regret. "It's just that we haven't had a chance to talk to many folks in the last few days."

Colin Webster frowned. There was definitely something wrong here, but he couldn't put his finger on it. Keeping his eyes on Zuniga, he drained the last of the coffee from his cup.

"Our thanks, ma'am, for your hospitality," Webster said. He swung into the saddle, sent a last look in Zuniga's direction, and rode out of camp. His men tipped their hats to Loralee, then followed after Webster.

Zuniga did not relax until he was certain they were gone, and then he looked at Loralee inquisitively. "Why?" he asked.

"I didn't want to see anyone get hurt," she answered, not meeting his eyes. "I don't want anyone killed because of me. Not even you."

Zuniga grunted, his expression thoughtful.

Loralee turned away from him, afraid he might see the truth in her eyes. Moving briskly, she smothered the fire and laid out their blankets. Slipping off her shoes, she crawled into bed and closed her eyes. Images of Zuniga rose in her mind . . . Zuniga sitting in her classroom, his deep voice filling the room as he read the story of Jack and Charles. Zuniga lying naked beside her at Shadow Lake, his mouth on hers. Zuniga smiling fondly at his grandfather. Zuniga standing beside the ashes of Nachi's lodge.

Zuniga. She had known him only a short time, yet he had become an integral part of her life. She carried his child beneath her heart.

17

After five days of hard riding, Zuniga reached his destination, a sheltered valley enclosed by the towering cliffs of the Dragoon Mountains.

He paused at the entrance, letting his eyes wander over the ancient Apache stronghold. It was a place rich in the history of his people. From here, Cochise had waged a long and bloody war against the whites—a war the white men started and the Indians had finished. It had all begun in 1861 when a band of Pinal Apaches kidnapped a white boy and rustled some stock. Cochise's tribe had been accused of the crime. Cochise had gone to parley with Lieutenant George Bascomb of the Seventh Cavalry near Apache Pass. Bascomb had demanded the return of the kidnapped boy, but Cochise had insisted that his people were not to blame. He had volunteered to help locate the missing boy, but Bascomb had called Cochise a liar and ordered his arrest. Cochise had managed to escape, but three of his warriors were captured.

In turn, Cochise captured several whites as hostages and demanded that his people be released. Bascomb refused, and hanged the three Indians. Cochise tortured his prisoners in retaliation, and the war was on. Cochise had been an amazing fighter. He had never lost a battle, outfighting and outwitting everyone sent against him.

The war might have lasted forever if it were not for the bravery of a man named Tom Jeffords. Jeffords was a New Yorker who had gone West as a young man. He had worked as a hunter and an Army scout, fighting against the Apache. He had also done some prospecting. During the Civil War, he had worked as supervisor of the United States mail. Cochise frequently attacked the mail coaches, sometimes killing the drivers. In a brave move, Jeffords went alone to see Cochise. The Apache chief admired Jeffords for his courage and honesty and agreed to let the mail coaches travel in safety.

Zuniga sighed as he thought of the old days, the good days. Cochise and Jeffords had become close friends, and Jeffords had been a frequent visitor at the stronghold. He had even married an Apache maiden. In 1871, General O. O. Howard, who was often called the "Christian General," came to Arizona for the purpose of arranging a peace treaty with Cochise. It was Jeffords who had guided the general to the Apache stronghold in the Chiricahua Mountains.

Nachi had been at that meeting. Many warriors had been against the peace, Nachi had said, and many had walked away, preferring to go on fighting against the whites, who, they said, could not be trusted. But Cochise had trusted Jeffords and the treaty had been made. Cochise kept the peace until he died in 1874. He was buried here, in the place he loved best, in a deep crevasse known to only a few ancient warriors.

Zuniga gazed at the mountains. Had peace been such a good thing? His people were no better off now than before. Personally, he would rather have died in battle than live in peace on the reservation, subject to the rule and whim of the whites.

He remained mounted for a long time, listening to the awesome quiet of the place. There were plateaus here, and canyons, and sheer cliffs that rose a thousand feet high. There was only one entrance to the rancheria. In the old days, ten well-armed warriors could have held off ten thousand invaders. . . .

He cocked his head as the wind soughed

through the ancient oaks, the sound like the whisper of ghosts long dead. He shivered as the inbred Apache fear of the dead rose within him, then shook the feeling away. The dead could not hurt the living, but the wind was talking to him again, singing like voices out of the past.

"Hi-disho," the wind seemed to say. "It is finished."

He gazed into the distance. Almost, he could see the ghost of Cochise walking along the wooded paths where the lodges of the Chiricahua had once stood. He saw the faces of warriors long dead, the smile of a maiden he had once thought to marry, the face of his mother as she laughed with the other women.

He glanced over his shoulder. There, beneath a gnarled oak, had stood the wicki-up where he had been born almost thirty-four years ago. Nothing remained now but a memory.

His gaze moved westward. There, in the distance, were the Chiricahua Mountains, site of Cochise's second stronghold. Memories, so many memories.

Loralee grimaced as she watched Zuniga dismount. No one would ever find her here. She was Zuniga's prisoner now, as surely as if she were bound to him by heavy chains, and she would remain so until her child was born.

The very stillness of the place seemed

ominous. Generations of Apaches had lived and died here. The great chief, Cochise, had walked this land, had likely stood on the very place she now stood. General Oliver O. Howard had come here to make peace over thirty years ago. Howard had described Cochise as being six feet tall, well-proportioned, with large dark eyes and a pleasant expression.

As Loralee surveyed the land that had once been the Apache homeland, she recalled an article she had read in an old copy of the *Arizona Citizen.*

"The kind of war needed for the Chiricahua Apache," the column read, "is steady, unrelenting, hopeless and undiscriminating war, slaying men, women, and children . . . until every valley and crest and crag and fastness shall send to high heaven the grateful incense of festering and rotting Chiricahuas."

She felt a sudden sadness for the Apache people. Their land was gone. Their way of life was gone. She looked at Zuniga, a man who hungered for the old ways. Was he also hearing the cry of spirits that had once walked this lonely valley? Was that the grieving wail of an Apache squaw, or only the wind sighing through the trees?

With a shake of her head, Loralee put such fanciful notions from her mind. The Apache and their destiny were not her problems now. She had her own problems, her own concerns.

She felt Zuniga's eyes studying her, and she met his gaze defiantly. She would not allow him to frighten her any longer. Though he no longer cared for her, she knew that he would not abuse her, or intimidate her. Not while she carried his child.

He grinned faintly, and Loralee wondered if he were reading her mind. He seemed to have an uncanny ability to know what she was thinking.

With a grunt, he removed the saddle and bridle from her horse, pulled the bridle from the stallion, and turned the horses loose to graze.

Loralee watched Zuniga. What now? she thought. They had no lodge to shelter them from the cold, no food save what little remained in the burlap bag. At least they would not die of thirst, she mused dourly. A shallow stream shimmered in the afternoon sun.

"Gather some wood," Zuniga said curtly. "Build a fire."

"I'm not your squaw," Loralee retorted. "Do it yourself."

"If you do not work, you do not eat," Zuniga replied flatly. "Gather some wood and build a fire."

Eyes flashing rebellion, Loralee wandered down the valley. It took only a few moments to gather an armful of dry wood, and in a short time she was sitting before a small, cheery fire.

She sat there, enjoying the warmth, while Zuniga cut several long branches. She continued to watch, fascinated, as he tied the long, slender poles together, fashioning the framework for a wickiup. He sent her a wry grin as he began to cover the framework with brush and yucca leaves, leaving a hole at the top to allow smoke to escape from the firepit which would be laid in the center of the lodge. A blanket was used to cover the narrow doorway.

Loralee smiled ruefully. It was the ugliest structure she had ever seen.

"Your house awaits," Zuniga remarked dryly. "Make yourself at home."

With a nod, Loralee gathered up her blankets and the burlap bag and entered the lodge. She was suddenly nervous, standing there in the alien dwelling. This crude hovel would be her home until her child was born. She would live here, sleep here, and give birth to her child here. For the next four and a half months, she would see no one but Zuniga. It was a sobering thought.

Suddenly needing to be busy, she spread her blankets at the back of the lodge along the right side. That done, she emptied the burlap bag, placing the cooking utensils in a neat pile on the left side of the lodge. Using a sharp stick, she dug a shallow firepit, then went outside to gather more wood.

Zuniga was nowhere in sight. Alarmed, she looked right and left, but he had vanished without a trace. Where had he gone? Why had he taken the horses? Surely he did not intend to leave her here to fend for herself until the baby was born?

Frightened, she gathered an armful of wood and returned to her wickiup. Lighting a small fire, she sat on her blankets, her eyes glued to the entrance of the lodge, her ears straining for some sound that would indicate Zuniga had returned.

Hours passed. The sky grew dark. Stars appeared. And still no sign of Zuniga.

She was too frightened to think of food, and she sat there, unmoving, until she fell asleep.

The raucous cawing of a crow roused Loralee from a deep sleep. It was just past dawn. For a moment, she stared at the inside of the wickiup, confused by her strange surroundings. And then, with a start, she sat up. Zuniga!

Rising, she ran out of the lodge and smack into his arms.

"You!" she shouted, backing away from him. "Where have you been? Why did you go off and leave me alone?"

Zuniga's brows rushed together in an angry frown. "Hold your tongue, woman," he admonished sharply. "I am not your husband, to be bullied and abused."

"Thank God for that!" Loralee snapped, her fright gone now that he was near. "But you might have told me you were leaving."

"Why? Did you worry?"

"Of course not, but I—"

"Fix breakfast."

"Don't you ever say please?" Loralee asked sulkily.

"No." He thrust a pair of rabbits into her hands. "Fix breakfast."

Loralee glanced at the rabbits in dismay. She had never cooked wild game, let alone skinned any. The very thought of cutting into fur and flesh made her stomach churn.

Zuniga made a sound of disgust low in his throat as he snatched the rabbits from Loralee's hands. White women, he mused sourly, and then sighed. She was pregnant, after all, and not accustomed to living in the mountains. She was used to living in a neat little house, cooking on a wood stove, sleeping in a bed.

He grinned wryly. She had wanted to help his people, to understand them. Soon she would learn more about Apache ways than she had ever wanted to know.

Loralee turned away, sick to her stomach, as Zuniga drew his knife and deftly skinned the rabbits, then spitted the carcasses over the firepit she had built the day before.

While the meat cooked, Zuniga scraped the remaining flesh from the inside of the hides and then stretched the hides between two stout sticks.

The aroma of roasting meat tickled

Loralee's nose, quickening her appetite. She had not eaten since lunch the day before and she was suddenly famished. She watched eagerly as Zuniga turned the meat. Juice dripped into the fire, sizzling loudly as it struck the hot stones.

It was the best food she had ever eaten, Loralee thought with surprise, or maybe it only tasted that way because she was so hungry. She amazed herself and Zuniga by eating most of one whole rabbit.

When the meal was over, Zuniga rose abruptly to his feet and went to his horse.

"Where are you going?" Loralee asked.

"Bisbee."

"Bisbee? Why?"

"We need supplies."

"Oh."

Zuniga felt a flicker of compassion for her. She sounded so forlorn. Almost, he was tempted to take her in his arms, to comfort her, to assure her that he would look after her until the baby was born. But then he remembered Schofield.

"I will be back late tonight," he said tersely. "Or tomorrow."

"Tomorrow." Her shoulder slumped dejectedly as she thought of spending another night alone. Two large tears welled in her eyes.

"Oh, hell," he muttered irritably. "I will be back tonight." Suddenly angry with himself, he swung onto the dun's back and rode away.

Loralee was overcome with loneliness as she watched him ride out of sight. And then it occurred to her that now was her chance to escape.

She looked around, hoping he had brought her horse back with him, and then she laughed a short, bitter laugh. Damn him. He had known she would try to leave if he left her alone. That was why he had hidden her horse.

With a sigh, she began to walk. She had no destination in mind, and she wandered aimlessly up a narrow trail that led to a plateau. She paused a moment, looking out over the valley below, trying to imagine what it had been like when Cochise and his band had lived here. Closing her eyes, she pictured hundreds of dome-shaped wickiups, smoke rising from the smoke holes, the aroma of roasting meat and ash cakes filling the air, the barking of dogs, the laughter of women and children.

Lifting her skirt, she climbed around the base of a tall tower, passing several deep crevasses. It was a quiet place, peaceful in the early morning sunshine.

Another half-mile along a winding trail brought her through small wooded glens. Farther on, she came to Treaty Rock where Jeffords, Cochise, and Howard had made peace and signed the treaty that ended the ten-year war started by Bascomb.

Here she sat down on the ground to rest, her chin cupped in the palms of her hands. The sun felt warm on her skin, the sky was a clear azure blue, the air was fragrant with the scent of pines. No wonder the Apache had loved this land. No wonder they had fought so hard to keep it.

Loralee smiled wryly. It was ironic, she mused, that this area was now called Cochise County. The Apache chief must be laughing in his grave to know that the whites had named the land after a man they had fought so hard to destroy. She thought about Tom Jeffords. He was an old man now, well into his seventies, living in peaceful retirement at his Owl Head Ranch. She thought she would like to meet Tom Jeffords. What stories he would have to tell!

She rested there for an hour, letting her thoughts wander where they would. She thought of her students. No doubt they were enjoying this unexpected holiday. She thought of her unborn child. And she thought of Zuniga. It hurt, knowing he hated her now. His eyes were cold when they looked at her. Cold, or cruelly mocking.

Rising, she made her way back to her wickiup. An apple and a slice of saltpork served as lunch.

At loose ends, she went to the stream. The water was cool, but she undressed and bathed as best she could, rinsing her hair in the clear cold water, letting it dry in the sun.

She spent the afternoon sitting in front of her lodge, watching the squirrels scamper from tree to tree. Birds twittered in the treetops. A skunk waddled along the stream.

The warm sun made her drowsy, and before long she was asleep.

Zuniga let the stallion pick its way down out of the mountains. For the first time in years, he felt alive, free. It was good to be back in the Apache stronghold, good to breathe air that was not fouled by the whites, to walk the land his ancestors had walked.

He reached Bisbee late in the afternoon. Leaving his horse on the outskirts of town, he wandered down the dusty street.

At the general store, he spent twenty minutes walking up and down the aisles before he began to take items from the shelves. He bought everything that caught his eye in the canned food section. Moving on, he bought a couple of bath towels, a few bars of soap since he was certain Loralee couldn't make soap out of a yucca plant like the Indians did. He bought a Dutch oven, a couple of knives and forks, a cook pot. As an afterthought, he shelled out seventy-five cents for a pair of levis for himself, and then bought a couple of white cotton shirts for Loralee to wear as her pregnancy advanced, as well as several yards of material, needles, and thread so she could make herself some skirts. He also bought two yards of linen, a bottle of iodine, and a pair of scissors.

The amount of his purchases took just over half of his money. The clerk as he made change threw Zuniga a questioning look. He thinks I stole the money, Zuniga mused, returning the clerk's gaze. And he's right!

Gathering up his bundles, he left the store, whistling softly.

When Loralee awoke, it was dark and cold. Shivering, she stood up, wondering what time it was. Running her hands over her arms, she went to the wickiup and pulled on her poncho. She searched blindly for the matches, and felt a little surge of relief when she found them. The night was less frightening with the lantern lit and a fire crackling cheerfully in the center of the lodge.

Beans and biscuits made do as dinner, and she washed it down with three cups of black coffee. Time and again, she went to the doorway to peer outside for some sign of Zuniga. No matter how she hated him, she missed his company. Every shadow, every night sound, conjured up visions of wild animals or evil spirits.

She laughed self-consciously. She was an educated woman. She did not believe in ghosts, and no flesh-and-blood animal was likely to enter the wickiup so long as a fire was burning. And yet there was something about the ancient Apache stronghold that inspired a belief in the supernatural.

She jumped, startled, as the call of an owl pierced the stillness. The Apache believed that owls came and called for the spirits of the dead. The Apache were strong believers in ghosts, hence their fear of the dead.

Sitting close to the fire, Loralee began to sing her favorite hymn, her voice shaky and a little off-key:

"Amazing grace, how sweet the sound, that saved a wretch like me, I once was lost, but now am found, was blind, but now I see. . . ."

Oh, God, she thought helplessly. *I'm so lost.*

A noise outside made her jump. Wrapping her arms around her body, she scooted closer to the fire. She wished suddenly that she didn't know quite so much about Apache beliefs and superstitions. It was so easy to imagine Indians long dead surrounding her wickiup, their sunken eyes filled with hate and accusation because a white woman had invaded their ancestral land and defiled sacred ground. She could almost see them standing around her, pale skeletons dressed in tattered bits of buckskin and feathers, their bony fingers pointing in her direction. She was the enemy, an intruder. She had come to take the children away from the true faith, to teach them to read and write the white man's language, to draw them away from the old ways, the old beliefs.

The wind began to blow, its low wail like the echo of spirit voices. A coyote howled in the distance, its melancholy lament filling Loralee with loneliness. Where was Shad? Why didn't he come? She made excuses for his tardiness. He had been detained in Bisbee. He had stopped for a drink at one of the saloons. He had forgotten something and had to go back. His horse had gone lame. He was hurt. He had found a woman. . . .

The thought of Shad making love to another woman cut into Loralee's heart like a knife. She was torturing herself with the thought when he stepped through the doorway, his arms laden with packages.

With a sob of relief, Loralee jumped to her feet. "Oh, Shad!" she cried, and threw herself into his arms. The packages clattered to the ground as he caught her.

"Don't ever leave me alone again," she begged, her luminous brown eyes pleading more eloquently than her words. "Please don't ever leave me."

Zuniga frowned as Loralee buried her face in his shoulder. Gently, he patted her back as she wept uncontrollably. Damn, but she felt good in his arms. So good, so right. He rested his cheek on the top of her head, inhaling the scent of her hair, feeling its silkiness against his skin. Her breasts were soft against his chest, sparking his desire in a quick surge of heat. He had not had a woman in months, not since the last time he had made love to Loralee. He forgot how that episode had ended and remembered only how good she had felt in his arms, how satisfying it had been to hold her, to touch her, how willingly she had responded to his caresses.

Without thinking, he removed her poncho. Then, claiming her lips in a long possessive kiss, he lifted her into his arms and carried her to her blankets. Carefully, he lowered her to the makeshift bed and stretched out beside her, his lips never leaving hers. She was woman, giver of life, and he was dying without her. With a low groan, he plundered her mouth, seeking the sweet refreshment within.

Loralee closed her eyes, letting the magic of his touch wash over her, chasing away the demons that had frightened her. She forgot about Mike, forgot she had once vowed to hate and despise Shad Zuniga until her dying day. All she knew, all she desired in that moment, was his mouth on hers, his hands fondling her breasts, stroking her thighs. She moaned softly as he took his mouth from hers, sighed with pleasure as he began to nibble her breasts. Her hands roamed over his neck and back and shoulders, her body straining to be closer to his.

With ease, he removed her dress and

undergarments, his dark eyes worshipping her body. Her breasts were swollen, her abdomen softly rounded with new life. Reverently, he placed his hand over her belly. His child was growing there, beneath her heart.

He gazed at Loralee. How beautiful she was. The firelight turned her hair to gold and made her skin glow like warm honey. She was lovely and wise, gentle and kind. He would want no other for the mother of his son.

His son. Emotions Zuniga had never known swelled in his heart. He would grow old and die, but he would not be forgotten. He would be remembered by his children, and grandchildren, should Usen let him live that long.

Loralee moved beneath his hand, urging him to take her. He needed little persuasion. He was on fire for her, shaking with the need to possess her. His hands were clumsy in his haste to remove his clothing and take her in his arms.

Civilization seemed far away now. He was primal man, and she was his woman. They had fire for warmth, a dry lodge for shelter, food and water. They needed nothing else.

He grasped her hair in one hand and slanted his mouth over hers in a kiss that branded her his for all time. He had vowed never to touch her again, but he knew it would be easier to give up breathing than deny the need he felt for this woman. She was his, would always be his. He would kill any man who tried to take her from him.

Moaning her name, he buried himself in her softness. . . .

18

When Loralee woke in the morning, she was alone. She stretched languorously, smiling as she remembered the way Zuniga had made love to her the night before. Surely he could not have made love to her so gently, so fervently, if he didn't care for her at least a little. His hands and mouth had touched and tasted every inch of her, and she had responded in kind, her hands glorying in his sleek bronze flesh, her mouth moving lazily over his eyes and nose, the curve of his neck, the hollow of his shoulder. Their bodies had strained together, as close as two people could be.

With a contented sigh, she rose to her feet and walked to the stream. She needed a bath, badly. The scent of their lovemaking covered her whole body.

The water was cold, but she held her breath and plunged in, letting the chill water flow over her. She scrubbed herself briskly, rinsed, washed her hair, and then stepped onto the bank. She was drying herself with one of the towels Zuniga had thoughtfully brought from town when he appeared.

Shad stopped in his tracks, his eyes moving over Loralee's body as she dried off. Her skin was the color of cream where she was untouched by the sun. Her face and forearms were a lovely golden brown. Drops of water sparkled in her tawny hair like delicate jewels. Her breasts were swollen, her belly round, her legs long and perfectly shaped. She had never looked more beautiful or more appealing, and he admitted to himself that he would probably have kidnapped her sooner or later even if she were not pregnant with his child, simply because he could not bear to live without her. She was warm and lovely and desirable, and his longing for her was something he could not ignore.

Loralee wrapped the towel around her middle, tucking the end between her breasts. She felt her cheeks grow warm under Zuniga's intense gaze. What was he thinking? Was he wondering how he could have spent the night making love to a woman with a swollen belly? Did she look repulsive to him now in the light of day? Her figure was no longer slim, her hands and feet were swollen. No doubt he was sorry he had made love to her. He was probably counting the days until the baby would be born and he would be rid of her.

She laughed a short, bitter laugh. She had come to this Godforsaken territory to teach the Indian children to read and write. Instead, she was barefoot and pregnant, living in the Dragoon Mountains with an Apache warrior. Why had she ever thought such a primitive life would be fascinating, even romantic? There was nothing remotely fascinating about living in a rough brush-covered hut; nothing the least bit romantic about cooking outside over a crude firepit, or huddling beneath an animal hide to keep warm. Why did the Indians long to return to such a life when houses and stoves and all the advantages of progress and civilization were there for the taking? It was beyond her comprehension. Perhaps they were only heathen savages, after all. Perhaps she had been wasting her time trying to teach the Apache children to read and write. No doubt the girls would grow fat and lazy, and the boys would turn into drunkards. She had only been kidding herself all along.

She glanced at Zuniga, who was walking slowly toward her. He was the root of all her problems, and suddenly she hated him with every fiber of her being. Why did he have to be so devastatingly handsome? Why had she succumbed so easily to the touch of his lips on hers, to the husky persuasion of his voice? He was nothing but a . . . a heathen savage, and now she was pregnant with his child. He had ruined her reputation, ruined her chance for happiness with Mike. In her anger, she forgot that she did not love Mike, that she had regretted her marriage. She remembered only that Mike wanted her and had given her a home, and now it was gone, and Mike with it.

A wave of self-pity washed over Loralee. She did not want to be here, living in the mountains like a squaw with a man who did not love her. She hated it here, and she hated Shad Zuniga most of all.

She drew back as Zuniga reached out to her. "Leave me alone," she hissed. "I hate you!"

Taken aback, Zuniga let his hands fall to his sides. Loralee had never looked at him like that before, her eyes glinting with hatred. His own eyes mirrored his confusion. Only last night she had been warm and willing in his arms. What had changed her into such a termagant?

Without a word, he turned on his heel and left her standing beside the river, alone.

A terrible ache blossomed in the pit of Loralee's belly, growing and spreading until the pain was more than she could bear.

Tears came then, flooding her eyes, washing down her cheeks. What had she done? Why had she lashed out at him like that? It wasn't his fault she was pregnant, not entirely. She could have said no.

She sobbed as though her heart would break, unable to stop the torrent of tears. Her emotions were so changeable, so near the surface these days. One moment she was thrilled with the baby, in love with Shad, glad to be with him, even if it meant hiding out in the mountains, and the next she was frightened and confused. Only her love for her unborn child remained constant.

She dressed slowly, feeling lethargic and melancholy. Nothing in her life had gone right since she met Shad Zuniga. Why hadn't she listened to Mike and stayed away from Zuniga?

The wickiup was cold and empty when she stepped inside. Where had Zuniga gone? The hours crawled by. At noon, she forced herself to eat something for the baby's sake.

She did not see Shad the rest of that day, nor did he show up for dinner that night.

The next few weeks were the longest and the loneliest Loralee had ever known. She saw Zuniga only rarely, and then for just a few minutes at a time. He hardly spoke to her, refused to meet her eyes, or tell her where he was spending his time. Every day or two she found fresh meat outside the wickiup. She became quite adept at skinning the small animals and birds he left for her, though it remained a task she despised. Once he left the hindquarter of a deer. Several days later she found a large supply of jerked venison and a deer hide that had been tanned until it was as soft as velvet.

She rubbed her hand over the smooth skin. It took hours of work to tan a hide until it was soft and pliable. Was it possible that Shad was as bored as she was? Tanning hides was considered woman's work. Had he condescended to such a task merely to pass the time? It was a lovely gift. Had he meant it for her, or for the baby?

To pass the time, Loralee took long walks. She sewed several rabbit skins together to make a blanket for the baby. She spent one whole day damming a section of the river, making it deep enough to swim in. She gathered stones and laid out a path from her wickiup to the river. She found a seedling pine and planted it beside the entrance to the lodge.

Spring was in the air, and she knew a moment of pleasure when the first flowers appeared along the river.

Zuniga was constantly in her thoughts. Where was he? Didn't he know she was dying for companionship? Didn't he realize she was frightened of the long nights, of the strange cries and calls that echoed between the high canyon walls? How could he leave her alone for days at a time? How could he be so cruel?

Zuniga sat on his haunches high in the hills, watching Loralee as she washed her hair and clothing. She seemed to grow more beautiful each day. Her advancing pregnancy had slowed her steps and thickened her waistline, but it had not detracted from her beauty. Her face was more lovely than ever. Often, her hands went to her abdomen and he saw her smile, the expression warm and loving as she felt her child move. He observed that the wickiup was well cared for, noticed the gently winding path she had laid out, the small tree flourishing under her tender care. Sometimes, when he saw her cry, he almost relented and went to her, but the hatred he had seen in her eyes and heard in her voice kept him away. And perhaps it was better so. He could not soften now. He had to stay strong, else how could he take the child? His child.

At night, alone beneath the starry sky, he ached with the need to hold her in his arms, to feel her body against his, to hear the passion in her voice as she cried his name. He sorely missed the lilting sound of her laughter, the warmth of her smile. He toyed with the idea of slipping into her lodge, of taking her in his arms and confessing his love. But he never did. He could not bear her rejection. And then, always between them

was the fact that she was married to another
man. Happily married, she had said. Well,
she could go back to her white man as soon
as the child was born.

Zuniga stopped in his tracks, his narrowed eyes searching the tangled under-
brush, his ears straining for some sound that
would betray the puma's hiding place. The
cat was wounded and must be put out of its
misery. The pelt, soft as tawny velvet, would
make a fine robe for his son.

He jacked a round into the breech of his
rifle, stepped warily into the shadowed forest. The cat's paw prints were clear and he
followed the tracks deeper into the trees, his
moccasined feet making no sound on the
soft earth. He moved cautiously, looking to
right and left before each step forward. A
wounded animal was always dangerous, and
he wasn't certain how badly his bullet had
hurt the cat.

The tracks disappeared at the base of a
tree. Zuniga's mind registered the meaning
instantly, and he took a quick step back as he
brought his rifle up. He was a fraction of a
second too late. With an angry growl, the
mountain lion sprang from an overhanging
branch, its weight driving Zuniga to the
ground. The animal's teeth and claws raked
Zuniga's back, neck, and shoulders. The cat
screamed, its cry sending a cold chill down
the Apache's spine as he reached for his

knife, struggling all the while to keep the
cat's teeth from tearing at his eyes and
throat.

With a mighty effort, he managed to get
hold of his knife, and he plunged the blade
into the cat's jugular vein. A river of warm
red blood spurted from the killing wound,
spraying over Zuniga's face and arm, splash-
ing over his chest as, with a last strangled
growl, the big cat went limp, its dead weight
dropping across the lower half of Zuniga's
torso.

For a moment, the Apache lay still, his
breath coming in hard short gasps. He was
soaked with his own sweat and blood, and
with the blood of the mountain lion. The
animal's weight soon grew too heavy to bear
and he struggled from beneath the carcass,
each movement requiring a painful effort.

His legs were weak and his body shook
spasmodically with each labored breath as
he stood up. With an effort, he choked back
the nausea that rose within him as he examined his wounds. His left shoulder was badly
clawed. The skin hung in shreds, and a large
chunk of flesh dangled from a narrow strip
of sinew on his upper left arm. There were
deep scratches on his neck, back, and legs; a
long gash ran the length of his right side.

Using his teeth and his right hand, he
tore a strip of material from his tattered shirt
and wrapped it around the grisly wound in
his left arm. The other wounds would have

to wait. He needed help, and he needed it now, before he passed out.

The stallion snorted and shook its head as Zuniga approached, its eyes rolling white as it scented blood. Zuniga spoke to the horse, his voice raspy with pain. If the animal bolted now, he was done for. But the stallion stood its ground, nostrils flaring, eyes wild as Zuniga pulled himself onto the animal's back.

The ride to Loralee's lodge was sheer hell. Each step the horse took created new waves of pain, pain that danced up and down the length of Zuniga's arm, pain that dulled his thoughts, until he forgot everything but the need to see Loralee just one more time, to hear her voice, see her smile.

It was near dusk when Loralee returned from her evening walk. Her heart skipped a beat when she saw Zuniga sitting astride his stallion in front of her lodge. At last, he had come to see her!

Almost immediately, she knew something was wrong. Zuniga's hearing was as keen as that of a wild animal, but he did not turn at the sound of her footsteps. It was then she noticed that he was not sitting proudly erect as usual, but was slumped over the dun's neck.

She ran the last few feet, then gasped aloud. There was blood everywhere—on Zuniga, on the stallion, on the ground. She uttered a hoarse cry of alarm when she saw the long scratches along the side of Zuniga's neck, the blood leaking from the gash in his side. How could a man lose so much blood and live? His face was gray and pinched, and she took a deep breath, willing herself to stay calm as she felt for a pulse in his right wrist. Dear God, what if he was dead? How would she ever get out of these mountains alone? How could she live without him?

She mouthed a prayer of thanksgiving when she felt a pulse.

"Zuniga. Zuniga!"

She shouted his name again. He had to wake up. There was no way she could lift him from his horse and carry him inside the lodge.

His eyelids flickered open and he stared at her, his eyes dark and filled with pain, but aware of who she was.

"Get down," Loralee said, speaking slowly and distinctly. "I'll help you."

He nodded slightly, his face going fishbelly white as he slid awkwardly to the ground, his right hand tangled in the stallion's mane for support.

"Put your arm around my shoulders," Loralee directed. She grimaced as he sagged against her. Lord, he was heavy. In seconds, the side of her dress was wet with his blood.

Step by slow step, they made their way into the lodge. Zuniga collapsed inside the doorway, grunting as he jarred his wounded side.

For a moment, Loralee could only stare at the blood on her hands, overcome by the magnitude of his wounds. She felt tears burn her eyes, and she willed them away. There was no time for tears. Not now. There was work to be done.

She was very busy for the next few minutes. She washed her hands, lit the fire, set a kettle of water over the flames, and searched for the first aid supplies Zuniga had brought from Bisbee. She spread a blanket near the fire, rolled Zuniga onto it, and removed his tattered shirt and blood-soaked trousers.

She gasped when she got a good look at the long gash in his side, and vomited the contents of her stomach when she removed the crude bandage from his shoulder and saw the chunk of flesh that had nearly been torn from his upper arm.

When her stomach settled, she rose to her feet. Moving like a sleepwalker, she found a bottle of whiskey Zuniga had bought for medicinal purposes. Uncorking the bottle, she poured herself a generous amount and downed it in a single swallow. She had never tasted strong spirits before and she gasped, choking, as the fiery liquid burned a path to her stomach.

With a grimace of distaste, she refilled the glass for Zuniga, who had regained consciousness. How did men drink such stuff? she mused, holding the glass for Shad. She knew that many men drank to excess, to the shame of their families, but she could not imagine anyone drinking for pleasure. The whiskey was bitter and vile.

Zuniga did not seem to find it distasteful. He emptied the glass and held it out for more. He drained the glass a second time, his eyes holding hers. I need your help, his eyes seemed to say, but I cannot ask for it.

Loralee let out a long breath, and then she got to work. Closing her mind to the fact that she was causing him pain, she began to wash his wounds. Don't think that he might have been killed, she told herself. Don't think that his wounds might become infected, that he still might die. Don't think.

Zuniga winced each time Loralee's hands touched him, but he never uttered a sound. Sweat poured down his face and neck, his hands were clenched into tight fists, but he remained silent as the hills.

Once, he closed his eyes and in his mind's eye he saw Nachi standing before him, tall and young and proud, as he had been in the old days.

"An Apache warrior laughs in the face of pain," the image declared in a voice like thunder. "Fear is unknown to a true warrior of the People. Death is but an adventure into another world."

The image faded as Loralee poured whiskey over his wounds to disinfect them. The pain was excruciating. To scream would have been a relief, yet he clenched his teeth until his jaw ached. A warrior laughed at pain.

Loralee was not so strong, and she wept openly over the pain she knew he must be going through. But she steeled herself. The wounds were clean now, disinfected with the whiskey. The gash in his side proved to be long but not as deep as she feared. The bleeding had stopped, and she had bound it with a length of linen. Likely, it would require no further attention. The scratches in his neck, back, and legs had been similarly treated. But the wound in his arm . . . she was uncertain how to proceed. Should she cut off that dangling hunk of flesh, or try to sew it back in place? Both ideas made her stomach heave.

In the end, she decided to sew it simply because she could not bear to cut a piece of living flesh from Zuniga's body.

Her hands were trembling so violently that it took several tries before she could thread the needle. What was she doing? She wasn't a doctor. She wasn't even a particularly talented seamstress. How could she sew living flesh?

She glanced at Zuniga. He was watching her through heavy-lidded eyes. Biting down on her lower lip, she began to sew the torn flesh. Was she doing the right thing? Were her stitches small enough? Tight enough? Would the thread hold the skin together?

Why hadn't Zuniga spoken to her? Why hadn't she spoken to him?

Zuniga watched Loralee's face as she began to sew the ragged edges of skin together. Perspiration dotted her brow, and her brown eyes were filled with anxiety as she took one neat stitch after another. Somehow the pain was not so bad when he looked at her. Perhaps she did care a little. Certainly she wouldn't look so worried if she didn't care, or would she? Perhaps it wasn't affection for him at all, but concern over her own future. She would not survive long in the mountains without him.

Loralee breathed a long sigh of relief when the task was done. Zuniga's eyes were closed. Was he sleeping? Unconscious? Gently she wiped the blood from his arm, covered him with a blanket, and mopped the sweat from his face. Then, thoroughly exhausted, she stretched out beside him and fell quickly asleep.

A low moan penetrated Loralee's dream, rousing her to instant wakefulness. The sound came again, a cry filled with pain. Sitting up, she turned toward Zuniga. She did not need to touch his forehead to know that he was burning with fever. His skin was flushed and he tossed restlessly from side to side.

Rising, Loralee poured some water into a bowl and began to sponge his face and chest with the cool water. Again and again she dampened the cloth, washing him down, praying he would not die.

Chills followed the fever, and she wrapped him in blankets, and when that didn't warm him enough, she put more wood on the fire. He mumbled in his sleep, his voice sometimes loud and angry, sometimes soft, entreating. She listened, hoping to catch a few words, but when he spoke, it was in garbled Apache and she could make no sense of his ramblings.

The fever came again and he thrashed about, tossing the blankets aside as old ghosts came to haunt him. He was a child again, young and confused, hurt by his father's irrational cruelty. He wanted to love his father, but he was afraid of him. He learned early not to cry, to stay out of his father's way when he was drunk on the white man's firewater. He watched, helpless, when his father abused his mother, vowing in his heart that one day, when he was older, he would avenge the pain his mother suffered at his father's hands.

His mother. She was a beautiful woman with hair like black silk and eyes as trusting and guileless as those of a child. Everyone in the stronghold loved and pitied her, but no one dared interfere between Nakai and Nadina.

Years passed. His mother grew thin and withdrawn. Nachi grew older, sadder. But Shad grew stronger, and as he matured, his hatred for the man who was his father grew stronger until that fateful night when he took his father's life with his bare hands. . . .

He cried out as his father's skeletal image rose up before him, eyes burning with hellfire, teeth bared in a death's-head grin, long bony fingers reaching out to grab him.

"No!" The word erupted from his throat like a primal scream of terror.

He bolted upright, eyes staring straight ahead at something only he could see.

Cautiously Loralee laid her hand on his shoulder and eased him back down on the blankets.

"It's all right," she murmured soothing-ly. "It's all right. Go to sleep."

He reached out for her blindly, his hand finding hers and clinging to it as if he would never let go.

Her voice penetrated the awful night-mares that swirled around him, keeping the demons at bay. His father's image evapo-rated like morning mist and he drew a deep breath, content to remain in the quiet dark-ness that hovered around him.

The voice came again, soothing and kind. He tried to open his eyes, to see her face, but as he struggled through the layers of darkness, the pain hit him again, and he retreated into the friendly peace of oblivion.

Loralee talked to him for over an hour, her voice soft and low. Once, she heard him mutter Nachi's name, saw tears glisten in his eyes as he stared, unseeing, at the dark patch of sky visible through the smoke hole.

The fever raged all that day. Loralee spent hours bathing him with cool water. Patiently she spooned broth into him, knowing he had to take some liquid to replace the blood he had lost and the fluids he was sweating away.

Evening found him sleeping peacefully at last. Loralee stood up, one hand pressed against her aching back. She needed a bath, she thought wearily, and a few minutes alone. She had not left Zuniga's side for more than three or four minutes in the last two days.

With a sigh, she stepped outside and walked slowly toward the stream. The water was cold and she washed quickly, then stepped onto the bank and toweled herself dry. How quiet the night was! Trees and shrubs were silhouetted against the darkness. She saw an owl take to the sky on wings as quiet as a sigh and she shivered with apprehension, then laughed self-consciously. She was getting as superstitious as the Indians.

Dressing, she walked back to the lodge and ducked inside. Zuniga was awake, his dark eyes clear, his face pale. She felt a surge of hope as she laid her hand across his brow. It was cool. The fever had broken at last.

Loralee cast about for something to say. Why couldn't she say what was in her heart? Why couldn't she tell him how worried she had been that he might die, that she was glad he was going to be all right? That she loved him.

"Are you hungry?"

Zuniga nodded weakly. He was hungry, but not for food. His eyes followed her every move as she put a pot of soup on the fire. His pride suffered when she insisted on feeding him. He was a warrior, not a child. It was galling, having to depend on a woman to care for his every need. He was being foolish, and he knew it, though he would not admit it, just as he would not admit that he was far too weak to lift the spoon.

Loralee seemed to understand how he felt. She spooned the good-tasting broth into him, never meeting his eyes, trying, in her way, not to make him feel helpless.

The broth warmed Zuniga through and through, making him feel better, stronger. Eating made him drowsy, and he closed his eyes and was soon asleep.

The next few days were like a dream for Zuniga. Loralee was an excellent nurse —feeding him, helping him relieve himself, bathing him. They rarely spoke. As Zuniga's strength returned, Loralee left him more and more to himself. She often went for long walks, her mind in turmoil. What was she going to do?

Once, while Zuniga was napping, she climbed onto his horse and started down the mountain. Zuniga was well enough to care for himself now. She could be far away before he awoke. She doubted that he was strong enough to come after her. She would find her way to Bisbee and wire Mike to come after her. She would have the baby and make the best of her marriage. Perhaps, in time, she would grow to love Mike as he deserved.

She was at the entrance to the stronghold when she reined the stallion around and started back to her lodge. She couldn't go. She couldn't leave Zuniga here alone. He needed her. But, more than that, she needed him. No matter that he didn't love her. No matter that he intended to take her child from her. She loved him with all her heart, and if these few months were all she had to spend with him, then so be it. She would stay until he sent her away.

19

Zuniga swam easily in the cool water, his strokes strong and even. It was a beautiful day in late April, and he had ridden to this place to be alone with his thoughts.

Since his fight with the puma, he had been living in Loralee's lodge. They ate together, took walks together, talked of inconsequential things like the weather and the flowers that were blooming on hillsides. She asked questions about his people, eager to learn more, to know more of the Apache ways and beliefs. She no longer asked for her freedom, nor did she ever mention the child growing in her womb. She cooked his meals, washed his clothes, kept the lodge tidy. Her hair was always clean and shining, like newly minted gold, and she always managed to look fragile and feminine, even in the too-large man's shirt she wore to cover her burgeoning belly. She smiled at him often, her eyes warm and gentle. She never complained, never argued. Indeed, she was the epitome of womanhood—warm, soft, feminine, agreeable, modest.

The nights were the worst part of the time they spent together. Lying alone in his bed across the fire from hers, his body burned with a fierce hunger. He yearned to bury himself in her sweetness, to confess how desperately he loved her, to beg her to forsake her marriage to the white man and be his woman. But his pride held him mute. He could not humble himself enough to beg for her love. She had chosen the white man to be her husband, and because Loralee cared about him, Zuniga decided he would let the white man live.

Leaving the stream, he shook the water from his hair and body and slipped into his buckskins. Taking up his rifle, he began to walk back to the lodge. The dun stallion trailed at his heels. It was quiet in the mountains, Zuniga mused, peaceful. He felt at home here, in the ancient land of his people. It was here he had been born. Here that the great Cochise had lived and died. Here that he had learned the ways of a warrior.

He took his time returning to Loralee's lodge. For all that he and Loralee lived together amicably, there was an underlying tension between them. It was something they did not speak of, just as they did not discuss Mike Schofield, or the baby.

Loralee was standing at the edge of the stream when he reached the lodge. Her hair shimmered like liquid gold in the light of the setting sun. A wave of heat surged through his loins and he moved toward her, wanting her. A voice in the back of his mind warned him to stay away. She belonged to another man, and any complications between them now would only make things more difficult later. But he could not turn away from her any more than he could keep the sun from setting.

Loralee turned as Zuniga padded up behind her, felt her heart leap with joy at the sight of him. He was so very handsome. His eyes were dark, intense, under straight black brows. Her eyes were drawn to his mouth. Would he kiss her? Could she make him kiss her just once? If only he would take her in his arms. If only she could find the words to tell him how much she loved him, how much she needed him. Couldn't he sense her need, see it in her eyes, hear it in her voice?

"Lovely evening, isn't it?" Loralee remarked, her heart pounding in her ears.

Zuniga nodded. He had never been a coward. Why couldn't he find the courage to admit how he felt?

"Dinner will be ready soon."

He nodded again. She was close. So

close. His eyes locked on hers, and Loralee nodded assent at the question she read in his steady gaze.

Time seemed to stop as Zuniga reached for her, and then she was in his arms, her lips tasting his, her nostrils filling with the rugged manly scent that was his alone. Her body strained against his, glorying in the strength of his arms and legs. Happiness welled up from the core of her being and flooded her eyes with tears as she surrendered to his touch. His hands roamed over her, kneading her back and shoulders, cupping her buttocks as his tongue plundered the sweet honey of her mouth. Carefully, he lowered her to the ground.

"Loralee." His voice was low and filled with desire. "I do not want to hurt you."

Her hands drew him closer, fearful he would slip away. "It's all right," she murmured. "Please, Shad."

Slowly he undressed her, his hands gentle, caring. Loralee blushed as his eyes moved over her body. She felt fat and ungainly, like a pregnant heifer. Would he be repulsed by what he saw? But no, his eyes smiled at her even as his hands, so big and brown, covered her swollen belly.

"You are beautiful, Loralee," he murmured. "More beautiful than ever."

"Oh, Shad," she whispered fervently, and melted into his arms, happier than she had ever been before.

She waited impatiently as he removed his own clothes, then stretched out beside her.

"Loralee." He breathed her name as he began to make sweet love to her, his caresses soft and tender, as though she were made of the most fragile porcelain and might shatter beneath his fingertips. She was breathless with desire when he entered her, filling her, making her complete.

She cried his name as he moved inside her, exciting her, lifting her to heights never before explored. It was so right to be in his arms, to feel his muscles tense and relax beneath her hands. She closed her eyes, losing herself in the magical rhythm of his loving. His skin was hot against her own, his mouth hungry and demanding, his tongue like solid flame. And then his seed poured into her, and for that brief moment of time, they were two bodies forged into one being.

Later, sated in body and soul, Loralee drifted to sleep cradled in Zuniga's arms.

Shad held her close, one hand lightly stroking the silky mass of her hair. She was so beautiful. So sweet.

He swore softly as he felt his child move beneath his hand. He could not take the child away from Loralee, he realized. He could not break her heart. She had not mentioned the baby, nor his plans to keep it, but he had seen the pain in her eyes. Well, she need worry no more. He would take

Loralee back to her husband in the morning. She would teach their son the way of the Apache, and he would be content with that.

He held her all night long, waking often just to look at her. He memorized each soft curve and plane of her face, the silky texture of her golden hair, her sweet womanly fragrance. How would he ever let her go?

Loralee woke slowly, a smile on her face. She had dreamed of Zuniga all night long, and now, as she opened her eyes, his face was the first thing she saw. The expression in his eyes drove the smile from her face.

"What is it?" she asked anxiously. "What's wrong?"

"Nothing," he replied quietly. "I am taking you back."

Loralee stared at him, certain she had misunderstood him. "What?"

"I'm taking you home, back to Schofield. It's what you want, isn't it? To go back to your white man?"

Loralee searched his eyes, but his expression was closed to her, impenetrable. His voice was cold, almost angry. What had she done? Why did he suddenly want to be rid of her?

"What about . . . what about the baby?"

"What about it?"

"I thought—" Her voice trailed off. Something was wrong, but what?

"Get ready," he said tersely. "We leave in one hour."

Thoughts rushed around in Loralee's mind like ants fleeing a disturbed mound. He was taking her back to Mike. Why? What had happened to change his mind since they had made love so sweetly the night before?

She gazed deeply into his eyes. Was she mistaken, or was it love she saw reflected there, beneath the stern visage? Was that the cause of his sudden change in plans?

Excitement flowed in Loralee's veins. For once, she was going to take a chance. For once, she was going to pour out her heart to him, beg him not to send her away. If he rejected her, she would learn to live with the hurt.

"Get ready," he repeated.

"I don't want to go back," Loralee said softly, her eyes intent upon his face. "I want to stay here. With you."

Disbelief showed in Zuniga's dark eyes. Disbelief and hope. "Why?"

"I love you. Haven't you guessed that by now?"

"I thought you were in love with Schofield."

Loralee shook her head. "No, never. I only married him because of the baby."

"Why did you not tell me you were pregnant? I would have married you."

"I couldn't. I thought you hated me, and my pride wouldn't let me beg."

317

"It did not keep you from marrying the white man," Zuniga accused.

"I didn't ask Mike to marry me. Mike loves me. He was willing to raise your child as his own to spare me the embarrassment of being pregnant and unwed."

"He must love you very much," Zuniga allowed grudgingly.

"Yes." She touched his arm. "I never slept with him, Shad. Never."

The words rang true, and Zuniga was filled with exultation as he took Loralee in his arms. She was his, only his.

He held her close for several minutes, his face buried in the wealth of her hair, his heart swelling with love. What a fool he had been, but fool he would be no more. She was his woman now, and he would live and die for her.

The days that followed were the most perfect Loralee had ever known. Nightly she fell asleep in Zuniga's arms. His face was the last thing she saw at night and the first sight to greet her in the morning. Living with Shad, sharing every hour of the day with him, she learned things about him she had never suspected.

She discovered, to her amazement, that he was deeply religious. Night and morning, he prayed to Usen. When he killed an animal, he said a prayer asking the animal's spirit to forgive him for taking its life. He never killed for sport, but always out of need. He had a deep and abiding reverence for all life, the plants and trees that grew in abundance in the hills and valleys, the squirrels and deer, the eagles and the sparrows. He opened her eyes to the grace and beauty of the animals and birds that inhabited the stronghold, and helped her gain a keener appreciation of the beauty around her.

Once, as she made her way to the stream to bathe, she saw Zuniga standing near the bank, his arms lifted toward heaven. She knew it was wrong to eavesdrop on such a private moment, but she could not tear herself away. He was praying, speaking in his native tongue, and Loralee listened intently, feeling her heart expand with love as she heard him pray for her health and for the health of their unborn child. He prayed for his mother as well, and entreated the Apache gods to grant his grandfather peace and happiness in the world of spirits.

He looked beautiful standing there, she mused, like a Greek god cast in bronze. The early morning sunlight caressed his arms and chest. His hair, shiny black as a raven's wing, fell over his shoulders and down his broad back. Yes, he was beautiful indeed.

That night, wrapped in his arms, Loralee asked Shad about his past. She knew so little about him, this man who had stolen her heart.

"What was it like, living here in the mountains?" she coaxed when he seemed reluctant to answer. "How long did you live here? Why did you leave?"

"It was a hard life," Zuniga answered quietly. "But we were free. There were only a handful of families still living in the stronghold after Geronimo surrendered, warriors who refused to go in because they did not trust the peace the white man offered. My uncle, Short Bear's father, was one of them. After my mother died, I went to live with my uncle and his family. We stayed in the mountains, raiding into Mexico for food and blankets and horses, until I was nineteen or twenty."

"Were you in many battles with the Mexicans?"

Zuniga nodded, a faraway look in his eye.

"Did you kill anyone?"

He shrugged as if it were of no importance. "A few."

Loralee grimaced. He sounded so unconcerned. "Didn't it bother you, killing those men?"

"No. They were the enemy."

Loralee nodded. The Mexicans and the Apache had always been enemies. "I'm glad I'm a woman," she remarked. "I wouldn't like to fight."

"Apache women often fight alongside their men," Zuniga said. "Sometimes they are more fierce than the warriors."

"Weren't you ever afraid?"

Shad smiled indulgently. "Afraid?" He shook his head. "There's no time to be afraid once the fighting starts. Your blood runs hot in your veins as you rush to meet the enemy, and your only thought is to drive your knife into his heart, to feel his blood on your hands."

He broke off as he felt Loralee shudder with revulsion. "I think I would have been glad to die in battle," he said softly.

"Why?"

"Because I knew what it would be like on the reservation, and I did not want to give up my freedom."

"After your people surrendered, did you go to the reservation?"

"No. I did not go in with the others. My uncle took Short Bear and my aunt, but I would not go. Short Bear was only a baby then, two or three years old. I hid out in the hills, sleeping in a cave during the day, scavenging for food at night."

"How dreadful. Surely living on the reservation with your people would have been better than living in the hills like a wild animal?"

"No. It is not better. Bread is not a fair trade for freedom."

"How long did you live like that?"

"A long time. Once, I went to Mexico and the *ruales* caught me stealing food from one of the cantinas. I spent two years in one of their prisons."

The look in Loralee's eye clearly expressed her horror. Mexican jails were reputed to be the worst in the world.

Zuniga nodded. "Living in a Mexican jail was worse than living alone in the hills, worse than anything I have ever known. I was beaten and starved. I spent a month locked in a dark cell with nothing to eat but stale bread and water and an occasional plate of fried beans."

"That's awful!"

"Awful. I thought I would go mad."

"How did you get out of there?"

"A woman came along. She was the captain's whore, and she liked to come down to the cells. She enjoyed watching the prisoners get punished, and she rarely missed a whipping or an execution. She was there one morning when I was being whipped for hitting one of the guards. She got mad when I did not scream and she took the lash into her own hands, determined to break my spirit. She said she would stop whipping me as soon as I cried out, but I refused to give her the satisfaction."

Zuniga laughed softly, ruefully. "It was a stupid thing to do. She was a stubborn woman, but I was young and proud and equally stubborn, and she whipped me until I passed out.

"When I came to, I was in her bedroom and she was bending over me, washing the blood off my back."

"Was she pretty?" Loralee asked. It was foolish to feel jealousy over a woman who had been so cruel, but she couldn't help herself.

"No. She had a heart like ice, and eyes as cold as death. She took care of me until my back healed. She said I was going to be her personal slave because I was as stubborn as she was, and she liked that. I went along with her until I regained my strength, pretending I liked doing her bidding, until the right opportunity came along and I escaped."

Zuniga paused briefly, as if looking back into his past, and then went on. "When I got back to Arizona, I went into the hills near the reservation. I spent a couple of days watching the place, hoping to catch a glimpse of Nachi. About a week later, Short Bear rode up into the hills. He was surprised when I stepped out in front of his horse. He told me that his mother had died and that Nachi was ill and there was no one to care for him. My uncle had lost his will to live and was no help to anyone. Short Bear was just a kid at the time, and he had a younger sister to look after."

"And that's when you surrendered?"

"No. I continued to live in the hills. I brought meat to Short Bear, sneaking in at night after everyone was asleep. When Nachi got better, I went wandering again. I drifted into Colorado and New Mexico, hoping to find a place where Indians still lived in the old way, but it was useless. There were no red men living free any more. They were all penned up on reservations. When I went back to see how Nachi was getting along, I learned that Short Bear's sister had died, and that my uncle was drinking more than usual. Short Bear had gone to live with his friend Yellow Deer, and Nachi was living alone. That was when I moved Nachi into the hills. The Army didn't like it, but we were still on reservation land, so they let us stay."

"How long ago was that?"

Zuniga shrugged. "Seven, eight years. Time has no meaning on the reservation."

With a sigh, Loralee snuggled against Zuniga. He had led a hard and unhappy life, but he would never be unhappy, or alone, again. Not if she could help it.

Her knowledge of the Apache language grew rapidly in the days that followed, and she felt herself slowly changing, becoming Indian in many ways. It was no longer a chore to cook outside over an open fire. Tanning a hide became easier with practice, and less disgusting, and she began to take pride in the fine robes and skins she turned into shirts and moccasins. She learned how to jerk venison, how to make ash cakes out of ground mesquite beans, tallow, and wild honey. She gathered acorns and sunflower seeds, pine nuts and juniper berries, wild plums and roots.

Each day was an adventure. She and Zuniga played together and worked together and made love beneath the bold blue sky and the quiet envious moon. Loralee's love for Shad Zuniga grew stronger, deeper, more intense with the passing of each day. They talked often of the baby, wondering aloud if it would be a boy or a girl, if it would be dark-skinned or fair. Loralee hoped for a boy that would look like Shad, and she counted the days until her child would be born, anxious to place their child in Zuniga's arms, eager to give him a son.

For Shad, each day was better than the last. Never had he known such happiness. He was living in the land he loved, living the life he yearned for. And he had Loralee at his side. Each day saw her becoming more Indian in her speech and beliefs, in her way of thinking. She would have made a fine warrior's wife in the old days, he thought, and could think of no finer praise for any woman.

The long lonely days when he had lived in the hills like a wild animal faded into the mists of time, almost forgotten. The years he had spent in prison no longer mattered. Loralee's love had healed all the old hurts, soothed his anger, and given him a reason to go on living.

20

Summer came, mild and balmy. The sky was a clear cerulean blue, the trees were green and fruitful, the river water cool enough to turn away the midday heat.

Their lodge was comfortable, just big enough for the two of them, and life had settled into an easy routine. Zuniga hunted or repaired his weapons during the day, looked after the horses, and made certain everything was secure. Loralee gathered wood and water, prepared their meals, and sewed tiny garments for the baby. In the evening they took long walks together, pausing to admire the way the setting sun turned the mountains and parapets to flame and touched the valley floor with gold. Life was perfect, and Loralee would have asked for nothing more save that her child be born strong and healthy.

By the end of May, their supplies were running low. Loralee knew a moment of panic when Zuniga told her he was going to town. They had been together night and day for weeks and she could not bear the thought of being parted from him, not even for a few hours. The baby was due in less than two months, and she grew more and more apprehensive as her time drew near. Childbirth was normal and natural, babies were born every day, but not to her. This was her first pregnancy, and doubts and fears plagued her mind. What if something went wrong? What if the baby was breech? What if she had no milk? What if she died? What if the baby came today, while Zuniga was away and she was alone?

She had never voiced her anxieties to Shad. He was so strong, so eternally sure of himself, she was afraid he would think her a terrible coward, unfit to be the mother of an Apache. Yet, as he held her in his arms, he seemed to know what was troubling her.

"I will be back before dark," he promised, caressing her cheek with the back of his hand. "Do not worry, Loralee. Everything will be fine. You are young and healthy, and I will be here to help you. Do not be afraid."

"I can't help it," Loralee murmured.

Closing her eyes, she held him tighter, trying to absorb his strength and confidence into herself.

"I have to go," Shad said gently. "We need supplies." He lifted her chin so he could see her face. "You do not want to live on nothing but meat, do you?"

Loralee shook her head. He was right, of course. They needed vegetables and fruit.

"I will bring back some seed," Zuniga remarked. "Perhaps it is not too late to plant a garden."

Loralee smiled. "Are you going to become a farmer, after all?" she teased.

Zuniga let out a long breath. "I cannot let the mother of my son go hungry," he said with a wry grin. "Maybe I will buy a few chickens. And a cow."

"Truly? Oh, Shad, that would be wonderful. We could have fresh milk and eggs."

"Have you ever milked a cow?" he asked, amusement dancing in his dark eyes.

"No."

"Such things are woman's work," he pointed out. "Shall I still bring a cow?"

"Yes," she said, laughing.

"Do not worry," he said as he kissed her cheek.

At the general store, he bought a large supply of canned goods, fruit and vegetables, a variety of seed. He bought some soft flannel for baby clothes, a jar of ointment for cuts and bruises, a bottle of carbolic.

329

He gave the shopkeeper the last of his cash to pay for the supplies. Outside, he lashed his purchases onto the back of Loralee's mare, then went down the street to the feed store. He had no money left with which to buy a cow or chickens, so he would just have to take them. You did not consider it stealing when you took something from the enemy. It was the Apache way of life. It was only stealing when you took from a friend.

He looked over the stock on hand, noted that the feed store closed at six o'clock, and then rode out of town. He found a good place to hide out until dark, tethered the horses in the shade, and stretched out to take a nap. He knew that Loralee would worry when he didn't show up before dark, as promised, but it could not be helped.

He napped until sundown, then sat up, knowing he would have to wait a few more hours before he dared go into town after the cow and chickens.

He gazed into the darkness, content to wait as Nachi had taught him to wait, until the time was right. Then, slow and silent, he made his way to the feed store. It was a simple thing to break a window. Inside, he grabbed a burlap bag, tossed three chickens inside, and climbed out the window. In the corral behind the store, he dropped a rope around the neck of a young heifer and led her out of the pen.

"That's far enough," a voice warned. "One more step, and I'll empty this scatter gun into your back."

Zuniga froze, his eyes searching the shadows. Three men materialized out of the darkness. One of them was the clerk from the general store. The second man owned the feed store. The third man was the town marshal.

"Get those hands up," the marshal ordered. "Clem, get his gun. Luke, put the cuffs on him."

Zuniga swore softly as the men walked toward him. It was now or never, he thought, and with a wild cry, he darted for the cover of the trees a few yards away.

"Luke, get down!" the marshal bellowed, and as the owner of the feed store hit the dirt, the marshal pulled both triggers.

Zuniga stumbled and went down as a dozen pieces of buckshot riddled the backs of his legs.

"Get him!" Luke shouted, and the three men had Zuniga surrounded before he could regain his feet.

Luke Croft was a vengeful man, and he grinned as he placed a well-aimed kick into Zuniga's ribs.

Shad gasped as the air was forcibly driven from his lungs. He heard a sharp crack through the red haze of pain that dropped over him and knew Croft had broken a rib.

331

"Luke, that's enough," the marshal warned.

"Is it?" Croft retorted. He grinned with satisfaction as Clem cuffed the Indian's hands together. "Dirty redskin thief," Croft growled, and drove his fist into the Apache's face. Blood spurted from Zuniga's nose and mouth.

"Luke, I said that's enough!"

"Dammit, Frank, the man tried to steal my livestock."

"I know what he did, Luke. And he'll get what's coming to him. Now let's get him over to the jail. Clem, help me get him to his feet."

Zuniga winced as Clem and the marshal grabbed him under the arms and yanked him to his feet. The backs of his legs felt as if they were on fire.

"Let's go, Injun," the marshal said. He jabbed his rifle barrel into Zuniga's spine. "Move it. And don't try anything funny."

Teeth clenched, Zuniga turned and started back toward town. Each step sent bright shafts of pain shooting along his ribcage and down the backs of his legs, but he kept moving. And all the while he was cussing himself for being a fool and getting caught. And for what? A couple of scrawny chickens and a slat-sided red heifer.

His trousers were soaked with blood when they reached the jail. The marshal locked him in a narrow, windowless cell, then sent Clem for the doctor.

With a low groan, Zuniga sank to the floor, refusing to sit on the cot that smelled of stale sweat and vomit. His legs ached and each breath was an effort, but he hardly noticed the pain. He had to get out of there. He had to get back to Loralee.

There was the sound of voices and laughter, and then the marshal and the doctor entered the cellblock. The doctor was short and thin, with a shock of wavy white hair and canny blue eyes. He paused at the cell door, and nodded to himself when he saw that the prisoner's hands were securely cuffed.

Zuniga scrambled to his feet and backed against the far wall as the doctor and the marshal entered his cell.

"Take it easy, son," the doctor said quietly. "I just want to help."

"I do not want your help," Zuniga hissed.

"That buckshot has got to come out," the doctor explained in a slightly bored voice. "You don't want an infection, do you? Could get ugly. Gangrene, maybe, and then you'd lose your legs. You don't want that, do you?"

Zuniga stared at the doctor, his distrust of white men showing in his eyes.

"I'm telling you the truth," the doctor said. "Why don't you drop your pants, then stretch out on that bunk on your belly and let me take a look?"

With a sigh of resignation, Zuniga did as bidden. He'd be no use to himself or Loralee until his wounds were taken care of.

"I'll need some warm water, Frank," the doctor said as he opened his well-worn medical bag and took out a pair of rubber gloves and pulled them on. "I'll need some whiskey, too, if you've got it."

The marshal nodded and left the cell, locking the door behind him.

"Not too bad," the doctor murmured as he examined the wounds. "Most of them aren't in too deep." Rummaging around inside his bag again, he withdrew a pair of long-nosed tweezers and began to remove the buckshot.

The marshal returned a few minutes later with a bowl of warm water and a bottle of rye whiskey.

"That's fine, Frank," the doctor remarked. "Give me a hand here, will you? Here, take this cloth and mop up the blood so I can see what I'm doing. Dammit, man, did you have to use both barrels? One would have stopped him."

Zuniga endured the doctor's ministrations in stoic silence. It was humiliating, being forced to lie on his belly with his pants down around his ankles while the doctor and the marshal took care of his injuries, talking and laughing as if he were a dumb beast who couldn't understand their crude jokes. One piece of buckshot had lodged deep in the muscle of his left calf and he clenched his teeth as the doctor probed around inside the wound.

Finally, with a little cry of satisfaction, the doctor finished the task. Hefting the whiskey bottle, he took a generous drink, then slopped the clear amber liquid over the backs of Zuniga's legs. It was all Zuniga could do not to scream out loud as the fiery liquor penetrated each wound.

"Hell of a waste of good whiskey, doc," the marshal lamented with a good-natured grin.

"Not really. We got all kinds of new ointments to stop infection, but I still think the old-fashioned way is best."

"Whatever you say, Ben, just save a little for me."

"To be sure, to be sure."

"Uh, Ben, you might check his ribs, too," the marshal muttered. "Luke gave him a pretty good kick. I think maybe he busted something."

Zuniga feared he might pass out as the doctor examined his ribs. Gritting his teeth, he fought the waves of nausea that engulfed him as the doctor's hands probed his side.

"Broken, all right," the doctor announced matter-of-factly. "Nothing to do but bandage him up tight and let nature take its course."

He pulled a strip of cloth from his bag, wound it tightly around Zuniga's ribcage, bandaged Zuniga's legs, picked up his little black bag, and left the cell, whistling softly.

"Put your pants on, Cochise," the marshal said with a sneer. Locking the cell door, he started after the doctor.

"Marshal."

The lawman stopped. "What is it?"

"My horses are about a half mile out of town."

"I'll take care of 'em."

Zuniga stood up slowly, cursing under his breath. What a mess he had made of things. Loralee would be worrying by now, wondering what had happened to him.

He swore aloud, tormented by the thought of her spending the night in the mountains alone. The chances of anything happening to her were slim, but there was always a chance.

Face grim, he lay down on the floor of his cell, willing the pain in his legs to go away, keeping his breathing shallow in an effort to subdue the ache in his ribs. There was no way to get comfortable. He couldn't lie on his stomach, and lying on his back was almost as bad. Damn, what a hell of a mess!

Loralee stared toward the entrance to the stronghold, her hands clasped to her breasts. Where was he? Why didn't he come? She knew, deep in her heart, that something had gone wrong. He was hurt, or dead, and she was alone. He had taken her horse to carry their supplies and she had no way to get out of the mountains except on foot, and she could not walk out. It was too far, especially for a woman in her condition.

She paced back and forth in front of the wickiup the whole night long, praying that God would help her. She had never felt so helpless, so alone. She kept the fire burning bright, but even the cheerful blaze could not lift her spirits. Shad, Shad, where are you? What am I going to do without you? She placed her hand over her abdomen as she felt his child give a lusty kick.

"Oh, Shad," she sobbed, and dropping to her knees, she buried her face in her hands and began to cry.

Mike Schofield stared at the telegram in his hand, frowning as he read the message for the second time. "Urgent. Come to Bisbee Jail immediately. Zuniga."

Schofield felt a hard knot of fear form in the pit of his belly. Something was wrong with Loralee. He knew it.

Twenty minutes later he was riding hard for Bisbee. If anything had happened to Loralee, Shad Zuniga was a dead man.

Zuniga stood up as the door to the cellblock swung open and Mike Schofield strode into view. It was an effort to stand.

Each breath brought new pain to his broken ribs, and the backs of his legs were sore and tender. But he did not allow his discomfort to show on his face. A warrior did not show weakness in the presence of a known enemy.

"Where is she?" Schofield demanded. He grabbed the iron bars in his hands, his knuckles showing white with the strain.

"At the Apache stronghold," Shad answered tersely. "In the Dragoons."

"The Dragoon Mountains?" Mike exclaimed. "Alone?"

"Yes."

Mike's face went white with fury. The Dragoon Mountains were a wild and deserted place, uninhabited except for snakes and mountain lions and an occasional renegade. And Loralee was there alone. Dear God! She must be frightened half out of her mind by now.

"You sonofabitch," Mike growled. He reached through the bars, his hands clawing for Zuniga's throat. "I'll kill you for this, you bastard."

With an effort, Shad managed to avoid Schofield's flailing arms. "You are wasting time," he said urgently. "She has been alone too long already."

Without another word, Schofield turned on his heel and stalked out of the jailhouse. Outside, he stepped into the saddle and rode out of town at a gallop. He pushed his horse as hard as he dared, his mind oblivious to everything but the need to find Loralee. *She has been alone too long already,* Zuniga had said. How long was too long? A day? A week? It had taken Mike a day to reach Bisbee, and the better part of another to reach the Dragoons, so she had been alone at least two days. Fear and anger warred in his heart. Two days alone in the mountains. Damn!

It was nearing dusk when he reached the old Apache stronghold. The short hairs prickled along the back of his neck as his horse picked its way along the narrow twisting pathway that led to Cochise's favorite hideout. In the old days, no white men except Tom Jeffords and Howard had set foot on this ground and lived to tell the tale.

Mike had never been superstitious, never been one to believe in ghosts and goblins, but he would not have been surprised to see one here. There was something eerie about the stillness of the stronghold. Long shadows danced on the faces of the rocks as the last rays of the sun faded and disappeared. A cool wind sprang up, stirring dust devils in his path. His horse spooked and shied as an owl took wing from a nearby tree.

He found Loralee asleep inside a roughhewn wickiup, her head pillowed on her arms. Her cheeks were stained with tears; there were dark shadows under her eyes, hollows in her cheeks.

"Loralee." He whispered her name, not

wanting to frighten her, and when she didn't respond, he shook her arm gently. "Loralee."

She came awake at his touch, a smile lighting her face. But it wasn't Shad bending over her. It was Mike.

She knew a moment of sweet relief. Shad was still alive. No one else could have told Mike where to find her.

The concern in her husband's eyes touched Loralee's heart and she murmured, "Oh, Mike, I've never been so glad to see anyone in my whole life."

Mike scooped her into his arms as she began to cry. My God, he thought, I'll kill Shad Zuniga for this if it's the last thing I ever do.

Mike studied Loralee while she wept. What had Zuniga done to her? Her beautiful blond hair was in braids, tied off at the ends with bits of ribbon. Her skin, once so fair, was a deep golden brown. Her hands, once unblemished, looked rough and red. There was a large blister on one delicate palm. Her clothing, though clean, was no better than what the squaws on the reservation wore. *White squaw.* The words crept into his mind, ugly and demeaning.

Loralee wept until she had no tears left, releasing all the fear and tension that had been her constant companions for the last two days. She had been fighting the urge to panic all that day, telling herself over and over again that Shad would come back for her. He would not leave her there alone. Soon, he would come to her. Soon. The day had passed slowly. She had tried to keep busy, but her panic had mounted with each passing hour, and when the sun had begun to set, marking her second night alone in the mountains, she had admitted to herself that he was not coming. She began to cry then, great wracking sobs that tore at her throat and shook her whole body, cried until exhaustion overcame her and she fell asleep. Mike had been the last person she had expected to find her.

Mike! He would know where Zuniga was. Raising her head, she looked into his eyes. "Shad," she whispered. "Where is he?"

"In jail," Mike replied caustically. "Where he belongs."

"Jail!" Loralee exclaimed. "Oh, no!"

The anguish in her voice tore at Schofield's heart. "He was caught stealing some livestock. He's in jail in Bisbee, awaiting trial."

Livestock, Loralee thought guiltily. He was stealing it for me, so I could have eggs and fresh milk. Oh, Shad, what have I done?

"What will happen to him?"

Schofield shrugged. "Who knows? I hope they hang him."

Loralee's stricken gaze filled Mike with

anger. Damn Zuniga! It was obvious Loralee still loved him, despite everything he had put her through.

"They won't hang him," Mike muttered, unable to endure the pain in her eyes. "He'll probably have to spend a few months in jail. Likely do some time on a road gang." Mike laughed shortly. "It'll be good for him to do an honest day's work for a change." He felt his anger rising at the look of sorrow on her face. "Dammit, Loralee, how can you worry about the bastard after the way he's treated you?"

"What do you mean?"

"What do I mean? Hell, look at you. Living like a squaw, probably doing all the work while that lazy bastard sat on his butt, too proud to lift a hand to help out. And you expecting a baby in just a few weeks. And then to go off and leave you here alone . . . I could kill him with my bare hands! I will kill him if I ever get the chance. Come on, I'm getting you out of here. Now."

He refused to let her take anything with her other than the clothes on her back. He tossed everything else into a pile in the center of the lodge and then set fire to the lodge, relishing the flames that quickly consumed the crude brush-covered hut and its contents.

A lump rose in Loralee's throat as she watched the wickiup burn. She had been happy there, truly happy. She and Shad had lain in each other's arms inside that wickiup, planning for the future. And now it was gone.

She did not protest when Mike placed her on his horse and swung up behind her. She was suddenly filled with apathy. It was over, all over.

Her spirits lifted as they made their way down out of the stronghold. They would have to stop at Bisbee for the night, and she would see Shad. One way or another, she would see him.

With a sigh of relief, she settled back against Mike and closed her eyes. Soon she would see Shad again.

It was late when they reached Bisbee. Mike drew rein in front of the hotel and helped Loralee to the ground. Inside the hotel, he signed for a room, then took Loralee by the hand and led her up the stairs. He ordered dinner while she bathed, washed up while she ate.

An hour later, Loralee slipped into bed, feeling full and refreshed. Tomorrow she would see Shad. With that thought in mind, she closed her eyes, but opened them abruptly as Mike slid into bed beside her.

"Mike! What are you doing?"

"Going to bed," he answered, frowning at her.

"Oh." Loralee swallowed the words of protest that rose in her throat. He was her husband, after all, and he had every right to share her bed. It was strange, she mused, but she had almost forgotten that she was legally married to Mike. In the last few months, she had started to think of Shad as her husband.

Loralee felt her insides grow tense as Mike took her in his arms and gently kissed the side of her neck.

"I've missed you," he whispered huskily.

"Have you?" She tried to keep her voice light, but she could not keep a note of panic from rising to the surface. Mike had promised he would never touch her unless she asked him to. Had he forgotten?

"Relax, Loralee," he murmured. "I just want to hold you. Nothing more."

She nodded and closed her eyes. But sleep would not come. She was all too conscious of Mike's body pressed against her own, of his desire for her.

Mike held Loralee all through the night, his emotions in turmoil. He had promised not to touch Loralee until she was ready, but what if she was never ready? He had not expected his self-imposed restraint to last forever. He wanted her. Despite all his promises to leave her alone, she was still legally his wife. Perhaps he had been too nice, too understanding. Perhaps it was time to remind her who was the head of the house. He had given her his name and a home, was willing to give his name to the bastard she was carrying. Perhaps it was time she did a little giving, showed a little appreciation.

Mike let out a long sigh filled with frustration. He had been so certain he could put Loralee out of his life, but now, with her here, in his arms, he knew he had to have her at any cost. No matter that she was carrying another man's child. No matter that she didn't love him. She was his again, and he would not let her go.

Loralee stared at Mike, completely baffled by his anger.

"What do you mean, I can't see him?" Loralee demanded, her own anger rising to the surface. "You can't tell me what to do."

"I am telling you," Mike said firmly. "You're never to see him again. Is that clear?"

"Mike, what's come over you?"

"I've finally come to my senses, that's what's come over me," Mike replied curtly. "You're my wife, and you're not running over to the jail to see that renegade. Not now. Not ever."

"You can't stop me!"

"Can't I?"

Loralee gazed at her husband, a baffled expression on her face. She had never seen Mike like this, angry and determined. He had always been so quiet and easy-going, so willing to do whatever she wished if it would make her happy. Why had he changed?

"Get dressed, Loralee. We've got some shopping to do. You can't go back to the fort looking like a damned squaw."

"Mike, please—"

"No." He closed the distance between them and took Loralee in his arms, his mouth closing over hers in a hungry kiss that demanded a response.

"Mike, stop." Loralee twisted out of his arms, confused and angry and a little afraid. "You promised!" she cried. "You said our marriage would be in name only unless I wanted it otherwise."

Mike nodded, his blue eyes growing dark with anger. "And you promised to be my wife. You broke that promise when you ran away with Zuniga. Did he make love to you, Loralee? Did you tell *him* no?"

"Mike, stop."

"I've been a fool," Mike said bitterly. "But no more. You're my wife, and when that baby is born, I intend to make you my wife in every sense of the word."

Loralee shook her head, too stunned to speak. She should have expected something like this, she thought dully. Mike was a man, after all. She had been a fool to think she could live with him and not fulfill her obligation as a wife. He wasn't a saint, and he loved her. It was only natural that he want to hold her and kiss her and make love to her. Truth

346

be told, she was surprised he had held out this long. Oh, but he had promised! What was she going to do?

"Get dressed," Mike said curtly. "I have to be back at the fort tomorrow night."

Loralee stared, unseeing, at the road ahead. Her thoughts were bleak, close to despair. Shad was in jail, would be a prisoner for months, perhaps years. And Mike was sitting beside her, a grim expression on his face. How quickly her life had turned upside down.

They had gone shopping the day before and Loralee was respectably attired in a blue traveling suit and matching bonnet. White kid shoes covered her feet, white gloves protected her hands, a lacy parasol blocked the sun. She looked every inch a lady. No one, seeing her now, would suspect that she had spent the past few months living in a brush-covered wickiup.

Mike had been most generous, and a small valise held several other dresses, all cut to allow for her expanded girth. She had not really been in the mood to shop, but Mike had insisted she buy whatever caught her fancy. She was an officer's wife now, and it was important to look the part.

Despite her lack of enthusiasm over returning to the fort, Loralee had been pleased by the prospect of new clothes. It had been so long since she had worn anything but a man's shirt and calico skirts. The new traveling suit complemented her hair and eyes, but she took little joy in her reflection. What difference did it make how she looked if Shad couldn't see her?

Shad. They had passed the jail on their way out of town, and her heart had ached at the thought of Zuniga locked away behind iron bars. She had gazed longingly at the jail. He was inside, separated from her by little more than six feet of dusty ground. She was tempted to leap from the buggy and fly across the street and up the three short stairs to the jail . . . sorely tempted, and only Mike's hand on her arm stopped her.

Now, sitting beside Mike, the town far behind, her thoughts were full of Zuniga. He was in jail, and it was all her fault.

21

Zuniga stopped his endless pacing to stare at the heavy oak door that separated the cellblock from the jail office. There was a small square window in the door that offered a tiny glimpse of blue sky. The handcuffs on his wrists rattled infuriatingly as he took hold of the bars of his cell. Impotent anger at being imprisoned gnawed at his vitals, and he gripped the bars until his knuckles were white. He had to get out of here, and soon, before he went crazy. Day after day, hour after hour, he paced the narrow cell, his frustration building until he thought he would scream with the need to be free. The air in the cellblock was stale, the view never changed: four gray walls and iron bars. He yearned for the sight of trees and hills, for the warmth of the sun on his face.

He thought constantly of Loralee. No doubt she was back at the fort with Schofield now. The thought of her being with another man was worse torture than being in jail. She had said Schofield had not touched her, but how much longer would that last? The man was flesh and blood, not a plaster saint. No man could be with Loralee day and night, day after day, without wanting her. Loralee and Schofield. The thought drove him wild.

But there was nothing he could do about it. He had been subjected to a brief trial, found guilty, and sentenced to six months at hard labor as soon as his ribs healed.

Six months in chains. He would surely go mad. He had never realized how much he loved the wild life, the mountains and hills that he had wandered as a boy, the freedom he had enjoyed. The sameness of each day in jail, the lack of activity or exercise, the physical restrictions placed on him by handcuffs and iron bars were wearing on his nerves. He was jumpy, irritable, eager for a fight.

And then there was the food. The marshal, a man filled with prejudice against Mexicans and Indians, served him the same menu every day: runny eggs and half-cooked bacon for breakfast, thin soup and brown bread for lunch, and beans and tortillas for dinner. Zuniga skipped breakfast, ate the bread for lunch, and wolfed down dinner, which was the only decent meal of the day.

He had spent just over four weeks in the jail cell when he was hustled out of the building and into the back of a slat-sided wagon. Shackles were placed on his feet, and the cuffs on his hands were secured to an iron ring in the side of the wagon. He took a deep breath as the wagon lurched forward. At last, he was outside again.

As the miles rolled by, he realized they were heading for the reservation. How Schofield would laugh, Zuniga mused bitterly, to see him in chains.

When they arrived at the reservation, Zuniga was locked in the stockade with a dozen other Indians who were being punished for a wide variety of crimes. The other prisoners were sullen-faced, querulous, and dirty. They eyed Zuniga warily until they recognized him, and then they laughed ruefully. So, the one remaining rebel had been caught at last.

Zuniga spent a sleepless night; at first light, he was rousted from the stockade and taken to the stables to muck out the stalls.

Anger was a tight fist in his gut as he shoveled horse manure into a wheel barrow. He had been working about twenty minutes when Mike Schofield entered the barn. Zuniga had just stepped out of one of the stalls and the two men glared at each other as they came face to face.

Zuniga was keenly aware of the chains on his hands and feet, of the sweat dripping down his face and back, of the manure clinging to his moccasins. Humiliation washed over him, but he held his head high, his expression remaining impassive.

Mike grinned broadly. So, Zuniga had been sent home to serve his time. He wouldn't be so arrogant after this. The boys and young men wouldn't look on him with such high regard after they'd seen him in chains.

Schofield glanced at the private who had been ordered to keep an eye on Zuniga. "Parker, you're dismissed. I'll keep an eye on the redskin."

"Yessir," Parker replied. Executing a salute, the private left the barn, glad to be relieved from such a boring detail.

"Get to work, Injun," Mike ordered curtly.

Rage boiled up inside Zuniga. For a moment, he thought of refusing. Instead, he shrugged and stepped into the next stall. It was foolish to provoke the enemy when he had the upper hand. It would have been easy to smash Schofield in the face with the shovel and make a run for it, but there was no place to go. The gates were closed, his hands and feet were shackled, and he had no weapon. In addition, there were soldiers everywhere.

It took two hours to clean the stalls, and when that was done, Schofield ordered Zuniga to curry his horse. Tight-lipped, Shad did as he was bid.

Schofield found a dozen other chores for Zuniga to do before returning him to the stockade.

Mike was in good spirits when he got home that night. It had been immensely satisfying, ordering Zuniga about, knowing how humiliating it was for the Apache to obey. Yes, he mused, the next six months were going to be interesting indeed.

The following day just after dawn, the Indian prisoners were herded outside the fort and put to work clearing the dry brush from the hills behind the back wall of the fort. It was hard, dusty work. The Apaches cursed under their breath. It was bad enough to be in chains, but to do woman's work was humiliation of the worst kind.

Zuniga was halfheartedly hacking down a fire-ravaged tree when he heard a snicker behind him. Turning, he saw Mike Schofield grinning impudently at him from the back of a raw-boned bay gelding.

Zuniga's hands tightened on the ax handle. It was humiliating, having your enemy see you in chains laboring under the hot sun, while he laughed in your face.

With lazy grace, Schofield lifted the crop in his hand and brought it down across Zuniga's chest. "Get to work, redskin," he said with a sneer. "I won't put up with any malingering while I'm on duty."

Anger flashed in Zuniga's eyes as he hefted the ax. It would be so easy to bury the heavy blade in Schofield's chest. So easy.

As if reading his mind, Schofield moved his hand to the gun holstered on his side, his fingers curling around the smooth walnut butt. "Go ahead," he challenged. "I'd love an excuse to cut you down."

Zuniga's mouth turned down in a wry grin. "No," he replied, shaking his head. "I am not ready to die. Not until I have seen my son."

"You'll never see him," Schofield vowed. His hand closed over the butt of his gun. "I'll kill you first."

"Perhaps." It was on the tip of Zuniga's tongue to ask about Loralee. Was she well? Was she happy? But he knew that Schofield would not tell him, and he could not humble himself enough to beg for an answer.

"Get to work," Schofield demanded, and turned away.

Zuniga stared after the lieutenant for a long moment. Then, with a sigh, he attacked the tree, unleashing all his pent-up fury as he destroyed what had once been a living thing, wishing all the while that it was Mike Schofield falling beneath the blade.

Loralee smiled stiffly at the ladies standing outside the sutler's store. She knew they talked about her constantly, gossiping about her unexplained absence, and the fact that she had been married only five and a half months and appeared to be due any day.

The ladies smiled and nodded, but their smiles did not reach their eyes, and as soon as she passed by, she could hear them whispering. Damn them, she thought angrily. Damn them all! They were strangers to her, wives who had come West to be with their husbands while she had been away. She did not know their names, but they knew hers. Indeed, they knew hers. She was certain they had nothing good to say, nothing at all.

She fought back the tears threatening to fall. She had never been so miserable in her life. Mike was a stranger. Whatever affection he had once had for her seemed to have withered and died when they reached the fort. He treated her well enough, but his eyes were guarded when he looked at her, and his attitude was one of contempt. And yet he still desired her. She could see it in his eyes sometimes, when she caught him staring at her.

When she got home, she put the few items she had purchased in the cupboard, then wandered through the house. Mike had forbidden her to leave the fort, but she needed to get away, to be in the open for a while.

Thirty minutes later she was driving out of the fort in a light buggy. The private who had harnessed the horse for her had been reluctant to do so, but he lacked the guts to argue with Lieutenant Schofield's wife.

Loralee sighed as the fort faded into the distance behind her. It felt good to be alone, away from walls and prying eyes and whispering tongues, away from Mike. He professed to love her, but she knew he would never forgive her for running away with Zuniga and liking it.

She drove for an hour, enjoying the open country, the clear sky, the cacti that were in bloom. She thought of her child soon to be born, but refused to think about Shad. It was too painful to think of him, too painful to picture him languishing away in prison, locked behind cold iron bars.

As she approached the fort again, she saw the road gang laboring on the side of the hill, hacking away the dry brush. She felt a twinge of sympathy for the prisoners. They were all Indians. Most were doing time on the road gang for being drunk and disorderly, or for stealing. It was hot, dusty work, and as she drew nearer, she could see that the men were sweating profusely. Forcing the Indians to work on the road gang on the reservation was supposed to deter the other

Indians from breaking the law, but she doubted it was effective. Certainly there was never a lack of men on the road gang.

She was about to rein the horse around and head for the front gate when she saw him. His shirt was off and his muscles bunched and relaxed with each swing of the scythe in his hands. A strip of red cloth kept the sweat from his eyes. Tears burned her eyes when she saw the shackles on his hands and feet.

For a moment, she could only stare at Zuniga, her eyes feasting on the sight of him even as she wondered how long he had been back on the reservation. Mike had never said a word. She gazed at Zuniga longingly, wishing she had the nerve to go to him. Almost, she reined the horse closer. And then she heard Mike's voice, cruel and taunting as he mocked Zuniga, belittling him because he was in chains.

Loralee cringed as she heard her husband make several derogatory remarks about Shad's honor, about how there was no pride in shackles or iron bars.

Loralee watched Zuniga's face. He seemed not to hear the relentless barbs, but she knew each taunt cut deep. How could Mike be so cruel?

She could not bear to watch any more. With a muffled cry, she started to turn the horse back the way she had come. At that moment she heard Mike remark that no doubt Shad's son would be proud to learn his father had once labored on a road gang with a bunch of two-bit thieves and drunkards.

It was the wrong thing to say.

With a wordless cry, Zuniga lunged forward, the scythe held in his hands like a club.

Loralee watched in horror as Shad struck Mike across the side of the head with the scythe's solid wood handle. Mike fell to the ground, blood oozing from his left temple. The other guard sprinted toward Mike. Drawing his service revolver as he ran, he fired a shot in Zuniga's direction, and missed. As the trooper took aim for a second shot, Zuniga grabbed Mike's sidearm from the holster and fired at the soldier bearing down on him. The bullet hit the man full in the chest, killing him instantly.

For a moment, Zuniga stood staring down at Mike Schofield. The man was still breathing. A cruel smile twisted Shad's lips as he raised the gun and thumbed back the hammer. He had killed one man already. What harm was there in killing two? They could only hang him once.

"Shad, don't!"

His head jerked up at the sound of her voice and he whirled around to see Loralee driving toward him.

"Don't!" she cried again, drawing the buggy to a halt beside him. "Please, don't."

With a curt nod, Zuniga shoved the pistol into the waistband of his pants, then dug the keys out of Mike's pocket before vaulting into the buggy beside Loralee. Taking the reins from her hands, he urged the horse up into the hills behind the fort.

The other prisoners stood staring after Zuniga and the woman, too stunned by the sudden violence to move. Then, realizing there was no one left to stop them, the Apaches melted into the scrub brush.

Loralee clutched the side of the buggy as it jolted over the rough, unbroken ground. There was no trail, and the wheels bounced over rocks and cactus, rocking wildly from side to side.

Once, glancing over her shoulder, she saw Mike lying on the ground far below. Was he dead? The other man had been killed instantly. She wondered if the shooting would be considered self-defense.

She looked at Shad. His face was taut, his mouth set in a grim line as he urged the horse to go faster.

"Shad, where are we going?"

"I do not know," he replied. He lashed the horse mercilessly. It would not take long for Schofield to regain consciousness and summon help. For a moment, he regretted not killing the man, and then he shrugged. It made no difference. He had drawn the blood of his enemy and that was coup enough. For now.

He slid a glance at Loralee. Her face was pale, her eyes wide and frightened, but he knew the fear she felt was for him and not for herself. She was a fine and brave woman, he reflected, worthy to be the mother of an Apache. She would have made him a fine wife in the old days, a fine wife, indeed.

He reined the horse to a stop at a place not far from the spot where Nachi's lodge had once stood. Dismounting, he released the horse from the traces and cut the reins to a manageable length.

"What are you doing?" Loralee asked in a small voice.

"I am leaving you here," Zuniga replied. Lifting her from the buggy, he took her in his arms and held her tight. "We cannot get away in this rig. It is too slow. And you cannot ride."

"Don't leave me."

"I will be back for you after the baby is born," he promised, stroking her hair. "Watch for me."

"I will."

Lowering his head, Zuniga kissed her long and hard. She felt good in his arms. So good. "Damn," he muttered. "I do not want to go."

"I don't want you to go," Loralee said. She reached up to caress his cheek. "I love you."

"I love you." He muttered an oath as he

unlocked the shackles from his hands and feet and tossed the irons away. "I must go."

"I know."

"Damn." He caught her in his arms and kissed her again, his mouth hard and insistent.

With regret, he let her go, only to stand there looking at her. How could he leave her?

"Go, hurry," Loralee said. "I'll be all right. I'll wait for you, no matter how long it takes."

One more quick kiss, and he was gone.

She did not try to contain her tears but let them fall freely, hoping they would ease the ache in her heart. He was gone from her again, but at least he was free.

22

Zuniga rode hard, climbing higher into the hills. He breathed deeply, drawing the clean fresh air into his lungs. Free at last. His hands and feet felt lighter than air now that they were freed of the shackles that had hampered his movements and galled his soul. He regretted that he had been unable to kill Schofield, but it was just as well. Loralee needed a man to take care of her, and she would be safe at the fort. Schofield would not turn her out. And when the baby was born, he would return and take Loralee and the child away with him. His plans went that far and no farther. He was a hunted man now, a fugitive. He had no money, no home, nothing to offer Loralee but a life of heart-ache and misery. And his child . . . what could he offer his son? Nothing.

He swore softly. He had made a mess of the whole thing. He should have served his time. At least then he would not be a wanted man. Now the Army would pursue him relentlessly for killing one of their men.

He drew the horse to a halt in a grove of aspens high in the hills and sat there looking back the way he had come. A distant line of blue told him the Army was already in pursuit.

With a grimace, he urged the horse deeper into the wooded hills.

Loralee sat beside Mike. He had been unconscious for three days, ever since Shad had escaped from the road gang. Mike's face was pale, his breathing shallow, and the doctor had said there was a possibility there could be complications. He did not elaborate on his diagnosis, and Loralee did not press him for details. What the doctor had inferred was too awful to contemplate.

With a sigh, she gazed out the hospital window. A squad of troopers were drilling on the parade ground. Sweat rolled down their faces and dampened their uniforms.

She lifted her gaze and stared at the distant hills. Where was Shad? How soon would he come back for her? Would he dare come back? He was a wanted man now.

"Loralee."

She gasped as Mike whispered her name. "Mike! Thank God. How do you feel?"

"Awful. My head—" He lifted a hand to the bandage swathed around his head. "What happened?"

"Don't you remember?"

"No."

"Zuniga escaped. He . . . he hit you when you tried to stop him."

"I don't remember a thing."

"Just lie still. I'm going to get the doctor." Smiling, she bent down and placed a kiss on his cheek. "I'm glad you're all right."

The doctor was pleased with Mike's recovery. Five days later Mike was discharged from the infirmary. His memory seemed fine except for the events of the day that Zuniga escaped. He had no recollection of that day at all. Two weeks later he was back to full duty.

Loralee woke up frowning, and then gasped as a contraction caught her unawares. The baby, she thought smiling. It's coming. She glanced at Mike, sleeping peacefully beside her, then slid out of bed. Drawing on her robe, she tiptoed into the parlor and sat in the chair by the window, looking out. The sky was cloudy, and even as she watched, it began to rain.

She sat there for an hour staring at the rain as the contractions gradually grew harder and more painful. Thunder rolled across the heavens, followed by jagged bolts of yellow lightning that lit up the sky like Fourth of July fireworks.

And still she sat there, her arms clasped around her belly, her eyes intent upon the raging storm as the pains grew steadily worse. She knew it was time to wake Mike, time to call the doctor, but she was reluctant to share this moment with anyone but Shad. He seemed close to her now. She could almost see his swarthy face in the storm, hear his voice in the thunder that rumbled across the cloud-blackened sky.

Tears filled her eyes as a sharp contraction threatened to split her in half. If only Shad were there to help her. If only she could see his face, hear his voice assuring her that everything would be all right. If only she could cling to his hand and make his indomitable strength her own. She knew she could bear anything if he were there beside her, but he was gone, perhaps for good.

The thought that she might never see him again was more painful than the contractions wracking her body as his child struggled to make its way into the world.

She closed her eyes, and a verse from the 34th Psalm whispered in her mind: "I sought the Lord and he heard me, and delivered me from all my fears."

She smiled faintly. If only she could be delivered of all her fears, and of the contractions that were growing unbearable. Delivered, she mused. That was the key word.

She screamed aloud as the hardest contraction of all knifed through her. The cry was filled with pain and despair because Shad was gone and she didn't know where he was, because she was frightened and alone.

Moments later, Mike ran into the room, his face ashen. "Loralee, my God, what's the matter?"

"The baby." She doubled over as another pain hit her. "It's coming."

Mike's face went white. The day he had dreaded was here. He felt a swift surge of anger. This was all Shad Zuniga's fault. Loralee whimpered softly and Mike's anger was forgotten as he saw the pain etched in her lovely face, saw the tears glistening in her eyes.

"Just relax," he said soothingly. "You'll be fine, just fine." Sweeping her into his arms, he carried her to bed and covered her with a clean sheet. "I'm going for the doctor," he said, giving her hand a reassuring squeeze. "I'll be right back."

"Don't leave me."

"I'll be right back, Loralee, I promise."

"Hurry!"

The next hour passed in a red haze of pain. She was only vaguely aware of Mike standing at her side, his face drawn with worry, as Zuniga's son came into the world.

She smiled weakly as the doctor placed the infant in her arms. It had been worth the pain, she thought wearily, to hold Shad's son in her arms. In the way of all new mothers, she counted tiny fingers and toes, marveling at such perfection. She touched the soft thatch of straight black hair, gazed in awe at the beautiful face, and fell asleep with Shad's name on her lips.

Mike Schofield swore under his breath as the doctor sent him a searching glance.

"It's the baby's name," Mike said quickly. "Shad Michael Schofield."

The doctor nodded dubiously. "Unusual name, Shad," he murmured. "Wasn't that the name of the Injun who killed Sergeant Blakely?"

"Good night, doc," Mike said abruptly. "Thanks for coming."

Face grim, Mike handed the doctor his bag and showed him to the front door. He stood there for a minute listening to the rain, his face bleak. Doc Hampton was the biggest gossip on the post. By tomorrow afternoon, everyone would know that the Schofields' baby was named after Zuniga.

Scowling, he shut the door with a bang. Moving to the kitchen, he poured himself a drink, then wandered back to the bedroom to stand staring down at Loralee and the child securely cradled in her arms. Damn, he thought bitterly, the little bastard looked Indian through and through.

23

Of course there were rumors. Mike told everyone the baby had been born prematurely, but it was obvious to everyone that Loralee had carried the child full term. He was too big, too healthy, to be premature.

It was just as obvious that the child had been sired by an Indian, though no one dared mention it aloud.

Stella Freeman made a bit of an effort to hide her shock and disgust when she made her obligatory call on Loralee after the baby was born, but her feelings were clearly etched in her eyes and in the stunned expression on her face.

Half-breed. The word seemed to hang in the air even though nothing had been said.

"He's . . . healthy looking," Stella Freeman finally remarked.

"Yes," Loralee answered. With an effort, she choked back her tears. The look of contempt in Stella Freeman's eyes hurt more than she would have thought possible.

"Well, I know you're tired," the colonel's wife said in a rush, "so I won't keep you. I just wanted to come by and . . . congratulate you. Good day."

Stella Freeman left the room as fast as her legs could carry her, and Loralee let out a sigh of resignation. By tonight everyone on the post would know that she had been pregnant when she married Mike, and that Mike wasn't the father of her child. How would she ever face Mike's friends again? How could she face Mike? He must be going through hell.

She tried valiantly not to cry, but she could not hold back her tears or banish the feeling of misery that washed over her. She would never be able to teach the Apache children again. Everyone would say she was unfit to teach. People would feel sorry for Mike. They would say she had used him to cover her sins. And they would be right.

No one would feel sorry for her. They would look at her with contempt in their eyes as they condemned her for what she had done. And the fact that she had been immoral with an Indian would make matters worse. Probably no one would ever speak to her again.

She gave her son a hug. Poor baby. He would suffer the most. People would shun him, or call him ugly names.

She stayed in bed for two weeks, spending every waking moment with her son, nursing him, singing to him, showering him with hugs and kisses so he would know he was loved. He became her whole life, the one person in all the world who loved and needed her.

She was surprised when Sally Stockman came to visit.

Sally smiled shyly as she handed Loralee a gaily wrapped package. "Congratulations, Loralee," she murmured. "I'd have come sooner, but Mike told me you weren't feeling well."

"I'm better now," Loralee mumbled, unwilling to meet Sally's eyes.

Sally gestured at the cradle next to the bed where the baby lay sleeping. "May I see him?"

"If you like."

Sally went to the cradle and peered inside, and Loralee felt herself begin to grow tense. Soon Sally would mumble some hurried excuse and leave. She had probably only come here to see for herself that the rumors were true.

"He's darling," Sally said, smiling at Loralee over her shoulder. "Aren't you glad he isn't bald? So many new babies are, but he has lots of hair. And such lovely skin."

Loralee studied Sally's face, looking for

some sign of derision or scorn, but found none.

Sally dragged a chair closer to the bed and sat down. "I love babies. I hope to have one soon."

Loralee nodded, touched by Sally's sincere good wishes and friendly smile.

"Open the present," Sally urged.

"All right." Loralee removed the ribbon and paper, lifted the lid, and gave a little cry of delight. Inside the box, wrapped in a layer of white tissue paper, nestled a lacy blue shawl with a long fringe, as well as a light blue sacque. "Thank you, Sally, they're lovely."

"Loralee?"

"Yes."

"I know we haven't been close friends, but I hope we can be. Don't let Mrs. Freeman intimidate you. You have many friends at the fort and on the reservation. Don't lock yourself in your room. You can't hide from the world forever."

"I'm so ashamed."

Sally shrugged. "We've all made mistakes, even Stella Freeman, though she probably wouldn't admit it."

"Is everyone talking about me?"

"Not everyone." Sally laughed softly. "Mrs. Cogan is quite shocked, of course, but she's just an old stick and probably jealous because she couldn't do any better than Tom Cogan."

Loralee laughed in spite of herself. Tom Cogan was one of the homeliest men she had ever seen. He was short and bald, with a bulbous nose, a receding chin, and close-set eyes. For all his lack of beauty, he was a kind and honorable man, and Loralee felt guilty for laughing.

"Loralee—"

"What?"

"Never mind."

"You're wondering, too, aren't you?" Loralee said. "Wondering who the father is."

"I'm sorry. I just can't help it. Curiosity is my worst fault. Forgive me."

"It's Shad Zuniga," Loralee confessed softly, and felt her heart twist with pain as she spoke his name aloud. Where was he? Would she ever see him again?

Sally saw the sadness in Loralee's eyes and heard the yearning in her voice. "You were in love with him."

Loralee nodded. "I don't know how it happened."

"No one ever does. I doubt that any woman alive could pinpoint the moment when she fell in love."

"He isn't like everyone says."

"I didn't know him, of course, but I saw him at the Agency several times. He was very handsome in a wild and rugged way. He scared me, though. I'm not sure why."

"I miss him terribly."

Compassion filled Sally Stockman's

heart as two fat tears rolled down Loralee's cheeks. Not certain if she was doing the right thing, she moved to the edge of the bed and put her arm around Loralee's shoulders.

Loralee sagged against Sally, letting all her unhappiness pour out in a flood of tears. It was good to know she had at least one friend at the fort, one person who did not condemn her.

Sally came to visit often after that and they quickly became good friends. Sally insisted that Loralee get out of the house, go for walks, go shopping, take the baby out for air. A few of the men eyed Loralee speculatively, wondering if the rumors were true, but they all treated her with respect. She was the wife of an officer, after all, and officers were all gentlemen.

Her relationship with Mike was strained. They spoke to each other only when necessary, and Mike spent most of his time away from home. Extra duty, he said. If he knew what people were saying about Loralee and the baby, he never let it show, though one night he came home with a black eye and bloody knuckles. Though he refused to say what had happened, Loralee suspected he had been in a fight, and that she had been the cause of it.

Mike made no attempt to touch her, but she knew that he was only waiting for the doctor's okay before he claimed his husbandly rights. What she would do then she did not know.

Six weeks after the baby was born, Mike insisted that Loralee accompany him to a dinner party at the colonel's home. Loralee pleaded to stay home, but Mike insisted she attend. It was one of the worst evenings of her life. Everyone was polite, but Loralee wanted to die of shame. Every time she saw two people with their heads together, she was certain they were talking about her.

Sally Stockman waltzed by on her husband's arm. They were an unusual pair, Loralee thought absently. Ken Stockman was a big man, with shoulders as wide as the Missouri and legs like tree trunks. Sally looked like a child beside him. But they were very much in love. Anyone could see that.

Sally smiled at Loralee. It was obvious that Lieutenant Schofield's wife was not having a good time. When the dance ended, Sally left her husband and went to chat with Loralee.

"Are you all right, Loralee?" Sally asked after they had exchanged greetings. "You look like you're about to be thrown to the lions."

"I feel like it, too," Loralee replied. "And Stella Freeman looks the hungriest."

"She does have sharp teeth," Sally allowed.

"Yes," Loralee agreed glumly. "She

looks at me as if I had a scarlet letter emblazoned across my forehead."

"Be brave," Sally coaxed. "Here comes Mike to dance with you. Smile now, and if Old Ironsides says anything, just spit in her eye."

Loralee laughed at that. Sally Stockman looked as timid as a field mouse, but she had more spunk than anyone she knew.

Loralee smiled at Mike as he took her onto the dance floor. They danced well together, Loralee mused as she sought for something to say, something light and airy that would take the haunted look from Mike's eyes. But she couldn't think of anything and she was glad when the music ended.

Later she danced with Colonel Freeman, who made it a habit to dance with every woman present at least once. He fancied himself to be quite an expert on the dance floor, but Loralee thought she would just as soon waltz with an elephant.

She was glad when the night ended. At home, she stared, unseeing, at her reflection as she brushed out her hair. If only she could put an end to the nightmare she lived every day. If only Shad would come and take her away. . . .

24

With a sigh, Shad Zuniga stepped from the saddle. Never in all his thirty-four years had he been so utterly weary or discouraged. The Army had pursued him relentlessly, never giving up, never slowing down.

Now, with darkness settling over the land, he bedded down in a dry wash, the dun tethered nearby. He grinned wryly. Soon after his escape from the road gang, he had made his way back to the fort, hoping to see Loralee. He had waited impatiently, counting the minutes until sundown, then made his way to Schofield's house, hoping to find Loralee alone. But his luck had been bad that night. Schofield had been at home, relaxing in an easy chair before the fire, his feet propped up on an ottoman.

Peering through the window, Shad had seen Loralee sitting on the sofa, leafing through a ladies magazine. So close, he thought. She was so close. He had stayed at the window a long time, his eyes drinking in the sight of her. Once, she had laid the magazine aside and placed her hand on her distended abdomen, a smile lighting her face as the baby moved beneath her fingertips. It had been all Shad could do not to burst into the room and sweep her into his arms. Soon, he had promised himself. Soon.

Zuniga had waited until the lights went out inside the house before he moved out of the shadows and padded noiselessly toward the horse corral. The horse he had been riding had gone lame the day before and he had been on foot since then. It had been his intent to steal a horse from the Army, preferably Schofield's big bay gelding. To his delight, he had found the dun penned in a small enclosure. Shad had grinned into the darkness. No doubt Schofield had brought the dun to the fort along with Loralee's mare when they returned from Bisbee. One day he would have to thank Schofield for returning his horse, he had thought wryly.

It had been no easy task, stealing the dun from the corral, but it had been worth the effort. There wasn't a horse in the territory that could match the stallion for speed or endurance.

Now, lying on the ground in the dry wash, Zuniga thought of Loralee, always Loralee. She was ever in his thoughts and her image came quickly to mind: hair like soft gold, eyes as warm and brown as mother earth, lips as soft and pink as the petals of a wild rose, skin like soft satin.

Thinking of her stirred his desire, and he groaned low in his throat, hungry for the sight of her. He had been long without a woman, he mused, far too long, but he knew that no other woman would ever satisfy him again.

Loralee. He cursed softly. It had been weeks since he had seen her last, and he didn't know when he would see her again.

Thinking of Loralee brought his child to mind. The baby would have been born by now, he mused, and wondered if he had a son or a daughter. The sex of the child was no longer important, so long as mother and infant were both well and strong.

His stomach growled loudly, reminding him that he had not eaten for two days. Muttering a mild oath, he gazed up at the stars wheeling against the midnight sky, willing his hunger to go away.

For the next three weeks, he stayed one jump ahead of the soldiers pursuing him. He ate whatever he could catch or steal, slept wherever he could find shelter. He grew thin and haggard, but still he ran. Better to live as a hunted man than to die at the end of a white man's rope, or spend the rest of his life rotting in prison.

In late August it rained for three days. Huge drops of water pelted the earth, pummeling man and beast like angry fists. Thunder rumbled through the heavens; great jagged bolts of lightning rent the sky. Zuniga murmured a quiet prayer of thanks to Usen as he made his way to the fort under cover of darkness. The rain would wash out his tracks. With luck, the Army would not find his trail again.

Tethering the stallion out of sight behind the fort, he padded across the muddy parade ground toward Schofield's house. A light burned in the front window. Peering inside, he saw Loralee curled up in the corner of a high-backed sofa, the infant nursing at her breast.

Zuniga stared at Loralee in wonder. She wore a white nightgown and fluffy white robe. Her hair fell around her face and shoulders like a soft golden cloud. She had never looked more beautiful.

With an effort, he drew his gaze from Loralee and glanced around the room. Where was Schofield? In another room? On duty? On patrol?

Muttering an oath, he rapped on the window.

Loralee glanced up, a frown furrowing her brow. She experienced a moment of alarm when she saw a face peering in the window, then felt her heart leap for joy as she recognized Zuniga.

Rising quickly, the baby clutched to her breast, she ran to the front door and flung it open. "Shad!"

He stepped inside, shut and locked the door. "Where's Schofield?"

"Out looking for you."

"When will he be back?"

"Not before tomorrow."

Zuniga grinned broadly, pleased to think of his enemy slogging around in the mud, following a cold trail. "Close the curtains and turn down the lamp."

"Get out of those wet things," Loralee admonished as she drew the curtains. "You'll catch your death." She turned down the lamp, then watched unabashed as Zuniga shed his rain-soaked shirt, pants, and moccasins. She felt a thrill of excitement as he drew her into his arms.

"I've missed you," Loralee murmured.

Zuniga nodded as he bent to claim her lips. They kissed until the baby began to whimper.

"You interrupted his dinner," Loralee remarked, laughing softly. "Why don't you go put on a pair of Mike's trousers while I feed your son?"

Zuniga nodded, unable to speak past the

lump in his throat. A son, he thought exultantly. I have a son!

A few moments later, seated in a chair across from Loralee, he watched while she nursed the baby.

"I named him Shad," Loralee said. "Do you mind?"

Zuniga shrugged. "It is a hard luck name, but maybe he will change it."

When the child finished nursing, Loralee laid it in Shad's arms. She felt her heart melt as Zuniga carefully inspected the boy from head to foot, his eyes alight with wonder.

"Isn't he beautiful?" Loralee asked, stroking her son's downy black head.

"Beautiful," Zuniga murmured huskily.

He held the child until it fell asleep, marveling at the infant's tiny fingers and toes, at the perfectly formed features, at the changing expressions that played across the child's face as it slept.

Loralee could not take her eyes off Zuniga. The love she saw reflected in his expression as he gazed at their son was the most beautiful thing she had ever seen. Unbidden came the memory of what Shad had told her about his father. Had Nakai once looked at Zuniga with that expression of love that bordered on adoration? Had he once carefully examined his son's hands and feet, gently stroked a black-thatched head, murmured tender words of endearment?

She felt her heart swell with tenderness as Zuniga bent to place a kiss on his son's cheek. How did such love turn to violence? What had caused Nakai's cruelty? Had he always been a mean-tempered, violent man? If so, how had Nadina fallen in love with him?

Zuniga raised his head and looked at Loralee. There was a bemused expression on her face, confusion in her eyes.

"What is it?" he asked, speaking softly so as not to disturb his son. "What is wrong?"

"Nothing. I was just wondering . . . nothing."

"Tell me."

"I was just thinking about your father."

"Nakai? Why?"

"Was he always mean to you?"

Zuniga stared past Loralee, his hand absently stroking the baby's hair. "No, not always. When I was very young, maybe five or six, I thought he was the most wonderful man in the world. He used to take me hunting in the mountains with him. He was a fine shot with a bow and arrow, and I wanted to be just like him. But then he changed. He began to accuse my mother of being unfaithful to him."

"Was she?"

"No! She never loved anyone else, but my father did not believe her. He started drinking heavily, and he never stopped. I was older then, and I was ashamed of him.

In my heart, I made Nachi my father. He was always there for me, always ready to listen. I could tell him anything without fear of being ridiculed or punished. It was Nachi who taught me to be a warrior, Nachi who was there to comfort me when my mother died in my arms. His heart was broken, too, but he put his grief aside to comfort me."

"He must have been a great man," Loralee mused softly. "I wish I could have known him better."

For a few moments, they were silent. Then Loralee stood up and Zuniga followed her into the nursery. Reluctantly he placed the child in its bed. For a moment Zuniga and Loralee stood side by side, gazing lovingly at the sleeping infant; then, with a low moan, Zuniga took Loralee in his arms. They clung together for a long time, content to be quietly close.

"You look thin," Loralee remarked sometime later. "Can I fix you something to eat?"

"I would like that."

"You look like you could use a hot bath, too."

Zuniga grinned wryly. He smelled worse than his horse.

The next hour was a busy one. Loralee draped Zuniga's clothes over a chair in front of the fire to dry out, prepared him something to eat while he took a long bath. She fixed enough for two, then said she wasn't really hungry and insisted that he eat it all so it wouldn't go to waste. He didn't argue, but wolfed down both portions. Belatedly she wished she had made more. He looked so thin, so tired. It tore at her heart to know that he had been living in the hills like a wild thing while she lived in a comfortable house, wanting for nothing except his presence.

She smiled at him as he pushed his plate away and sipped a cup of coffee. "I can be ready to leave in twenty minutes," she said lightly. "Less than that, if you're in a hurry."

"No."

Her smile stayed in place, but lost its glow. "You're not in a hurry?"

"Loralee . . . damn."

"Isn't that why you're here?" she asked anxiously. "To take us away with you?"

"I cannot, Loralee. Not now. I have got nothing to offer you. No home, no future, nothing."

"But you promised."

"Loralee, I am a wanted man."

"I don't care."

"I care. I cannot drag a woman and a baby around in the hills. I have not been able to stay in one place for more than a few hours at a time. There are nights when I have nothing to eat. I sleep on the ground."

"I don't care. Please take us with you," she begged, but she was frightened by the way of life he was describing to her. For herself it wouldn't matter, but she had the baby to think of now. Still, even knowing he was right, she couldn't bear to be parted from him again.

"Loralee, do not make this any harder than it is. I cannot run forever. Sooner or later the Army will catch up with me. I do not want you to be there when it happens. I will come back and see you when I can."

She nodded, tears filling her eyes as she gazed up at him, silently pleading with him to make things right, to figure out a way for them to be together. Always she had known he would come back for her, that they would have a life together somewhere, somehow. It was all she'd had to cling to, the only thing that had made life worthwhile when missing him grew unbearable.

Her tears tore at Zuniga's heart. Murmuring her name, he walked around the table and took her in his arms, one hand lovingly stroking her hair.

"I'd take you with me if I could," he said quietly. "You know that, don't you?"

"I know."

"I want to make love to you," he whispered.

His words, soft and low, were the words she longed to hear. Taking him by the hand, she led him into the bedroom. Then, slowly, she removed her robe and gown.

Zuniga sucked in a deep breath as she stood naked before his eyes. Her body was more rounded, the curves lush and womanly. Her breasts were fuller, heavy with milk, her stomach was almost flat again. Slowly she held out her arms, beckoning him.

"Is it all right?" he asked huskily. Not for anything would he hurt her.

Nodding, she drew him close, lifting her head for his kiss. Fire shot through her veins as their mouths came together and they sank to the bed.

Zuniga shed Schofield's clothes, and then he lowered himself over Loralee, his mouth kissing her nose and eyes, the curve of her throat, the delicate lobe of her ear.

They had been too long apart and they came together in a rush, eager to possess and be possessed, eager to be one flesh, if only for a little while.

Loralee savored each moment, each caress. Soon, too soon, he would be gone again and she would be alone. She could not bear the thought, and she cried his name, tears welling in her eyes as he brought her the fulfillment she sought.

Moments later, Zuniga shuddered to a halt, his breath warm on her neck, his weight a welcome burden. When he would have rolled away, she held him tight, not wanting him to move, wanting to be a part of him for a little longer. Zuniga shifted his weight to the side a little so that she was not supporting his whole body, and that was how they fell asleep.

* * *

Dawn was streaking the horizon with brilliant slashes of gold and vermillion when Loralee awoke. For a moment she lay still, smiling faintly as she remembered the night past. It had not been a dream this time, she mused happily. She placed her hand on the pillow Shad had slept on. It was cold to her touch, and she sat up, heart pounding with despair. Surely he had not left!

Throwing back the covers, she jumped out of bed and ran into the parlor, only to come to an abrupt halt when she saw him standing before the fireplace, his arms raised toward heaven, his lips moving in a silent prayer.

What an enigma he was, Loralee thought, watching him. Was the real Shad Zuniga the violent man who had killed his own father? The tender lover? The angry warrior? The proud father? Or this quiet man standing before her, naked, primal, as he supplicated his god?

Zuniga dropped his arms as he became aware of Loralee's presence.

"I'm sorry," Loralee said. "I didn't know you were praying. I was afraid you'd gone."

Zuniga smiled at her, his eyes filled with love and sadness. "Without saying good-bye?"

Loralee shrugged. "I was afraid you might not want to say goodbye."

"It is not really goodbye," Zuniga said, drawing her to him. "For us, there will be no

388

goodbyes. I will always come back to you, Loralee, as long as there is life in my body."

He was leaving her, and she felt as though her heart would break. The hardships he had described the night before, the danger to herself and her child, no longer seemed important. He was her life, and he was going away.

"Take me with you." She knew he would refuse even before she spoke the words.

"I cannot," he said heavily.

Loralee smiled wistfully. "I know. Promise me you'll be careful."

Zuniga nodded. "Fix me some coffee, and then I must go."

He dressed quickly. Going to the nursery, he bent over the crib and stroked his son's cheek. It was hard to leave, but he had stayed too long already. Soon, the fort would come to life.

He drank the coffee Loralee offered him in three hasty swallows, kissed Loralee deeply, and slipped out the back door. Silent as a shadow, he ghosted around the corner of the house, vaulted over the back fence, and ran to where the dun was tethered.

He heard the clear notes of a bugle playing reveille as he put the stallion into a lope.

Mike came home just before sundown, looking beat. He gave Loralee a wry smile as he shrugged off his uniform shirt and pulled off his boots. They had been trailing Zuniga for weeks, but they hadn't been able to catch him. Like a will-o'-the-wisp, the Apache managed to slip through their fingers.

Mike cursed under his breath. None of the Indians would scout against one of their own. He had offered to let them name their own price, but to no avail. Zuniga was the last hero they had, and they would not ride against him, not for any amount of money, not even for whiskey.

Mike went to bed immediately after dinner, his dreams haunted by visions of Shad Zuniga laughing at him and at all the men who had ever worn Army blue.

Loralee sat up late that night, the baby cradled in her arms. How much longer could she stay here with Mike? How much longer could she go on hurting him? Mike had never done anything but love her, and what had she given him in return? Nothing. She lived in his house, ate his food, slept in his bed. And repaid his kindness by loving another man.

Loralee hummed softly as she sewed a new gown for her son. Mike was out on patrol again, searching for Zuniga. He was becomming obsessed with the need to capture the Apache. His obvious hatred for Shad, his single-minded goal to capture Zuniga at any cost and see him hanged for the killing of Sergeant Blakely, frightened

Loralee and put a new strain on their already strained relationship.

It was a subject they never mentioned, and the fact that they couldn't talk about it made other conversation uncomfortable. Mike knew that Loralee hoped he would never capture Shad, that he would give up the hunt and let him go. But that was something he had vowed never to do. The need to see Zuniga destroyed haunted Mike like a demon, driving him to spend long hours combing the hills. Often he did not come home at night. His men grumbled under their breath. For all they knew, the Apache could have left the territory by now. But Lieutenant Schofield refused to give up.

Loralee sighed as she put her sewing aside for the evening. It was almost time to feed little Shad.

She felt his presence even before she felt his hand on her shoulder. Heart pounding, blood singing, she rose to her feet and melted into his arms.

"I could not stay away," Zuniga murmured, his lips moving in her hair. "I started out for Mexico, then circled back and hid out in the hills."

His words warmed Loralee's heart through and through. With a sigh, she laid her head against his chest, content to be held in his arms, to know he missed her as much as she missed him.

"When will he be back?"

"I don't know. Not before tomorrow night."

Zuniga nodded, his arms hugging her tight.

They made love before the fireplace, bathed together, shared a cup of coffee, and made love again. Later, when the baby woke for its midnight feeding, Zuniga sat beside Loralee while she nursed their child, his arm around her shoulder.

Loralee's heart ached with a bittersweet pain. How right it felt to have Shad at her side, to be able to reach out and touch him, look at him. For this moment, they were a family as they were meant to be. It was a moment to be treasured.

When her son finished nursing, she changed his diaper, then placed the boy in Zuniga's arms. "You two should get acquainted," she said, smiling.

Zuniga nodded. The child was small and fragile, and he felt awkward cradling the infant in his arms. Still, it was a good feeling, holding his son. He had cared for only a few people in his life: his mother, Nachi, Loralee, and now this tiny scrap of humanity that he had created without thought or consideration. The baby caught hold of Zuniga's finger, clasping it tightly in its small fist, and Zuniga felt a rush of love for the boy. This was his son, flesh of his flesh, and he would live and die for the child, and for Loralee.

He held the baby until it fell asleep in his

arms, then gently placed the child in its bed. Loralee was waiting for him on the sofa, her soft brown eyes warm and loving.

He made love to her one more time before slipping out of the house, promising to return when he could.

Mike came home the following night, his face drawn, his eyes weary and filled with discouragement. They had ridden for hours, hoping to pick up Zuniga's trail, but all in vain. The rain had washed out his tracks completely, and Mike was at a loss as to where to pick it up again. Where would the bastard go? Back to the Dragoons? To Mexico? Into the Sierra Madres? Who the hell could say what an Indian would do?

He bathed and changed into a pair of clean trousers and a shirt, then went into the kitchen. Loralee was warming a pot of soup for him. Taking a seat at the kitchen table, he watched her as she stirred the soup, poured a generous amount into a large bowl, sliced a loaf of fresh-baked bread, and poured him a cup of coffee. She looked different, he mused thoughtfully. There was a sparkle in her eye, a bounce in her step that had not been there before.

She sat at the table with him while he ate, filling him in on the latest news at the fort. The Colonel's wife had ordered a whole houseful of new furniture from an Eastern catalog. Sally Stockman was pregnant.

Mike nodded absently. He didn't care if Stella Freeman ordered a new house from the East, couldn't care less if Sally Stockman had one child or twenty, but he did care about Loralee, and he knew her well enough to know that something had happened while he was away.

"What did you do while I was gone?" he asked, keeping his tone casual.

"Oh, the usual things. Cleaned the house and looked after the baby. You know, like always."

Nodding, Mike left the kitchen and went into the parlor to stand before the fireplace. He stared into the cold hearth, eyes thoughtful, and then swore softly as a bit of color caught his eye. Bending, he picked up a narrow piece of buckskin. He stared at it for a long moment, not wanting to believe what he knew to be true.

He did not turn around when Loralee came into the room.

"So you did the usual while I was gone," Mike said in a tight voice. "Cleaned the house and looked after the baby." He whirled around, thrusting the bit of buckskin into her face. "And played the whore for that bastard Indian!"

Loralee stared at the piece of fringe dangling from her husband's hand, her heart in her throat. What could she possibly say to defend herself?

"How many times has he been here?" Mike demanded angrily.

"Mike, please."

"How many times?"

"Twice."

"Slut," Mike hissed through clenched teeth. "You slept with him here, in my house. Didn't you? Didn't you?"

"Mike—"

He threw her a look of disgust, then strode into the bedroom. Moments later he emerged dressed in a clean uniform. Snatching his hat from the back of a chair, he stalked out of the house, his face a dark mask of rage.

With a sob, Loralee sank down on the sofa, her face buried in her hands. What a mess she had made of everything. Mike had every reason to be angry. She wept for an hour, then crept into her son's nursery to be sure he was covered. How precious he was.

Still weeping softly, she went to bed, only to lie awake listening as the clock struck the hours.

It was just after midnight when she heard the front door swing open. Footsteps. A crash and a vile curse, and then Mike was silhouetted in the bedroom doorway, a Mike she had never seen before. His uniform was rumpled and stained, his hair mussed, his eyes glazed with drink.

"You." He sneered the word, his expression twisted with anger and disgust. "You wouldn't share my bed," he accused drunkenly. "I wasn't good enough for you. I loved you, gave you my name, provided a home for you and that bastard, and you repaid me by sleeping with that dirty redskin."

"Mike, don't. Please don't."

"Shut up, you tramp. Tonight you'll play the whore for me, by damn, for me!"

He lurched into the room and staggered toward the bed, removing his shirt as he crossed the floor. There was a cruel, determined look in his eye, and Loralee shrank back against the bed, her heart pounding with fear. She had never seen Mike drunk before, or this angry. He looked as if he hated her, as if he wanted to hurt her, and she could not blame him. She had wronged him horribly.

She grimaced as he fell on top of her, his breath foul with the odor of stale whiskey. His hands grasped her breasts, hurting her, as his mouth closed over hers, his lips grinding against hers until she felt her lower lip split. She tasted blood in her mouth and she began to thrash about, trying to free herself from the rough hands that roamed over her flesh.

"Mike, no!"

"Mike, yes!" he shouted. Grabbing her hands in his, he imprisoned her body beneath his own, holding her helpless as he kissed her again and again. Transferring both her hands to one of his, he ripped her nightgown from her body, his blue eyes hot with drunken lust as he fondled her breasts.

Loralee began to cry helplessly as Mike unfastened his trousers. He was going to rape her and there was nothing she could say or do to stop him. Indeed, she had no right to stop him. He was her husband, after all, and entitled to love her whenever he wished. Only this wasn't love. . . .

She felt his manhood probe between her thighs, felt his lips brush her cheek, and then he was still, his breathing heavy and loud.

Loralee went limp with relief as she realized he had passed out. With an effort, she managed to inch out from under him, then she lay there, sobbing quietly, wondering what she was going to do.

25

Mike was withdrawn and cold toward her in the morning. He dressed slowly, carefully, and Loralee knew he was suffering from a terrible hangover. He made no comment about the night before, and neither did she.

When she offered to fix him breakfast, he refused with a curt shake of his head. Picking up his hat, he started for the door.

"Where are you going?" Loralee asked.

"After Zuniga." Mike faced her, his blue eyes as cold as ice. "I won't be back until he's dead."

From his vantage point, Zuniga watched Mike Schofield ride out of the fort, followed by twenty heavily armed men and several mules packed with supplies. They headed southwest. Zuniga frowned thoughtfully. Were they headed for the Dragoons?

He stayed where he was throughout the day, dozing fitfully. He had intended to light out for Mexico and lie low for a few months, then return for Loralee and the baby when the child was older and fit to travel. But the thought of being away from Loralee for longer than a few days was more than he could bear. The thought of seeing her, holding her, drew him like a magnet and he was powerless to resist.

With the inborn patience of a warrior, he squatted in the shade of a high bluff, waiting for night to fall. He sat there for hours, unmoving, his mind emptied of all thought. A squirrel darted past him. A lizard crawled over his foot. And still he gazed straight ahead, willing the hours to pass.

Darkness fell, covering the land like a dark cloud. Rising, he led the stallion to water and let him drink his fill. Then, swinging aboard the stud's back, he headed toward the fort. Dismounting some twenty yards from the first outbuilding, he tethered the stallion to a tree, then padded toward Loralee's house, blending into the shadows as he passed the other homes along the way.

He paused briefly at the front steps, his eyes darting warily from side to side. Too late, he sensed he was not alone.

He whirled around and ran silently back

the way he had come. He had gone only a few feet when the bullet slammed into his back, knocking him off his feet. He heard the sound of the report, then a victorious cry as Mike Schofield stood up on the roof of his house and jacked another round into the breech of his rifle.

Zuniga muttered an oath as he scrambled to his feet and began to run.

From up and down Officer's Row, doors were thrown open and men raced outside, pulling on their boots and pants as they looked around for the source of the gunshots. From somewhere in the distance, a woman screamed. Lights went on all over the fort.

"Get him!" Schofield hollered. He sighted down the barrel, squeezed the trigger, and cursed loudly when his shot went wide.

Loralee stood at the window, her hand at her throat, as she watched Zuniga melt into the shadows.

Breathless, his back soaked with blood, Zuniga grabbed the stallion's reins and climbed into the saddle. He drummed his heels into the animal's flanks, wrapped one hand in the stallion's mane as the horse broke into a gallop.

Mike Schofield hurried down from the roof and ran to where Zuniga had fallen. He smiled triumphantly as he saw the blood that stained the ground. "I got him!" he shouted gleefully. "By damn, I got him!" He laughed out loud. "He walked right into my trap," Mike said excitedly, speaking to the men who were gathering around him. "I knew he'd come back here. I knew it. All I had to do was wait!"

Loralee turned away from the window, her heart aching. Mike had set a trap for Shad, and she had been the bait. If Zuniga died, it would be all her fault.

She stood in the middle of the parlor, staring into the cold fireplace, listening as Mike called his men together and set out after Shad. In minutes the parade ground was quiet, the lights were out, and it was as though nothing had happened.

Loralee went back to bed, but she couldn't sleep. Every time she closed her eyes, she saw visions of Shad, wounded, bleeding, dying.

Just before dawn she fed her son, bundled him up in a warm blanket, dressed herself, and slipped out of the house.

Sally Stockman frowned when she saw Loralee standing on her doorstep. "What's the matter?" she asked. "Is anything wrong?"

"I don't have time to explain, Sally. Can you watch the baby for me for a few days?"

"Of course, I'd love to, but . . . why? Where are you going?"

"I can't tell you. Not now."

Sally smiled as she took the sleeping

infant in her arms. "I'll look after him as though he were my own," she promised. "Don't worry."

"Thank you, Sally. You'll never know how much I appreciate this."

"Loralee, does this have something to do with the shots we heard last night?"

"Yes."

Sally nodded. "What shall I tell Mike if he comes looking for you?"

"Don't tell him anything. And don't let him take the baby. Promise me."

"I promise. Be careful."

Loralee gave Sally's shoulder a warm squeeze of affection, kissed her son's cheek, and left before she could change her mind.

Back at home, she saddled Lady, then rode purposefully toward the reservation and Short Bear's lodge. Dismounting, she rapped loudly on the lodge flap. What would she do if he wasn't home? What if he refused to help her?

Short Bear threw back the lodgeflap and glared at Loralee. "What do you want?"

"Zuniga's been shot. I need your help."

"I'll be right out."

Loralee waited impatiently, each second seeming like an hour. What could be taking the boy so long to get ready? Why didn't he hurry?

Short Bear emerged from his lodge a few minutes later. "I need a horse," he said, and walked off toward a corral located some yards away. Loralee fretted as Short Bear threw a bridle over the head of a stocky gray quarterhorse and swung onto its back. Every minute of delay could be costing Shad his life.

Dawn was brightening the horizon when they rode away from the lodges of the Apache. Short Bear spent a few minutes at Loralee's house, studying the ground where Shad had been wounded, and then they began riding westward. Short Bear paused now and then to study the ground, checking for a sign.

"Here," Short Bear said a little over an hour later. "He is on foot. The soldiers went that way," he said, pointing south. "They are chasing Zuniga's horse. It will not take them long to realize their mistake."

Loralee's heart began to pound. How far could Shad go, wounded and on foot? Short Bear dismounted and scouted the trail. Loralee saw nothing to indicate that anyone had passed this way, but Short Bear went steadily onward, his sharp eyes picking up clues where she saw only dirt and rock.

They were in the foothills now. Brush and stunted trees covered the rocky slope, cacti were plentiful. They climbed steadily upward. Once, Loralee saw a dark smear on the face of a rock. She didn't need Short Bear to tell her it was blood.

When they reached the top of the slope,

Short Bear paused, his dark eyes scanning the ground intently. To the left the land stretched away flat as a tabletop. To the right were a series of small hills crowded with boulders and gray-green shrubs.

Short Bear turned to the right and began slowly picking his way up the side of the first low hill. Loralee followed, urging Lady up the rocky slope.

Near the top of the second hill there was a small cave, barely visible behind a screen of brush.

"In here," Short Bear said.

Quickly Loralee grabbed a bag from her saddle horn and dismounted.

"Wait," Short Bear admonished. Carefully he walked to the mouth of the cave. "Zuniga," he called softly. "It is Short Bear." He hesitated, waiting for an answer. "Zuniga? Are you there?"

Still no answer.

"I'm going inside," Loralee said.

Short Bear nodded. Fearful of what they might find, he followed Loralee into the cavern.

Zuniga was lying face down in the back of the cave, unconscious. His shirt and pants were caked with blood.

"Start a fire," Loralee directed. "There are matches in the bag. Hand me the scissors, will you, and then heat some water."

Loralee concentrated on the task at

hand, refusing to consider the possibility that Shad might die. His breathing was erratic, his face as pale as death itself.

She willed her hands to stop shaking as she began to cut away his shirt and pants. In many places dried blood had glued the fabric to his skin, and when she pulled the material away, the wound began to bleed again. She stanched it with a strip of cloth, disinfected the wound with carbolic, washed the wound, and disinfected it again before she bandaged the ugly hole. Thank God the bullet had gone through flesh only.

When the wound in his back was carefully bandaged, she dipped a strip of cloth in warm water and began to wash the dirt and dust from his face and body. As she worked, she prayed, pleading with God to spare Zuniga's life.

When she had finished bathing him, she covered him with a blanket and sat down to wait.

Short Bear studied the white woman as she tended his cousin's wounds, and his respect for her increased tenfold. She was not squeamish, like the other white women he had known. She saw what had to be done and she did it. Her hands were gentle and yet firm. Her movements were quick and sure, and she did not cringe at the sight of blood. He was suddenly sorry for all the snakes and grasshoppers and bugs he had tormented her with.

When Zuniga was resting comfortably, Short Bear stood up. "I will go back to the reservation now," he said. "I will see what I can find out. Tonight I will be back with food and water."

"Thank you, Short Bear."

A quick nod, and the boy was gone.

Loralee sat beside Zuniga all that day, his head cradled in her lap. He slept so soundly that she feared he might not regain consciousness. She stroked his hair, ran her fingertips over his forehead, and bent from time to time to brush his lips with her own. And always, in the back of her mind, a prayer lifted toward heaven.

Just after sundown he began to thrash about, and Loralee held him down, afraid his wound would reopen. He had lost too much blood already, she thought in despair. He could not afford to lose any more.

Once, his eyes flickered open, but he did not see her. He drank greedily when she offered him some water, then closed his eyes and was quickly asleep.

Sitting there in the dusky cave, she wondered where it would all end. Holding his hand, she willed her strength into him, wishing she could absorb some of the pain he was suffering, wishing she could work a miracle.

Zuniga began to mumble in his sleep, his words sometimes coherent, sometimes rambling and unintelligible.

She began to weep softly when he murmured her name.

Mike Schofield pushed his men relentlessly. Mile after mile, they searched in ever-widening circles, looking for some clue as to where Zuniga had gone.

"It's like he disappeared from the face of the earth," one of the troopers muttered under his breath.

"He hasn't disappeared!" Mike snapped angrily. "He's flesh and blood like anybody else, and I'll find him if it's the last thing I do!"

At nightfall Mike called a halt. They would make camp for a few hours to rest the horses. His men slept, but Mike did not. He paced the dark night, fretting over the time that was being wasted. *Not this time*, he promised himself. *This time he won't get away.*

At dawn his men were back in the saddle.

Mike rode like a man possessed by the devil. Where had Zuniga gone? How could a man vanish without a trace, especially a man who had been wounded? It wasn't possible.

Playing a hunch, Mike led his men back to the fort, then started out again. Two sets of tracks led away from the blood-stained patch of ground near the house.

Mike grunted softly. Two sets of tracks, he mused, where before there had been only one. Someone was following Zuniga, someone from the reservation. He followed the second set of prints, certain he was on the right path at last. Someone had gone after Zuniga, and that someone would lead him to the man he sought.

But the new trail gave out at the base of the foothills. Mike sat his horse for a long time, his eyes moving over the hills and the desert. Someone had erased both sets of tracks. That much was obvious. But who? And where had they gone?

His eyes returned to the hills. "Sergeant, take the men back to the fort."

"Sir?"

"Do as I said, Carter. I'm going the rest of the way alone."

"Is that wise, sir?"

"I don't know," Mike murmured, spurring his horse up the hill. "I don't know."

He rode up the hillside, his eyes carefully searching the ground for sign. Cactus and catclaw snagged at his uniform, but he was too intent on his search for sign to notice. His instincts told him he was getting closer to his quarry, and the blood pounded hot in his veins.

Midway up the hill, he dismounted and took up the search on foot. It was a steep hill, and he was breathing heavily by the time he neared the top. Pausing, he removed his hat and mopped the sweat from his face and neck.

Moving on, he studied the ground, the rocks, the bushes and trees. Nothing, he mused angrily. Not a hoof print, not a rock out of place, not so much as a strand of horse hair. Visions of Shad Zuniga sitting back on his heels and laughing at him drove Mike steadily onward.

He almost passed by the cave, but a gust of wind brought the scent of smoke. He followed the smell of roasting meat to the entrance to a small cave that was very nearly invisible.

A thrill of exultation brought a smile to Mike Schofield's face. His quarry was inside. He knew it as surely as he knew the sun would set in the west. It was a good feeling.

With a tight smile, Mike Schofield went back to his horse and headed for home.

Zuniga woke with a groan and tried to sit up. A soft hand settled on his chest and gently pushed him down.

"Lie still," Loralee said. "You need to rest."

He looked at her in surprise. "I thought you were a dream," he murmured, covering her hand with his. "What are you doing here?"

"Short Bear brought me. How do you feel?"

"Better, now that you are here. But you cannot stay. It is not safe."

"I'm not leaving," Loralee said firmly, "so let's not discuss it."

"Where is the baby?"

"Sally has him." Loralee picked up a bowl and offered him a spoonful of beef broth. "Eat," she urged. "You've lost a lot of blood and you need to eat as much as you can."

"I am not hungry."

"I said eat!"

Zuniga smiled weakly, then obediently opened his mouth. The broth was good and its warmth spread through him, making him drowsy again.

He was almost asleep when Short Bear entered the cave.

Loralee smiled at the boy, but the smile quickly died away when she saw the expression on his face.

"What is it?" she asked anxiously. "What's wrong?"

"Schofield knows you are here."

Zuniga struggled to sit up, the pain in his back forgotten at the mention of his enemy's name.

"Shad, lie still," Loralee admonished.

"I am all right." He sat up, his eyes intent upon his cousin's face. "How does Schofield know where we are?"

"I don't know, but he gave me a message to give to you." Short Bear glanced at Loralee, then back at Zuniga. "Schofield says you are to meet him at Shadow Lake tomorrow at dawn. You are to come unarmed, and to bring Loralee with you."

"And if I refuse?"

411

Short Bear looked at Loralee again, his eyes dark and sad. "Schofield has your son."

Zuniga stood up, his face terrible to see. "What are you trying to say?"

"The two of you must go to Shadow Lake," the boy repeated. "Schofield will be there, with the child."

Loralee wanted to scream, to lash out and smash her fist into something, but she was too numb to move. Mike's threat was all too clear. If they didn't show up at the lake, he would do harm to her son. She could not believe he would be so cruel, yet they dared not take a chance. Not when their son's life was at stake.

"Shad." She looked at him, hoping he could think of something that would make everything turn out all right.

"We will do as he says," Zuniga told Short Bear. "We have no other choice. Go tell him we will be there."

"I will go with you," Short Bear offered. "I will stay out of sight, in case you need help."

"No. Thank you for your offer, but I can't take any chances, not with Loralee and the baby there."

"I found your stallion," Short Bear remarked. "He's tethered outside."

Zuniga clasped his cousin's forearm. "Thank you for your help. Go now."

The two men embraced briefly, and then Short Bear left the cave.

"He's going to kill you," Loralee said in a voice cold and flat. "You know that, don't you?"

"He'll try."

"And if he succeeds? Shad, what will I do without you?"

"Do not weep for me, Loralee. Not now. I cannot bear your tears."

He took her in his arms and held her close, so close she could scarcely breathe. She lifted her face and he began to kiss her, soft, gentle kisses that soon grew deeper and more intense. After tonight he might never see her again, never hold her again. But for now, she was his, totally his, completely his, and he made love to her as never before. Made love to her all through the night, now tenderly and sweetly, now violently, until, utterly spent, Loralee fell asleep in his arms.

But for Zuniga there was to be no sleep that night. He held Loralee close, his eyes never leaving her face. If he was to die tomorrow, so be it. He was not afraid to die, but he meant to take the memory of her face with him into the Afterworld. Once, he had laughed at the thought of death. Once, he would have welcomed it, but no more. Life was suddenly precious to him, as precious as the woman in his arms, as precious as the child she had borne him.

He woke her the hour before dawn.

It was time to go.

26

The sun rose over the valley, painting the pale gray sky canvas with graceful plumes of pink and lavender and gold. Sunlight danced on the quiet blue lake and transformed the dew into thousands of tiny, many-faceted diamonds.

Loralee was unaware of the spectacular sunrise as she drew Lady to a halt, nor was she aware of the chill in the air. Her eyes filled with unspeakable horror as she gazed at Mike. He held her son in the crook of his left arm; in his right hand he held a gun—a gun that was pressed against her child's forehead.

She glanced at Zuniga beside her. He was sitting tall and proud astride the big dun stallion, his handsome face void of all expression. Only the slight twitch of a muscle in his jaw betrayed his anger.

Mike looked at Loralee and felt a twinge of remorse for what he was about to do. And then he looked at Zuniga, proud, arrogant, the cause of all his unhappiness, and new resolve surged through him.

"Get down," Mike ordered tersely. "Both of you."

Wordlessly, Zuniga swung down from the back of his horse, dropped the stallion's reins to the ground, then walked around and helped Loralee dismount.

Mike Schofield grimaced as Zuniga's hands closed around Loralee's trim waist and lifted her from the back of her horse. He did not miss the way her hands rested lovingly on Zuniga's shoulders for *just* an instant, or the little caress she gave his cheek before they turned to face him.

"Here." Mike tossed a length of rope at Loralee's feet. "Tie his hands behind his back."

"Mike—"

"Do as I say!"

Loralee's hands were trembling visibly as she picked up the rope and tied Shad's hands behind his back.

Zuniga offered no resistance as Loralee bound his hands. His whole attention was focused on Mike Schofield, and the gun that still rested against the baby's head.

Mike nodded as Loralee tied the last knot. "Move away from him."

Loralee stepped to the side, and Mike checked the knots she had tied. Satisfied, he holstered his revolver, then drove his fist into Zuniga's back.

Shad grunted as Mike's fist smacked into his wound, breaking the thin scab so that a trickle of blood oozed down his side.

Grabbing Zuniga by the shoulder, Mike forced the Indian around so that they were standing face to face, less than a foot apart.

"So," Mike said. "We're all here at last. The unfaithful wife. The lover. The bastard child. And the fool." He laughed humorlessly. "And I was a fool, wasn't I, Loralee? A fool to think I could make you love me."

"Mike, I never lied to you about how I felt."

"Oh, I know that. I knew you were in love with Zuniga. I knew it, but I kept hoping I could make you love me instead. I tried, Loralee. God knows I tried." He stared down at the child squirming in his arm. "Do you have any idea what it's been like, knowing that the men are talking about me behind my back, calling me an idiot for loving a woman who would sleep with a damned Indian? That's the worst of it, you know. I do love you, but it doesn't matter now. Nothing matters now."

Fear's cold, clammy hand coiled around Loralee's insides. She did not like the note of despair in Mike's voice, or the ominous expression that lurked in the back of his eyes, an expression that boded ill for someone, but who? Herself? Zuniga? Her son, perhaps? Each possibility filled her with greater trepidation.

"Mike, we can try again. I'll do whatever you want, I swear it." She would promise him anything if it would spare the lives of the two people she loved most in all the world. She would promise Mike anything, and gladly do what he asked, if he would only put that gun away.

Schofield shook his head sadly. "No. It's too late for that now."

"What are you going to do?"

"I'm going to give you your freedom," Mike said, but his words did nothing to ease the fear growing in Loralee's heart. She glanced at Zuniga. He was standing quietly, his whole body tense, his fathomless black eyes riveted on Mike's face.

Loralee licked her lips nervously, afraid to move, afraid to speak, for fear of what was to come.

Mike smiled at her. It was a decidedly cruel, spiteful smile. "Of course," he mused aloud, "freedom has always come at a high price."

"A price?" Loralee asked, puzzled. "What do you want—money?"

He seemed not to hear her. "Yes, a high

price. Sometimes blood must be shed, but if it's for a worthy cause, you count the cost as blood well spent."

"Mike, I don't understand."

"Don't you? Then I'll spell it out for you. You can't buy your freedom with anything as mundane as money. Instead, you must choose." Mike grinned wickedly. "It isn't fair for me to be left with nothing while you have everything, so you must choose, wife of mine."

"Choose?" Loralee frowned. "Choose what?"

"It is for you to choose who will live and who will die," Mike explained triumphantly, "the little bastard, or the big one."

For a moment, Loralee could only stare at him, unable to believe her ears. Was this the man she had once thought of as her friend, the same man who had always been so kind and thoughtful, so fair and compassionate? Surely he could not be serious! How could he expect her to make such a dreadful choice?

"Well?" Mike drawled, obviously enjoying his moment of victory. "Who will it be?"

Loralee turned tormented eyes toward Zuniga. "Shad," she wailed miserably. "What should I do?"

"You know what to do," Zuniga answered, his eyes never leaving Mike Schofield's face. "Do it."

"What will happen to Shad if I choose that my son shall live?" Loralee demanded, suddenly angry.

"I'll kill him," Mike replied coldly. "A little piece at a time."

"And if I choose Shad?"

"The little bastard dies in his place."

"You'd kill an innocent child," Loralee exclaimed, unable to believe her ears, unable to believe that anyone could be so cruel, so heartless.

Mike glanced at the child cradled in the crook of his arm, and felt nothing. All he saw was a tiny version of the man who had ruined his life. "I could kill this one with pleasure," he assured her.

Loralee gazed lovingly at her son. He was whimpering softly, upset by the strange arms that held him, and by the tension he sensed in the air. And then she looked over at Shad, who had not moved so much as a muscle in the last few minutes. How could she choose between them when she loved them both with all her heart?

"Shad."

He heard the sorrow in her voice, and his eyes filled with love as he returned her gaze. "Take care of my son, Loralee," he said quietly. "Don't ever let him be ashamed of what he is. Who he is."

Loralee nodded, unable to speak past the lump in her throat. Tears blurred her eyes as she stepped forward and took her son from Mike. With a sob, she pressed the child to her breast, her lips gently brushing the top of his head as he snuggled against her.

Summoning all the composure she could manage, Loralee walked over to Zuniga, stood on tiptoe, and gave him a last heartfelt kiss goodbye.

"I love you," she murmured brokenly. "I'll always love you."

Zuniga nodded, his dark eyes expressing the feelings he could not put into words.

Loralee was walking toward her horse when Mike's voice reached out to her. "Where do you think you're going?" he demanded.

"Home," she answered succinctly. "To pack."

"Not until it's over."

Loralee glanced over her shoulder. "I can't stay, Mike. Please don't make me."

"You'll stay until it's over," Mike said relentlessly.

"Let her go, Schofield."

Mike glared at Zuniga. "You keep out of this," he warned.

"What are you going to do if I don't?" Shad challenged. "You can only kill me once, white man, no matter how long it takes."

"Please, Mike," Loralee begged. "Don't make me stay."

Schofield raked his hands through his hair. He had planned everything so carefully, right down to the last detail, but now that his hour of vengeance had arrived, he was finding it difficult to pursue. He had wanted to hurt Loralee as he had been hurt when he realized he had lost her for good, but he could not bear to see the agony in her eyes as she begged him to let her go.

"All right, all right," he relented. "Get out of here."

Loralee sent a last look at Zuniga; then, clutching her son close to her breast, she ran for her horse. She did not look back.

Zuniga stared at Schofield, his heart pounding as he waited for the lieutenant to fire the first shot. He clenched his fists, his fingernails digging into the palms of his hands so hard that he drew blood. He was not afraid to die, he was not afraid of the pain, only that he might not be strong enough, brave enough, to die as a warrior should. He recalled the stories he had heard in his youth, stories of Apache warriors who had been tortured to death, but who had died with courage and honor. The blood of those warriors flowed in his veins, and he lifted his head a little higher, determined not to bring shame to his ancestors, to prove that he was as much a warrior as any Apache who had ever lived.

Every muscle in his body went rigid as

Mike Schofield drew his service revolver and eased back the hammer. The snick of the gun being cocked echoed like thunder in Zuniga's ears.

"I've waited for this for a long time," Mike mused aloud. "Every time I thought about you and Loralee together, I vowed to kill you for it."

"So do it and get it over with," Zuniga rasped.

"All in good time," Mike retorted, and squeezed the trigger.

The bullet struck Zuniga high in his left shoulder, the impact almost knocking him off his feet. He grimaced as hot, burning pain lanced through his shoulder and down the length of his arm. Blood trickled from the wound, warm and wet, as his eyes bored into Schofield's.

Mike frowned. He had expected to feel exhilaration at his enemy's defeat, a sense of victory, or at least a sense of satisfaction. Instead, he felt only self-disgust at what he had done, and for what he yet planned to do. He stared at the blood dripping onto the ground at Zuniga's feet. It was very red, he mused absently, very red indeed.

"Do your worst, Yudastcin!" Zuniga rasped through clenched teeth. "She will never be yours."

The truth of Zuniga's words hit Schofield hard, and he cocked his weapon a second time, wanting to strike out at the man who had taken away the only woman he had ever loved. . . .

Loralee had gone about a quarter of a mile when the first gunshot rang out, clear and loud in the stillness of the hills.

"I'm going to kill him," Mike had said. "A little piece at a time." The words echoed and re-echoed in her ears.

The sound of the second shot seemed to rip through her own flesh, and she doubled over as though in physical pain as her mind conjured up grotesque images of Shad's body being riddled with bullets until, in the end, he lay in a pool of his own blood, slowly dying.

She urged her horse into a gallop. The noise of the hoofbeats pounding over the hard ground combined with the harsh rasp of her sobs to smother every other sound.

At home, she turned Lady loose in the corral, then went into the house to feed young Shad. That done, she bathed him and changed his diaper and dressed him in a clean gown. Hugging him to her breast, she held him until he fell asleep in her arms.

After putting him down for his nap, she took a quick bath and changed into a freshly laundered dress. She had performed the routine tasks like a sleepwalker; her heart was dead within her. She had to pack, she thought dully, had to be gone before Mike came home. She could never face him again, but somehow she lacked the energy to begin. Instead, she stretched out on the bed and tried to sleep, but sleep would not come and she paced the floor, her steps listless, her heart heavy, numb with grief. Time and again, she went into the nursery to gaze down at her son.

His son.

She had condemned Shad to death. She had chosen their child and now Shad was dead. But what else could she have done? She could not let Mike kill her child, Shad's child.

She wept quietly, unable to stop the flood of tears as morbid thoughts crept into her mind: images of Shad's body lying out in the open, prey to vultures and coyotes; visions of Shad lying in an ever-widening pool of crimson, barely alive, helpless, slowly bleeding to death while Mike stood by, laughing fiendishly.

"All my fault," she moaned softly. "All my fault."

Mike stepped from the saddle, his face drawn. At last, it was over. He had hated Shad Zuniga intensely, and now, with his revenge taken, he felt drained, empty. Ashamed. How could he have behaved in such a barbaric fashion? He had known from the day of his marriage that Loralee loved the Indian. He had been wrong to try to keep them apart. But that was all over now. Over and done.

Removing his hat, he ran a hand through his hair, hoping Loralee had not yet packed up and left.

Entering the house, Mike stopped just inside the door. Loralee was standing in the middle of the parlor, staring blankly into space.

Mike swore under his breath, stunned by Loralee's appearance. Never in his whole life had he seen anyone who looked so desperately unhappy, so completely lost and forlorn. Her eyes, always so bright and alive, seemed empty of life. Her face was pale and haggard; there were dark circles under her red-rimmed eyes, making her look as though she had not slept for days. Even her lovely golden hair seemed tarnished and dull.

"Is he dead?" Loralee asked tonelessly. "Have you come to gloat because you've won at last?"

"Loralee, don't—"

"Don't talk to me!" she shrieked. "You've ruined my life, killed the only man I'll ever love." Tears welled in her eyes and coursed down her cheeks. "Haven't you done enough? Go away!"

"Loralee, listen to me, please."

"No!" She was screaming now, overcome with pain and rage because Shad was dead.

Muttering an oath, Mike grabbed her by

the shoulders and shook her. "Loralee, for God's sake, listen to me. He's not dead."

Loralee stared at Mike blankly. Not dead? But she had heard the gunshots.

"He's alive," Mike said. "Do you understand?" Good Lord, why was she looking at him like that? Had she lost her mind?

She went suddenly limp as Mike's words penetrated her grief.

"He's alive," Mike repeated, "and he needs you. Go to him, Loralee."

"I don't understand," she said slowly, afraid to believe. "I heard gunshots."

"He's wounded, but he'll be all right."

He'll be all right. The words wiped the despair from her eyes and filled her heart with hope. Zuniga was alive! Thank God, he was alive.

"I've got to go to him!"

"Your horse is saddled and waiting."

"Thank you, Mike." She was running into the nursery as she spoke. She threw the baby's things into a bag, grabbed the boy in her arms and gave him a hug. "He's alive," she murmured, the joy mounting with each moment. "Alive!"

Mike sighed as Loralee burst into the parlor. She looked like the old Loralee again, her eyes shining and vibrant, her smile bright and beguiling. How could he have ever thought to hurt her or cause her pain? He had known from the day he married her that she would never truly be his. She was the kind of woman who loved only once, and she loved Shad Zuniga. Any fool could see that.

"Thank you, Mike," she said fervently. "Thank you a thousand times over."

"Be happy, honey," he murmured, and she was gone.

Loralee rode as she had never ridden before. Young Shad howled at the top of his lungs, frightened by the speed of the horse, and by the tight grip his mother had on him. For once, Loralee ignored his cries as she urged Lady to go faster, faster. Zuniga was wounded, and he needed her. She kicked Lady, willing the horse to go faster still, unmindful of everything but the fact that Shad was alive and in pain. She breathed a sigh of relief as the lake came into view.

She found him lying beneath a tree, his eyes closed. The dun stood beside him, grazing peacefully on the sparse yellow grass. The stallion's head went up as he scented Loralee's mare and he whickered softly. A moment later, Zuniga sat up, his eyes wary as the sound of hoofbeats reached his ears. He relaxed visibly when he saw it was Loralee and the baby.

"Shad!" Dismounting, she placed the squalling child on the ground, then threw herself into Zuniga's arms, her eyes searching his face. "Are you all right?"

"I am fine, Loralee. Honest."

"Oh, Shad." She touched the blood-stained cloths tied around his left shoulder

428

and right forearm. "Lord, I never knew anyone who got himself shot up as much as you do."

"I am all right." He touched his wounded shoulder with his fingertips. "The bullet went clean through. And this," he gestured at the bloody rag tied around his forearm. "It is just a scratch. Hey," he chided softly, "it is all over now. Do not cry."

"I can't help it," she wailed, and burst into tears. He was so dear, and she had come so close to losing him forever. She wrapped her arms around his waist and held on as if she would never let him go.

Zuniga stroked her hair, loving the feel of it in his hands, the way it always smelled faintly of lavender. Holding her close put a strain on his wounded shoulder, but he would not have let her go for anything in the world. He glanced at his son and saw that the child had cried itself to sleep.

"What happened?" Loralee asked when her tears subsided. "Why did Mike change his mind?"

Zuniga shrugged. "Who can say? Perhaps he realized that killing me would not really solve anything. He loves you, Loralee."

"I know."

Zuniga smiled wryly. "You cannot pick and choose the people you love," he murmured. "It just happens."

Loralee grinned as Zuniga repeated the words she had once said to him.

"I love you, Loralee," Shad said fervently. "I guess I have loved you ever since the first time I saw you hanging up that load of wash."

"And I love you. So much."

"I know, but will you be happy spending the rest of your life with a man like me?" He shook his head ruefully. "I have no money. I have no home to offer you. I am wanted by the law."

"I have a little money," Loralee replied softly. "And I'll make you a home wherever you wish." She kissed him on the cheek, then let her lips wander to his nose and eyes and chin before returning to his mouth. They kissed for a long time.

"We could go to California," Shad said, thinking aloud. "A man I know there offered me a job a long time ago. He said the offer was good any time."

"What kind of job?"

"As a cowboy," Zuniga answered gravely, then burst out laughing.

Loralee laughed, too, her eyes shining with happiness. "I'd love to go to California," she said enthusiastically. "I've always wanted to see Los Angeles and the Pacific Ocean and San Francisco."

"I think you would go anywhere I asked," Shad mused.

"Anywhere."

Loralee's smile was radiant as Zuniga took her into his arms once more. "We'd better get started," she suggested, then shuddered with pleasure as Zuniga's hand began to stroke her thigh in a lingering caress.

"Tomorrow," he said huskily.

"Tomorrow!" Loralee exclaimed. "Why not now?" Her eyes sparkled with mischief as she waited for his answer.

"You know why not now," Zuniga murmured, and Loralee willingly surrendered to the touch of his hands and lips as they began to work their familiar magic on her willing flesh.

Tomorrow they would start for California. Shad would get a job and they would build a home and a life together.

Tomorrow.

But for now, she wanted only to bask in his love, to hear his voice, husky with longing as he whispered,

"I love you, Loralee, for now and evermore."

Make the Most of Your Leisure Time
with
LEISURE BOOKS

Please send me the following titles:

Quantity	Book Number	Price
_____	_____	_____
_____	_____	_____
_____	_____	_____
_____	_____	_____
_____	_____	_____

If out of stock on any of the above titles, please send me the alternate title(s) listed below:

_____	_____	_____
_____	_____	_____
_____	_____	_____
_____	_____	_____

Postage & Handling _____

Total Enclosed $_____

☐ Please send me a free catalog.

NAME_____
           (please print)

ADDRESS_____

CITY _____ STATE_____ ZIP_____

Please include $1.00 shipping and handling for the first book ordered and 25¢ for each book thereafter in the same order. All orders are shipped within approximately 4 weeks via postal service book rate. PAYMENT MUST ACCOMPANY ALL ORDERS.*

*Canadian orders must be paid in US dollars payable through a New York banking facility.

Mail coupon to: **Dorchester Publishing Co., Inc.
6 East 39 Street, Suite 900
New York, NY 10016
Att: ORDER DEPT.**